EVERY MAN...
KEN CASEY'S PAST AS DED AXTON—
NOTORIOUS GUNSLINGER,
SANCTIFYING PRIEST—IS DEAD. . . .

★

"Ded Axton! We thought you was dead!"

"Did you, now?"

"Look, Cap'n, we didn't find out until later that your wife and boy was kilt," Loomis said.

"Whether or not you knew that my wife and child were among those you killed doesn't matter. You killed nine people that day. The sin is no less."

"Sin? Ha!" Colby said. "What do you mean sin? What are you going to do, Preacher Man? Save our souls?"

"No," Ded answered. "I'm about to lose my soul, so why should I give a damn about yours?"

"You know, Loomis, I believe the cap'n wants to fight," Colby said with a broad grin.

"We don't have to fight," Ded said. "You can come with me down to the marshal's office, confess your sins, and I'll donate these coffins to the county so they'll have them available for you after you both hang."

WHEN HELL CAME TO TEXAS

ROBERT VAUGHAN

POCKET BOOKS
New York London Toronto Sydney New Delhi

Pocket Books
A Division of Simon & Schuster, Inc.
1230 Avenue of the Americas
New York, NY 10020

This book is a work of fiction. Any references to historical events, real people, or real places are used fictitiously. Other names, characters, places, and events are products of the author's imagination, and any resemblance to actual events or places or persons, living or dead, is entirely coincidental.

First Pocket Books paperback edition June 2013

POCKET and colophon are registered trademarks of Simon & Schuster, Inc.

For information about special discounts for bulk purchases, please contact Simon & Schuster Special Sales at 1-866-506-1949 or business@simonandschuster.com.

The Simon & Schuster Speakers Bureau can bring authors to your live event. For more information or to book an event, contact the Simon & Schuster Speakers Bureau at 1-866-248-3049 or visit our website at www.simonspeakers.com.

Designed by Kyle Kabel

Manufactured in the United States of America

10 9 8 7 6 5 4 3 2 1

ISBN 978-1-4767-1583-4
ISBN 978-1-4767-1584-1 (ebook)

For my agent, Frank Weimann:
    Thanks, Frank.

PROLOGUE

★

"Can't you hurry Davy along, Mary? How would it look for the priest to be late for church? This is Pentecost Sunday."

"I know it's Pentecost, Ded, that's why it's taking so long. Davy is looking for something red to wear."

"Well, do hurry, will you?"

Mary came over to kiss her husband. "Aren't you the one who always says that the Lord loves a patient man?"

Ded smiled. "It's not fair to use my own words against me."

"Look, Daddy, I'm wearing a red shirt!" Davy said, running into the room with his arms up.

"Indeed you are," Ded said. He picked Davy up and swung him around, rewarded with the little boy's giggles.

"Now, we must go, or I believe Mr. Byrd will decide to start without us."

"He can't do that. You're the priest," Davy said.

"Your daddy isn't just the priest, Davy, he's the most

handsome priest in the world," Mary said, smiling broadly at her husband.

"You're just trying to butter me up so I won't get on you for being late."

"Don't worry, we'll be there in plenty of time."

Ded, Mary, and Davy walked from the rectory to the church, which, conveniently, was just next door. Once there, they greeted the arrivals.

"You're not wearing red," Davy accused one of the parishioners. "This is Pentecost. You're supposed to be wearing red."

"Davy!" Mary said, embarrassed by the comment. "It isn't your place to tell people what they should wear."

The parishioner chuckled. "You're right, young man, I just forgot. I promise you, I'll remember next year."

Organ music spilled from the church as Miss Peterson began playing the offertory hymn.

"Remember the words of the Lord Jesus, how he said it is more blessed to give than to receive," Ded said, and as the ushers started the collection, the congregation began to sing, the hymn floating through the open windows on the warm, spring day.

> *And make within our souls thy home;*
> *Supply thy grace and heavenly aid*
> *To fill the heart which . . .*

Suddenly the back doors burst open and six armed men rushed into the church. The organist, startled by the intrusion, stopped at once, the last note of music hanging in a discordant chord.

"Ded Axton! Your day of atonement has arrived!" one of the men shouted, then all six men began firing indiscriminately.

Women screamed, men cursed, and children cried. Miss Peterson and several of the parishioners went down under the fusillade, and blood was running in the aisle and on the pews.

Ded Axton, unarmed and in liturgical garb, leaped over the altar rail and onto one of the intruders. He wrestled the gun away from the gunman and shot him point-blank. Then, using the gunman's weapon, he shot two more before he was shot.

When Ded regained consciousness, he was in his own bed in the rectory. For a moment he thought it might have been a bad dream, but when he looked over, he saw that Mary was not lying beside him. He saw, also, that he was wrapped in bandages.

"Mary!" he called. "Hey, Mary, where are you?"

In response to his shouts, the doctor came into the bedroom and looked down at him. "You're awake."

"Yes."

"You've had a rough go of it, Padre. For a while there, I didn't know if you were going to live or die. But I think you've come through the worst of it now."

"Where is Mary?"

"Father Ded, do you not remember what happened?"

"Yes. Some armed men came into the church while we were having services, and they started shooting."

"That's right. I wasn't sure you would remember. Often when something like this happens, the memory of it is lost for some reason."

"Where is Mary? Where is David? Where are my wife and child?"

"You . . . you don't know?" The doctor pinched the bridge of his nose, lowered his head, and closed his eyes. Ded knew then, without having to be told, that his wife and child were dead.

"No," Ded said. "God in heaven, no!"

"I'm sorry," the doctor said. "Besides Mary and David, Miss Peterson was killed. So, too, were Mr. and Mrs. Kelly, Mrs. Baker and her two children, and Mr. York."

"The church?"

"It was burned to the ground," the doctor said. "I don't understand it. They didn't rob anyone. All they did was shoot up the place, then they set fire to the church. Carl Byrd pulled you out of the church when it caught fire. Why would anyone do such a thing?"

"What about the men who did this? Did they all get away?"

"Two of them were killed and a third was wounded. I'm told that you are the one who shot all three of them. I patched up the one who was wounded. He's over in the jail now."

"Is he going to die?"

"I don't think so. His wounds aren't as serious as

yours. The two that were killed have been standing up in front of the undertaker's for the last two days, but nobody has been able to identify them."

"Two days? You mean this happened two days ago?"

"Three days ago," the doctor said. "You've been in and out of consciousness for the entire three days."

"I don't remember any of those three days."

"I wouldn't expect you to."

"You say the church was burned. What about Mary and David? Were they . . . uh?"

"They weren't burned," the doctor answered, anticipating the question. "They got them out too. The undertaker has been holding them, waiting for you to either bury them or be buried with them."

The funeral for Mary and David was held the next day. Though most people thought that Ded would conduct the funeral, he asked Reverend Bass of the Hunter Memorial Presbyterian Church to lead the service. Then, even as the funeral was being conducted, Ded leaned over to speak to Carl Byrd.

"I'm leaving town," he said.

"After the funeral?"

"Now."

"Father Ded . . ."

Ded held up his hand. "Don't call me that anymore."

Byrd watched in shock as Ded got up from the back pew, then left the church.

Ded hadn't said anything to anyone, but he knew

who the attackers were. He had recognized them the moment they burst through the doors.

Nearly everyone in town had gone to the funeral, so the streets of Estacado were empty as Ded walked from the church. He went first to the mortuary, where he saw two men strapped to a board to hold them up.

"Petrie and Filbert," he said.

Petrie had a shock of straw-colored hair and a pock-marked face. Both eyes were closed, and there was a bullet hole in his cheek, just under his left eye. His mouth was also closed.

Filbert's hair was dark, and so was his beard. Both his eyes were open, but the lid was half-closed on one eye. The eyes still showed their brown color, but they were opaque. He had a bullet hole in his chest, just over his heart.

Ded looked around and, seeing that there was no one watching, held his hand out toward them, making the sign of the cross.

"'To we who are alive, may He grant forgiveness, and to all who have died a place of light and peace.'"

Ded stared at the two bodies for a moment longer, then walked down to the jail.

"Father Ded, what are you doing here?" Deputy Grimes asked, surprised to see him. "Is the funeral over already?"

"Marshal Spears wants to see you, Deputy."

"Really? What does he want—do you know?"

"I don't know; he didn't say."

"All right," Grimes said, taking his hat from the hook. "Oh, Father Ded, I'm just real sorry about ever'thing."

"Thank you," Ded said.

After Grimes left, Ded went back to the cell. There was only one prisoner in the jail at the moment, and he was sitting on the cot.

"Hello, Cap'n Axton," the prisoner said. "I'm surprised to see you here. They told me you was about to die."

"As you can see, I didn't die. Would you step up here to the bars, please? I'd like to talk to you."

"You can talk to me from there, can't you?"

Ded shook his head. "I'm afraid if I talk to you from here, I'll just wind up yelling at you. I don't want to yell."

"All right, Cap'n." The prisoner walked up to the bars and stood there with a smirking smile on his face. "What have you got to say?"

Suddenly and totally unexpectedly, Ded reached in between the bars, grabbed the prisoner by his hair, and pulled his head against the bars, slamming it hard enough to knock him out.

When the prisoner came to a little later, he was staring into the muzzles of a double-barreled shotgun. His feet and one hand were tied to his bunk, and a rawhide cord from his other hand was tied to the triggers of the gun.

Ded was sitting on a stool beside the bed with a feather in his hand. "Hello, Asa," he said. "When did you boys get out?"

"Last month," Asa said.

"And the first thing you did was come to see me?"

"Yeah, why shouldn't we have come to see you? You betrayed us, Cap'n. You not only told the Yankees what we was goin' to do, you was there with 'em."

"Asa, I'm going to ask you a few questions," Ded said, not responding to Asa's charge of betrayal.

"Ask anything you want, I ain't tellin' you nothin'," Asa said.

"Oh, I think you will." Ded held up the feather. "I'll just bet you are wondering what I'm doing with this feather," he said.

"Ha! You can stick it up your ass, as far as I'm concerned."

"Before we proceed, I think I should explain to you that if you move that right hand of yours by so much as an inch, you will pull the triggers, and half your head will be blown off."

Ded put the feather under Asa's nose, and Asa started to move his hand to scratch, but realized at the last minute what would happen.

"Wait . . . what are you doing?"

"Where can I find Nate Walker?"

"I don't know."

Ded tickled Asa again, and again Asa almost moved his hand to scratch at the irritating feather.

"Stop that, it's driving me crazy!"

"I'm going to ask you again," Ded said calmly.

When Deputy Grimes returned to the jail, he called to the back. "Father Ded, you still here? You must've been mistaken. Marshal Spears didn't want to see me."

"Help!" a voice shouted from the back. "Deputy, get back here, fast! Hurry!"

Puzzled by the shout, Deputy Grimes hurried to the back of the jail. The first thing he saw was the open cell door.

"What the hell . . . Who left that open?"

"Get in here! Hurry!"

Deputy Grimes saw the prisoner with one hand and both feet tied to the bed. He also saw his other arm up in the air, a cord around his hand, looping across an overhead pipe, then tied to the triggers of a double-barreled shotgun.

"Get me loose from this contraption!" the prisoner begged.

"How did you wind up like this?"

"Cap'n Axton did it. Please, get me loose!"

Grimes hurried to the shotgun, then broke it down. He laughed.

"What the hell are you laughing at?" the prisoner shouted.

"There ain't no shells in the gun," he said. Grimes laughed again. "He left you all trussed up like a . . . damn! You've done peed in your britches!"

"That son of a bitch! That son of a bitch!" the prisoner shouted. "I'm going to kill him! I'm going to kill him!"

"How do you plan to do that?" Grimes asked. "Seein' as you'll more'n likely hang within another week."

BOOK ONE

★

DED AXTON

CHAPTER ONE

★

Coy Axton owned Twin Hills Ranch, and Darren Walker owned the adjacent ranch, which he called Doubletree. They were good friends who often ran their cattle together, as they were able to tell which cow belonged to which rancher both by mutual trust and by their brands. When a cougar took down a couple of steers, the ranchers sent their two sons, Ded Axton and Nate Walker, out to track down and kill the cat.

Ded and Nate were only fifteen years old, but they were both big for their age, and both had done a man's work for the last three years. Good friends, they were also competitive, often engaging in shooting contests, riding contests, and foot races. Despite their competitiveness, there had never been a fight between them.

The two boys, carrying food enough for three days, set out in search of the cougar. They lost the trail just before dark on the first night, but picked it up again in the morning. They had been taking turns riding in the lead, and for the moment Nate was in front, following the fresh tracks. Nate held up his hand calling for a stop, then dismounted and examined something on the ground. He looked back with a big smile.

"We're real close," he said. "He just took a shit and it's still soft."

As Nate was delivering his report, Ded saw the big cat creep out onto a flat rock about ten feet above Nate's head. The cougar was getting ready to leap.

"Nate, look out!" Ded shouted. He had been holding his rifle across the saddle in front of him; fortunately, the gun was primed and loaded. He raised the rifle to his shoulder and fired just as the cougar leaped.

"Ahh!" Nate called out as the cat landed on him. "Get him off, get him off!"

Ded dismounted and, pulling his pistol, started toward the struggling Nate. Then, before he reached him, he was surprised to hear Nate laughing.

"Nate!"

Nate rolled out from under the cat, then stood up. There wasn't a scratch on him. The cougar was still on the ground, not moving.

"Are you all right?" Ded asked.

"Yeah," Nate said. "You hit him plumb center. He's dead. He was dead when he fell on me."

"You scared me to death," Ded said.

"*I* scared *you*? What were *you* scared about? *I* was the one the cat jumped on."

Ded chuckled. "He didn't jump on you. He fell on you."

"Yeah, I guess that's right." Nate pointed at Ded.

"All right, you saved my life, but don't let it go to your head."

"Ha! I should have let him take a bite out of your hide before I shot him," Ded said. "That might make you a bit more beholden to me."

The two boys skinned the cougar and were on their way back when they saw smoke coming from a small house.

"Isn't that the Chandler place?" Nate asked.

"Yes, I think it is. Maybe we had better get over there and see if we can help."

The two started toward the burning house and were close when they heard gunfire.

"Whoa! What's going on?" Nate asked.

"Comanche!" Ded shouted, pointing.

"Let's get out of here!"

The two boys turned their horses but saw more Comanche behind them. They heard shooting coming from the barn and, assuming that was where Chandler was holed up, fighting the Indians, rode toward the barn as fast as they could. They were surprised to see the barn door open just as they approached.

"Get in here, fast!" Chandler shouted.

As soon as they rode in through the open door, Chandler closed and barred the door behind them.

"Are we glad to see you!" Chandler said. "Where are the others?"

"What others?" Ded asked. "There are only the two of us."

Looking around the barn, Ded saw Ben and Mrs. Chandler, Boston Chandler, their six-year-old son, and Dooley Hayes, their hired hand.

"The Injuns come down this morning," Chandler said. "At first I only seen a couple of 'em tryin' to steal my horses. I took a shot at 'em and they run off, but they come back a few minutes later with about twenty of 'em. They set the house on fire, but we managed to get here."

"Boss, there's about three of 'em tryin' to sneak up on us," Hayes said. "I think they're goin' to try an' set fire to the barn."

"Where are they?"

"They're over there, squattin' down behind the waterin' trough," Hayes said.

Hayes, Chandler, Ded, and Nate all aimed at the trough.

"Don't nobody shoot till all three of the heathens show themselves," Chandler said.

"Maybe we ought to pick out who we're going to shoot, so that we don't all shoot the same one."

"Good idea," Chandler said. "I'll take the one on the left."

"I'll take the one in the center," Ded said.

"That leaves me the one on the right."

"Which one should I shoot?" Hayes asked.

"Pick out one, it won't make any difference."

"No, don't shoot until after we do," Ded suggested. "That way, if one of us misses, you can take him."

"Good thinking," Chandler said.

The defenders in the barn waited for nearly a minute, then the three Indians rose as one and started toward them. The one in the middle—the one who Ded had selected as his target—was carrying a flaming torch, intending to set fire to the barn.

"Now!" Chandler shouted, and all three fired as one. The three Indians went down.

"I tell you the truth, boys, I'm near 'bout out of powder and ball," Chandler said. "I don't know how much longer we can hold 'em off."

"I've got an idea," Ded said. "I'm going to turn my horse loose. He'll run back to the ranch. If Pa sees him without me, he'll likely come see what happened."

"Wait," Mrs. Chandler said. "I took this from the house before we left."

She opened a box and took out a piece of paper, a bottle of ink, and a pen. "If you're going to send the horse back, let him take a message."

Ded nodded, then wrote: *Pa, trapped by Indians at the Chandler place, running out of powder and ball. Come quick. Ded.*

"Where are you going to put it on the saddle to keep it from falling off?" Nate asked.

"I've got some glue out here I was using to make saddle repairs," Chandler said. "We'll glue the paper to the saddle."

Slathering the back of the paper with glue, they stuck it on the saddle, then smoothed it down. When they were sure there was sufficient adhesion between the paper and the saddle, Ded led his horse over to the back door and waited while Chandler opened it.

"Go home, boy! Go home!" Ded said, slapping the horse on the rump.

The horse galloped away, and through a window Ded watched until it was out of sight.

Over the next couple of hours, the Indians attacked several more times. But they prefaced each charge with ungodly screeches and yells, and that enabled the defenders to get some rest in between their assaults.

"If we can just hold them off until your pa gets here . . ." Chandler said.

"I know how we can slow 'em down," Hayes suggested.

"How's that?" Chandler asked.

Hayes pointed through the window. "That fancy-dressed son of a bitch sitting on that horse seems to be in charge of 'em. I've noticed he starts whoopin' and hollerin' and pointin' before they attack. If we could kill him, it would least slow 'em down."

Chandler looked toward the Indian Hayes had pointed out, then shook his head. "He's too far away."

Ded looked as well.

"No he's not."

"What do you mean, he's not?" Chandler asked.

"Take a look, Nate. What do you think? You think you could hit him from here?"

"Maybe," Nate said. "But he's so far away, the ball might not penetrate even if it did hit him."

"What if we put a double load of powder in and both of us shoot at the same time?" Ded suggested. "One of us might hit him."

"Yeah, if the gun doesn't blow up on us," Nate said with a little laugh.

"I'm willing to give it a try if you are," Ded challenged.

"All right, let's do it," Nate said.

For the next several seconds the boys prepared their rifles, pouring in twice as much powder as they normally used. Then they packed down the wads, then the balls.

"There's no way these barrels aren't going to split wide open," Nate said.

"Maybe only one of them will," Ded suggested.

"Yeah, but which one?"

"I guess we'll see. Are you ready?"

"I'm ready."

The two boys picked up their rifles then and rested the barrels on the windowsill. They aimed, then lowered their rifles and adjusted their sights, picked them up, aimed once more, then lowered the rifles for one last adjustment.

"Let's fire on the count of three," Ded suggested.

"I'll count," Nate said.

Nate counted, and on the count of three both rifles roared and kicked back against their shoulders. A great deal of smoke billowed up in front of them.

"Well, the barrels didn't burst," Ded said.

"Damn!" Hayes shouted. "You hit him!"

"I knew I hit him," Nate said.

"Ha! How do you know I wasn't the one who hit him?" Ded challenged.

"It doesn't matter which one of you hit 'im," Chandler said. "They're leavin', and they're carryin' his body with 'em."

"Now we'll never know if both of us hit him or just one of us," Nate said.

"Why don't we just say both of us did?" Ded suggested.

"Agreed."

It was another hour before Coy Axton, Darren, and Nate arrived at the Chandler place with two dozen cowboys. They were warmly welcomed, even though by now the Indians had left. They trailed after the retreating Indians, returning when they were sure that they were well gone.

Within two weeks, the neighbors had rebuilt the Chandlers' house for them, and at the celebration party over the house raising, Ben Chandler stood to thank everyone for coming to help them rebuild.

"But I especially want to thank two boys—no, by their action they proved they aren't boys, they are young men—I especially want to thank the two young men who came to our rescue. If it hadn't been for Ded Axton and Nate Walker, there wouldn't have even been a need for a house raising, because the Indians would have gotten us for sure. Ded, Nate, stand up so we can all get a look at you and give you a round of applause."

Nate and Ded stood; then, as the others applauded, they shook hands and smiled.

JUNE 5, 1855

Ded and Nate were sitting in the stagecoach depot at Whistler, when a peddler came in.

"Lemonade! Lemonade! Fresh lemonade here!"

"Want a glass of lemonade?" Nate asked.

"I don't know, I've got a long trip in front of me, I probably should watch my money," Ded answered.

"Ha, I'll buy it. It'll be my going-away present to you."

"All right, my mouth is kind of dry, a glass of lemonade would go well now."

"I'll be right back."

True to his word, Nate returned a minute later carrying two glasses of lemonade. He handed one to Ded.

Ded took a swallow, then wiped the back of his hand across his mouth. When he did, he got a drop of lemonade on the trousers of his suit.

"Oh, I hope that doesn't leave a spot."

Nate laughed. "What do you care? Soon as you get to West Point, you'll be getting one of those fancy cadet uniforms."

"I wish you were coming with me, Nate. It's not too

late. Why, I bet if you had your pa write to Senator Sam Houston, he'd be able to get you right into the same class as me."

"Being a soldier is your idea, Ded, not mine. I'm going to the University of Mississippi, where I plan to study the fine arts."

Ded laughed. "What can you do with a degree in fine arts?"

"Why, don't you know, Ded? I'll be a gentleman. I'll be owning Doubletree someday, I already know all I need to know about ranching. I just need to learn to be a gentleman."

Ded laughed and punched him on the shoulder. "Nate Walker a gentleman? Why, they would have to assign you your very own professor to do that."

"Coach is a-comin'!" someone shouted, and Ded and the other three passengers stood. Ded reached for his bag but Nate held his hand out and reached for it himself.

"Better let me carry that out for you. From what I've heard about West Point, they'll have you running and such from the moment you get there. You'd best get all the rest you can while you can."

Ded and Nate followed the others out to the coach, and Nate handed the bag to the driver, who stowed it in the boot.

Nate reached out to take Ded's hand. "You might write to me now and then," he said.

"I will," Ded said.

"All right, folks, climb aboard so we can get under way," the driver said as he climbed up onto the box.

Ded got a seat next to the right rear window and looked out at Nate, who was still standing there, waiting to watch them leave.

"A gentleman, huh?" Ded called out with a big smile. "Well, I'm going to be an officer *and* a gentleman."

"Heyaah!!" the driver called, and he snapped his whip over the head of the team. The coach started forward.

"We'll see!" Nate called after him. "We'll see!"

CHAPTER TWO

★

Ded Axton grew to be exactly six feet tall, with pale gray eyes and a chiseled face. He graduated from West Point with the class of 1859, and was appointed a second lieutenant in the U.S. Army; but when the Civil War started, Ded gave up his commission in the U.S. Army to accept the rank of captain in the Confederacy.

His first action was under General Leonidas Polk, then in command of Confederate troops at Columbus, a small town in Kentucky, on the Mississippi River. There was also a Confederate camp on the Missouri side of the river at Belmont, and that was attacked by Union forces under Ulysses S. Grant.

Grant succeeded in capturing and destroying the camp, but Polk sent more soldiers across the river and they were able to rout the Union forces, retaking Belmont, and sending Grant and his troops fleeing back up north on riverboats. Captain Axton had fought particularly well in that battle and afterwards General Polk asked to see him.

"You did well, Captain," Polk said.

"Thank you, General."

"You are a Texan, aren't you?"

"Yes, sir, I am."

"Captain, I have a request from General Albert Johnston that may interest you. The general wants me to find someone who can lead a company of irregular soldiers. You would model your tactics after those of Quantrill's Raiders."

"Quantrill? General, Quantrill is no better than a murderer. With his raids against civilians, he has done more harm than good for the Confederacy."

Polk, who was a rotund man, held up a stubby finger. "Ah, Captain, but we want you to model your *tactics* after Quantrill, not your activities. You should limit your attacks to military objectives only."

"Where is this unit of irregulars now, General?"

"As of this moment, there is no such unit. Your directions are to return to Texas and raise the unit. You will be given five thousand dollars to get you started, but after that you will have to fund your own operation. Not only your own operation, but you will also be expected to make a significant contribution to the operating funds of the Confederate Army. As a matter of fact, your sole purpose will be to raise funds for the Confederacy."

Ded raised his eyebrows in response to the general's comment. "I beg your pardon, General, but how am I to fund my operation—as well as the Confederate Army?"

"With Yankee money," Polk said with a chuckle. "With Yankee money."

Armed with letters of authorization from General Polk and President Jefferson Davis, Ded returned to Texas to recruit those who would ride with him. The first person he spoke to was his old friend Nate Walker. At the time Nate was a sergeant in Sibley's Brigade of the Fifth Texas Cavalry.

"I thought you went to school to be a gentleman," Ded teased. "And here you are, a soldier."

"I couldn't very well sit by and let someone else do my fighting, could I?" Nate replied. "Now look at me. All dressed up like a soldier, but we've done nothing but drill."

"How would you like to do something besides drill—and be an officer and a gentleman to boot?"

"What do you mean?"

"I've been authorized to organize a troop of raiders, Nate. We'll make our own tactics and fight our own war. Would you like to join me?"

"Hell yes, I'll join you," Nate said. "I swear, we haven't done anything but drill since I joined up. And I didn't join the army to drill day in and day out."

"All right, Lieutenant Walker, you are now part of the Texas Raiders."

"Lieutenant?" Nate asked. "I'm a lieutenant?"

"Unless you would rather stay a sergeant."

Nate laughed. "No, I can get used to being a lieutenant. But, as my first suggestion as a lieutenant, I think we should change the name of the unit to Axton's Texas Raiders."

"You don't think that would be sort of self-serving?" Ded asked.

"No, not at all. I think men like to be able to identify with the unit, and with the commander. Look at Sibley's Brigade."

"You may have a point. All right, Axton's Texas Raiders it will be," he said.

"I think we should keep the unit small, and very mobile," Nate recommended, and Ded agreed.

Never larger than a dozen men, Axton's Raiders soon earned a reputation with their quick strikes, often behind enemy lines.

JULY 9TH, 1863

The Ohio River was a wide, dark gash in front of them, visible only by the winking glimmers of reflected moonlight. Ded and his raiders were on the Kentucky side of the river. On the Indiana side were two Yankee gunboats that had been shelling Confederate positions at will. Ded was given the task of eliminating the gunboats.

Ded planned to cross the river in two rowboats, with five men in each boat. Nate would be in one of the boats and Ded in the other.

"What I want to know is, what the hell are we wrappin' cloth around the oars for?" Logan Petrie asked.

"Because it deadens the sound of the oars in water," Nate explained.

"Yeah, well, it don't make no sense to me."

"Just do it and quit your bellyachin'," Nate said.

Fifteen minutes later, with all the paddles wrapped, the boats put in. It took another fifteen minutes to cross the river where they landed just upriver from their targets.

Moving quietly, the ten men followed the bank of the river until they reached the two gunboats. The boats were being guarded not by regular soldiers but by members of the Indiana Militia, none of whom had seen any battle.

The plan was to slip up to the boats, then attack, making as much noise as possible, with the idea that the untested militiamen would abandon their posts. When they were in position, Ded stood up and shouted.

"Baker's company to the left! Anderson's company to the right! Attack!"

There were, of course, not two companies, but when firing commenced immediately after the orders were shouted, the militia guards, as Ded had believed they would, threw down their arms and abandoned their posts.

Ded had been told that the riverboats themselves were not manned when they were moored, and as it turned out, the intelligence was correct. Ded waited onshore while Nate Walker took the others aboard the two boats, where they poured kerosene around, then set both of the boats on fire.

The flames were just taking hold when the men started scrambling back down the gangplanks. Ded was watching when he saw Nate suddenly draw his pistol, point it toward him, and fire. Ded heard the whiz of the bullet passing by, as well as the sound of the bullet hitting flesh behind him.

Turning, Ded saw a Yankee soldier sprawled on his back, a dark bullet hole in his forehead. In his hand was a knife. When Ded turned back to look at his friend, Nate held the pistol up and smiled.

JUNE 1864

CLEVELAND COUNTY, ARKANSAS

For three years, Ded Axton had commanded Axton's Texas Raiders, which, because it was a guerrilla group, was independent of any organized Confederate unit. Though some Northern newspapers regarded the Raiders as no better than Quantrill's men, Ded went to great lengths to differentiate his command from the groups led by Quantrill and "Bloody Bill" Anderson. Unlike Quantrill, who acted entirely on his own and sometimes even at cross purposes with the goals of the Confederacy, Ded coordinated all his operations with regular Confederate units.

A skirmish with a Yankee soldier a year earlier had given him a scar, a purple streak of lightning that ran down his left cheek from below his eye to just above the corner of his mouth. That encounter left Axton permanently scarred; it left the Yankee soldier permanently dead.

Ded was temporarily attached to the First Arkansas Cavalry Regiment under Confederate general Fagan for the fight at Marks' Mills. Fagan attacked a Union supply train, routing the Union soldiers, and capturing most of the supplies; but one coach, known to be carrying as much as twenty thousand dollars in gold, escaped the ambush.

Shortly after the fight, Ded met with General Fagan in the house of Clyde Barnes. Barnes was a local whose sympathies—as were the sympathies of nearly all the locals—lay with the South.

"You are sure the coach is carrying money?" General Fagan asked Barnes.

"Yes, sir, twenty thousand dollars. I seen 'em put the money on there myself," Barnes said. "The coach escaped the attack by goin' south. But it has to go to Little Rock, and that means somewhere it'll be turnin' around, an' more'n likely takin' a different road back."

"Is there an army detail with the coach?" Ded asked.

"Yes, sir, there is."

"How many men are there?" General Fagan asked.

"I counted at least twenty," Barnes said. "There mighta been a few more. Warn't no less, that's for sure."

"How many men do you have, Captain?" General Fagan asked.

"I have ten, counting Lieutenant Walker and myself, sir."

"Oh, that won't do," General Fagan said. "You'll be badly outnumbered."

"That's not a problem, General. We'll have the element of surprise and cover."

General Fagan chuckled. "All right, Captain. I must say, I do admire your confidence."

"Thank you, General."

"Tell me, Mr. Barnes, do you have any idea what route the coach will take back to Little Rock?" General Fagan asked. He spread out a map on Barnes's dining room table.

"More'n likely they'll turn around in Rison, then come up by the Dixon Pike," Barnes said. Using the map, he pointed to a place on Dixon Pike. "Right here, the road makes a hard turn to the left."

"What's on the side of the road here?" Ded asked, pointing to the hard turn.

"Cotton on this side, and a pecan grove on the other," Barnes said.

"Maybe you can hide your men in the pecan grove," General Fagan suggested.

"Yes, sir, that's just what I was thinking. I'd better get started right away," Ded said. "I want to make certain that we are all in place before the coach gets there."

PECAN GROVE ON DIXON PIKE

It was very cold, and as Ded stood alongside the road, he pulled the collar of his coat up around his neck to ward off the chill. They were all wearing a red band tied around the left arm of their uniforms. Ded had suggested the red armband, and was surprised at how quickly the men took to it, not only because it identified them as part of Axton's Texas Raiders, but also as a badge of pride.

"Damn, when I signed up to fight, I thought maybe I might get shot," Nate said. "But I sure didn't plan on freezing to death."

"Nate, I swear you would complain if they used a new rope to hang you," Ded teased.

"Would you blame me? New ropes are stiff," Nate replied with a little chuckle.

"Cap'n! Lieutenant! The coach is a-comin'!" Logan Petrie called.

"All right, get the fire started," Ded ordered.

A large pile of deadwood and trees had been piled up in the middle of the road. The brush was soaked with kerosene, then set afire.

Ded, Nate, and the others got into position on either side of the road, knowing that when the coach encountered the fire, it would be forced to stop.

Ded could hear the coach and its escort approaching, not only by the squeak and rumble of the vehicle itself, but also with the jangle of every harness and bit, as well as the drumming of hooves.

"Are we going to call out for them to stop, or just open fire?" Nate asked.

"They almost have us outnumbered, two to one," Ded said. "I think if we called for them to stop, they would open the battle, then we would lose our advantage. We'll just open fire when they come in range."

Nate smiled and nodded. "Yeah," he said. "I figured it would have to be something like that."

Ded pulled his pistol, then called out to the others.

"When you hear me shoot, pick out a target and open fire," he said.

"Ded, we need to shoot one of the coach horses, just to make sure it doesn't get away," Nate said.

"I know," Ded said. "I really hate to do that. The horses have no say in this war. But you are right: that will stop the coach."

"I know you're squeamish about shooting horses, so I'll do it if you want me to."

"Yes, go ahead."

Now the coach and outriders were close enough that Ded could hear the driver's whistles and shouts to the team. He waited until the first two soldiers were just about even with him. One of the soldiers, he noticed, was a lieutenant, and that lieutenant became Ded's first target.

Ded fired, and the lieutenant, hit just in front of the ear, was knocked from his horse.

With Ded firing the first shot, the rest of his men opened fire as well. Out of the corner of his eye, Ded saw the first, off-side lead horse stumble, then go down. As Nate had predicted, that brought the coach to an immediate halt.

The Union soldiers tried to return fire, but with their leader dead and with no enemy in sight, they weren't quite sure what to do. They simply fired wildly into the woods, shooting without a specific target. Within the opening seconds, the coach driver and at least eight of the soldiers were down.

"Let's get out of here!" one of the Union soldiers shouted, and although it was a private who had made the suggestion, the remaining soldiers complied as if it were an official command. There were twelve left alive—twelve out of the twenty soldiers who had accompanied the coach—and they galloped down the road, not in any kind of military formation, but in a wild and frenzied dash.

Ded's men cheered, then ran out onto the road, urging the retreating soldiers on with catcalls and jeers.

"Keep me covered, Nate," Ded said. "I'll get the strongbox."

Ded hurried over to the wagon and, using the spoke of the front wheel to gain a foothold, climbed up onto the driver's box. Looking down into the well of the splashboard he saw not a heavy box but two canvas bags. The bags were sealed shut and locked, and when he picked them up, he could tell by their weight that they held the gold they had come for.

"Here it is, boys!" he called, holding one of the bags up for the others to see.

The men cheered, and Nate Walker, now mounted, rode over to the coach, leading Ded's horse. Then, after handing one of the bags to Nate, Ded, carrying the other one, stepped from the coach, onto his horse.

"Ded," Nate said quietly. "Have you ever thought about just riding away?"

"What do you mean?"

"You know what I mean. I'm talking about just keeping the money, all of us dividing it up, then riding away."

"Why would we do something like that?"

"Well, just think about it, Ded. Hell's fire, there's twenty thousand dollars here. You keep six thousand for yourself, I'll keep six thousand, and we'll divide the rest of it up among the men. They'll get a thousand dollars apiece that way, and you know damn well that there isn't a man among them who's ever had a thousand dollars of his own."

"That's less than they would get if we were honest with them," Ded said.

"If we were truly honest, we wouldn't even be talking like this a-tall," Nate said. "We'd turn the money over to General Fagan like we said we would."

"And that's exactly what we're going to do."

"Why?"

"Because there is such a thing as honor."

"Hell, Ded, the way this war's going, it will be over

soon and you know it. This business of stealing money, then just giving it over to the failed Confederacy, has nothing to do with honor and everything to do with stupidity."

"I won't argue with you, Nate, because it could be that you are right," Ded said. A slow smile played across his lips. "But I still consider it honor . . . and, of late, honor is all most of us have left in this world."

"All right, Captain, if you say so," Nate Walker said. Ded couldn't help but notice that Nate had called him "Captain" instead of "Ded."

Mounted now, and with pistols drawn, Axton's Texas Raiders went around checking all the Union soldiers, just to make certain they were dead and wouldn't suddenly rise up against them. A few more shots sounded off in the damp air, the echoes rolling back from the trees on either side of the road. The air smelled strongly of gun smoke.

Ded counted the bodies of the Union soldiers. There were eight of them. Eight dead men who had done nothing to him. Eight men who were husbands, fathers, brothers, and sons who died only because they were wearing the wrong color uniform on this day.

This was the fourth year of the war, and Ded was well aware that there had been many, many days just like this one.

CHAPTER THREE

★

It was one year after the fight at Marks' Mills, and Ded and Nate were planning a train robbery when they learned that the war was over. As soon as he was given the news, he called off the strike.

Nate Walker and a handful of others wanted to go through with the robbery, but Ded said no.

"But don't you see, Ded? This isn't the way it was before, when you said you felt honor-bound to give the money we took to the Confederacy. We can do this job just as we had planned, and we keep the money for ourselves. We are violating no code of honor now that the war is over. Besides, it seems to me that those damn Yankee bastards owe us something."

"The war is over, Nate. Robbing a train during the war was a military operation. Doing it now is criminal larceny. So my answer is no."

"All right," Nate agreed. "I guess I can see your point. What are you going to do now that the war is over?"

"To be honest with you, I don't have the slightest idea. I went to West Point, planning a military career. But that's over. I guess I'll just have to see what turns up. What about you? What do you plan to do?"

"I don't know, I haven't made up my mind," Nate said. "I can't go back to Doubletree: my brother Dagan has run the ranch all through the war, so it rightly belongs to him."

"At least there still *is* a Doubletree," Ded said. "Ma and Pa both died during the war and Twin Hills is gone, taken for taxes." He shrugged. "But the truth is, I didn't want to go back to ranching anyway."

Ded mustered out of his unit, shook hands with everyone and wished them good luck, then he rode away with no destination in mind beyond the next hill.

Within a month after the war ended, a coach carrying a payroll for the occupying Union soldiers was robbed, using the exact plans Ded had drawn up for wartime raids. Furthermore six robbers were said to have been wearing red armbands. Knowing it had to be members of his old group, Ded sought them out and ordered them to stand down.

"You are bringing dishonor on every honest man who fought with the South," Ded said.

"It's like you said, Ded," Nate Walker said. "The war's over. And that means you are no longer in command. You can join us if you want to, but you can't order us to stop."

Ded looked at the men, all of whom had ridden with him, and called them by name. "Nate, Petrie, Filbert, Blackman, Colby, Loomis, Wyman, don't do this. You are making a huge mistake."

"You are the one that made the mistake, Ded," Nate said. He pulled his pistol and pointed it at Ded.

"Nate!" Ded called out in alarm. This wasn't anything he had expected. "You would pull a gun on me?"

"I'm sorry it has to be this way, friend."

"Nate, if you go through with this, our friendship is over. Do you understand that?"

"That's your call, Ded. Now, strip down to your long handles."

"What? Why do you want me to do that?"

Nate pulled the hammer back on his pistol, the click sounding ominously loud.

"Just do it," he ordered.

Responding to the order, Ded stripped down to his long-handled underwear. Then they put him on his horse and sent him away.

SIX MONTHS LATER

Like many veterans of the war, Ded was unable to rid himself of the ghosts of battle. He began drinking, just enough to keep a balance between being numb and being drunk. He did it to forget things he wanted to forget, but he never let himself get so drunk that he couldn't function. Since the war he had supported himself in half a dozen jobs, with his only ambition being to have enough money to eat, pay for a room, and drink.

Most of the time he found work as a cook, having discovered that he had a talent for it.

"Cap'n Axton?" someone said from just behind his bar stool.

Ded recognized the voice of someone who used to ride with him, but instead of turning toward him, he continued to stare into his half-empty glass of whiskey.

"Cap'n Axton?" the voice said again.

"I'm no longer a captain," he said.

"But you was my cap'n, and far as I'm concerned, you still are."

Ded tossed down the rest of his whiskey, then turned to look at the speaker. He saw a young man in his early twenties, smooth-shaven, with blond hair and light blue eyes.

"Hello, Wyman. I'm surprised to see you here."

"Yes, sir, well, what the lieutenant done to you, makin' you strip down like that, wasn't right," Wyman said. "There wasn't nothin' right about it."

"You were with them, Wyman."

"Yes, sir, I was. And I'm real sorry 'bout that."

"Your apology is accepted," Ded said. He started to turn back to the bar.

"That ain't the only reason I come to see you," Wyman said.

Ded turned back to him. "What is the other reason?"

"I thought you might like to know what the lieutenant and the others is plannin' on doin'."

"What would that be?"

"They're plannin' on holdin' up the bank in Allenton."

"How do you know?"

"Because they think I'll be with 'em," Wyman said. "But I ain't goin' to be."

"Why won't you be?"

"So far purt' nigh the only thing we've done is rob the Yankees. But when we start robbin' banks, why, that's robbin' our own people. Besides which, if the lieutenant don't stop robbin', the Yankees ain't never goin' to go back north and leave us alone."

"That's probably right. I don't suppose you know when this robbery is going to be, do you?"

"Yes, sir. It's goin' to be about ten o'clock in the morning of the fifteenth."

"Why did you come to me with this?" Ded asked.

"You're my cap'n," Wyman said. "I didn't know nobody else to go to. Besides which, I know you tried to stop 'em once before. I figured, maybe if you know'd exactly what they was plannin' on doin', why, maybe you could tell someone about it."

"If I get it stopped, they may know that the information came from you," Ded said.

"That won't bother me none. I'm goin' to California," Wyman said. He stuck out his hand, and Ded accepted it. "I wish you good luck, Cap'n."

Two days later and two days sober, Ded went to a temporary military camp just outside the town of Painted

Cave. The commandant of the camp was Major Mike Lindell. Ded and Lindell had been classmates at West Point.

"Axton?" Lindell said when a sergeant led Ded into the office. "Ded Axton! Well, well, you are a sight for sore eyes!" Lindell stood and extended his hand.

"Hello, Mike," Ded replied, taking the proffered hand.

"Axton's Texas Raiders. That was you, wasn't it?"

Ded nodded. "I'm ashamed now to say that it was," he said.

"Well, it was war," Lindell said. "I reckon we can't always be proud of everything we do in a war."

"No, we can't."

"So, where have you been keeping yourself?"

"Anywhere I can find someone who will put up with me."

"Hey, you remember Merlin Casey, don't you?" Lindell asked. "He was in the class ahead of us."

"I remember him."

"He was killed at Gettysburg."

"A lot of good men were. Do you remember Ken Kirby?"

"Yes, I remember Kirby. He was a class behind us. Like you, he joined the Confederacy, didn't he?"

"Yes. Kirby was killed at Antietam."

"We lost a lot of good men," Lindell said.

"We did indeed."

"Come on down to the Silver Dollar with me and I'll buy you a drink," Lindell offered.

"I never turn down a free drink."

Inside the Silver Dollar, Ded and Lindell were met by a young woman as soon as they pushed through the batwing doors. Her painted face and scanty attire bespoke her profession. She may have been pretty once, but the dissipation of her line of work had taken its toll, and she looked older than her years.

"Do you gentlemen want a lady friend to drink with you?" she asked with a practiced smile.

"No, thank you," Lindell replied with a pleasant smile. "We appreciate the offer, but we have some old times to talk about."

"If you change your mind, just ask for Shelly," the woman said.

"We'll be sure to," Lindell said.

Lindell ordered two shots of whiskey at the bar, and he and Ded took their drinks to a table in the farthermost corner of the saloon.

"To fallen comrades," Lindell said, lifting his glass.

"On both sides," Ded answered, lifting his own glass.

"Yes, on both sides," Lindell agreed.

The two men downed their drinks, then Lindell wiped his mouth with the back of his hand.

"All right, Ded, what brings you to see me? I'm flattered by the visit, but I have a feeling it isn't just a class reunion."

"Some of the men of my old command have taken to the outlaw trail," Ded said.

"Well, hell, Ded. That's pretty much what you were doing for the whole war, wasn't it? Riding the outlaw trail?"

"I know some Yankee newspapers called us outlaws. But I prefer to think of us as irregular soldiers. No different from Ethan Allen and the Green Mountain Boys of the Revolutionary War," Ded said.

"You have a point," Lindell conceded. "But what do you mean that some of your old group has taken to the outlaw trail?"

"I've recently learned that Nate Walker, who is leading the group, intends to rob the Bank of Allenton at ten o'clock on the morning of the fifteenth."

"Isn't that information that is more for civilian authority than for the military?"

"In the first place, the sheriff doesn't have enough deputies to handle them. I know these men, they are tough and determined. If they are going to be stopped, it will require the military. Besides, you have the authority, we are still under martial law."

"That's true. Why are you telling me this, Ded? Why are you turning on your own men like this?"

"It's bad enough having to deal with a world that doesn't know the difference between Quantrill and me," Ded said. "I'm not going to make matters worse by having people think I'm still doing this. Also, Nate Walker is an old friend of mine. I'm hoping we can stop them without anyone being killed."

"Do you want to be in on it when we stop them?"

Ded thought of the humiliation of having been forced to strip down to his underwear.

"Oh, yeah," he said, nodding. "I very much want to be in on this."

Their quiet conversation was interrupted by a woman's scream, and when they looked toward the source, they saw that someone had grabbed Shelly. Her assailant had his arm around her neck. He was holding his pistol to her head, but he was yelling at three men who were sitting at a card table.

"You been cheatin', mister! You been cheatin' from the moment I sat down here. And this here woman has been helpin' you."

"What are you talking about? I haven't done anything!" Shelly said, her voice breaking with fear.

"The hell you ain't. Do you think I don't know how you been sneakin' around behind me, tellin' him what cards I was holdin'? Now, all of you, get up from the table and leave the money on it. I aim to get back what I was cheated out of."

Ded pulled his pistol and stood up.

"What are you doing, Ded?" Lindell hissed. "That son of a bitch is crazy. Don't get him any more riled than he already is."

Ded raised his pistol and aimed it at the man who was holding Shelly, then started walking toward him. The man didn't even notice Ded approaching until Ded was within ten feet of him, then he jerked around, still holding his gun to Shelly's head.

"Stop right there, mister!" he called out angrily. "What do you think you're about to do?"

"I think I'm about to kill you," Ded said, his voice flat and completely emotionless.

"What do you mean, you are about to kill me? Are you blind? Don't you see that I have a gun pointed toward this woman's head?"

"Yes, and that's your problem. Your gun is pointed toward her, my gun is pointed toward you."

"Drop the gun, mister. Drop it now or I'll kill the girl."

"Go ahead," Ded said easily.

"What?" the man asked, shocked by Ded's response. "Look, you don't understand. If you don't drop the gun now, I'm going to kill her!"

"No, *you* don't understand. The woman means nothing to me, so I don't care whether you kill her or not. Go ahead and do it, then I'll kill you."

The man who was holding Shelly looked at Ded and saw the black hole at the end of Ded's pistol pointing straight at him. His eyes grew wide in fear, and small beads of perspiration popped out on his forehead and his upper lip.

"I'll give you to the count of three to make up your mind," Ded said. "One . . ."

"You're crazy!"

". . . two . . ."

"No, no!" the man said. He dropped his gun and took his arm away from Shelly's neck. Quickly, and with a little cry of relief, Shelly darted away from him to join the other bar girls, who, like everyone else in the saloon, had been drawn to the drama.

Two of the men who had been playing cards jumped up to grab the now unarmed man.

Ded put his pistol back into his holster, then went back to the table he had been sharing with Lindell. Lindell's mouth was open in shock.

"Tell me, Ded, how the hell did you know he wasn't going to kill that woman?" Lindell asked.

"I didn't," Ded replied easily.

CHAPTER FOUR

★

On the morning of the fifteenth, Ded, Major Lindell, and ten soldiers came into town. Lindell was in uniform, but the other soldiers were wearing civilian clothes. Their job was to take up places of concealment around the bank so as not to be noticed when Nate and the others arrived. There was some discussion as to whether they should stop the robbers before they went into the bank, but it was decided that if they did that, no crime would have been committed, and thus an arrest wouldn't hold up in court.

"We have to let them actually take the money," Lindell explained.

"What if the teller gets killed?" one of the others asked.

"You know Nate Walker, Ded. Do you think he'll kill the teller?"

"If the teller cooperates with him and gives him the money, I don't think he will," Ded said.

"All right, let's go in and get things set up," Lindell said.

When Ded and Lindell went into the bank, there

were two customers waiting. C. D. Matthews, the president of the bank, was talking to one of the customers, and when he saw Lindell, he smiled.

"Good morning, Major," he said.

"Mr. Matthews, I wonder if we could speak to you for a moment. It's very important."

"Yes, of course," Matthews replied, excusing himself from the customer. "You want to come in to my office?"

Ded and Lindell followed Matthews into his office, which was located at the back of the bank. "What can I do for you?"

Ded explained that his bank was going to be robbed at approximately ten o'clock.

"It is very important that the teller give them the money they ask for, without any resistance," Lindell said. "This is not only to protect the teller but also to give us enough evidence to put these men away."

Lindell explained that he had men in position all around the bank. "There will be no chance that they'll get away with the money, because we will stop them as soon as they leave the bank."

"All right," Matthews said. "I'll tell Mr. Pollard to cooperate with them fully."

"In the meantime, we need to get the townspeople all off the street, just in case there is any shooting," Lindell said.

At a quarter to ten, Nate Walker and five other men came riding into Allenton. The street, which would normally be busy with morning commerce, had very few people.

"What the hell? Is this Sunday?" Loomis asked.

"This is Friday," Nate replied.

"Then how come there ain't nobody out on the street?"

"What do you mean, there's nobody out? There's some men over there playin' checkers," Blackman said. "Damn, that must be some game. They got six men watching it."

"Yeah, and there's some more men over there, sittin' out on the porch in front of the store," Blackman said.

"There's a bunch down there at the blacksmith's, pitchin' horseshoes," Colby said.

"How come there ain't no women out walkin' around and gabbin'?" Loomis asked.

"They're all in the stores, spendin' their husbands' money," Petrie said, and the others chuckled.

"There's the bank," Nate said, pointing to a small building.

"Hell, look how little it is," Filbert said. "How do we know it even has any money?"

"It's a bank," Petrie answered. "Banks have people's money."

"Except this bank has *our* money," Loomis said with a big smile.

"Hah! This is goin' to be 'bout the easiest job we ever done," Blackman said.

"I don't know," Nate said.

"What do you mean, you don't know?"

"I don't know what I mean. It's just that I have a rather disquieting feeling about it."

"Lieutenant, you're the damnedest talker I ever knew," Colby said. "What does that mean, you're feelin' quiet?"

"Disquieting. It means that there is something about this that's bothering me."

"What?"

"As I said, I don't know," Nate replied.

"Well, we ain't goin' to back out, are we? I mean, we *are* goin' to do it, ain't we?" Blackman asked.

"Yes, we're going to do it."

The six men rode up to the front of the bank, swung down from their horses, and handed the reins over to Blackman, who stayed mounted. Blackman held the reins of his own horse and the five others with his left hand, while in his right he held his pistol, though he kept it low and out of sight.

As soon as Nate and the others were inside, they pulled their pistols. Nate was carrying a cloth bag.

"This is a holdup!" Nate shouted. "You, teller— empty out your bank drawer and put all the money in this bag!" He handed the bag to the teller.

"You aren't going to shoot, are you, mister?" the teller asked as he began putting the money in the bag. "They told me if I cooperated with you that you wouldn't shoot."

"What? Who told you?" Nate asked suspiciously.

"*I* told him," Matthews said, stepping out of his office then. "I told him that if we are ever robbed to cooperate fully. We can replace money. We can't replace a life."

"Yes," Nate said. "That's a most reasonable position for you to take."

With shaking hands, the teller handed over the sack, now filled with money.

"Let's go," Nate said as, with guns drawn, he and the four men with him backed toward the door, then turned and stepped outside.

"You men drop your guns!" someone demanded in a loud voice.

Looking up, Nate saw that Blackman had dismounted and was holding his hands in the air. Their horses had been led away, and there was a semicircle of at least twenty men in front of the bank. Every man was armed and pointing his pistol toward Nate and the others.

"Do it, Nate," Ded said. "We've been friends a long time. I wouldn't want to see you killed right in front of my eyes."

"Drop your guns, boys, they've got us," Nate said.

"Thank you," Ded said. "That was the intelligent thing for you to do."

"*Et tu, Brute?*" Nate asked, looking toward Ded with an angry expression on his face.

Nate Walker, Logan Petrie, Moe Filbert, Asa Blackman, Carl Colby, and Todd Loomis were brought to trial in San Antonio, Texas. The six men were sitting at two tables in the courthouse, with three of the accused at each table. An armed guard stood at either end of each table. There was only one lawyer for all six men, a court-appointed attorney who was doing his best to defend them.

The judge, A. J. Heckemeyer, was bald except for tufts of gray hair above his ears. His glasses had a habit of sliding down his nose, so that he had to continually push them back up.

Robert Dempster was the defense counsel and he was giving his closing argument to the jury.

"You are all Texans," Dempster said. He pointed to some of the men. "Pete, you served with Allen's Regiment of the Seventeenth Volunteer Infantry. John, you were with Elmore's Regiment of the Twentieth. Carl, you rode with the Lone Star Defenders of the Third Cavalry. And, Marty, you were with Moseley's Seventh Field Light Artillery Battery.

"Like all of you, these men were soldiers for the Confederacy. Most of the money on deposit in the bank they robbed was money on deposit by the Yankee soldiers who are currently occupying the South. And in taking money from the Yankees, they weren't doing anything more than they had done for the entire war when, led by Ded Axton, they cut a swath of larceny and killing across the entire South."

Dempster looked over at Ded Axton, who was sitting in the front row of the gallery. During the trial Ded had been a damning witness for the prosecution.

"Now, let us consider Ded Axton, shall we? Ded Axton was a man that Nate Walker, Logan Petrie, Moe Filbert, Asa Blackman, Carl Colby, and Todd Loomis served with loyalty and affection." Dempster pointed to his defendants. "There is not one man sitting at those tables who would not have given his life for their leader. And at any time in his life, if you had asked Nate Walker who his best friend was, he would have proudly stated, 'Ded Axton.'

"But how did Axton repay this loyalty, service, and friendship?"

Dempster pointed to Ded, then boomed out the next line: "*He repaid them with treachery! Ded Axton is a traitor who betrayed the very men he once led!*"

With those words hanging in the air, Dempster took his seat.

Dan Norton was the prosecuting attorney, and he had made a strong case during the trial, bringing forth a dozen witnesses to the bank robbery. Now he stepped up to the jury box to make his closing statement.

"Marty, you were with the artillery. Today, would you set up one of your guns and start firing shells into a town?"

"Why, no, sir, of course not!" Marty said.

"What if it was a Yankee town—say, one up in Kansas?"

"No, sir, that wouldn't matter none. I wouldn't do it."

"John, you were in the infantry, and I know you saw

a lot of battle at Antietam, Fredericksburg, and Franklin. You shot at Yankee soldiers then. Would you do that today? Would you lie behind a bush somewhere and start shooting at Yankee soldiers?"

"No, Dan, you know damn well I wouldn't do anything like that. The war is over."

"No, and neither would Pete nor Carl," Norton said. "But in calling upon your war experience, Dempster would have the folks believe that you're no different from these men." He pointed to the prisoners at the table. "These men are guilty as sin, and that's pure and simple. The only thing to do with them is find them guilty and send them to prison."

The jury was out for less than fifteen minutes. When they trooped back into the courtroom, they kept their eyes straight ahead, glancing toward neither the gallery nor the defendants.

"Gentlemen of the jury," Judge Heckemeyer said when all were seated, "have you selected a foreman?"

A man with bushy white hair and wire-rimmed glasses stood.

"We have, Your Honor. I am Jerome Witherell."

Witherell didn't have to identify himself: he owned Witherell's Mercantile and everyone in town, including the judge, knew who he was.

"Mr. Witherell, has the jury reached a verdict?"

"We have, Your Honor."

"Would you publish the verdict, please?"

Witherell pulled a piece of paper from his pocket, unfolded it, then cleared his throat.

"We the jury find the defendants," this was where he referred to the paper in his hand, and began reading the names, "Nate Walker, Logan Petrie, Moe Filbert, Asa Blackman, Carl Colby, and Todd Loomis, guilty as charged."

"Thank you, Mr. Foreman, you may be seated for the penalty phase. Defense Counselor, would you and your clients stand, please?"

Dempster stood and, with a wave of his hand, signaled for the others to stand as well.

"Mr. Walker, Mr. Petrie, Mr. Filbert, Mr. Blackman, Mr. Colby, and Mr. Loomis, you have all been found guilty as charged. It is the sentence of this court that you be taken to the maximum-security prison in Huntsville, Texas, and there to be incarcerated for a period of twenty years."

"Twenty years? I'll be an old man when I get out!" Loomis shouted angrily.

"Sheriff, take charge of your prisoners," Judge Heckemeyer said. He banged his gavel against the bench. "This court is adjourned."

"Let's go," the sheriff said to his prisoners as he and his deputies escorted them back to the jail to await transportation to the state penitentiary in Huntsville.

As they left, Nate looked over at Ded, fixing him with a withering stare.

"I'm sorry, Nate," Ded said.

Nate didn't respond, but he held Ded in his disapproving gaze until he was led out of the courtroom.

Ded wished Nate had spoken to him, even if it had only been to curse him out. Although he knew he had done the right thing, he felt a tremendous sense of guilt, as if he had betrayed his lifelong friend.

Later that same day, Ded stopped by the sheriff's office to get permission to speak with Nate.

"I don't know why you would want to talk to him," the sheriff said, "but go on back."

Ded walked into the back of the jailhouse and down a long aisle that stretched between two rows of cells. The prisoners were in three cells, two per cell.

"What are you doing here, you son of a bitch?" Loomis shouted angrily. Colby's greeting was just as vitriolic.

Ded walked all the way to the last cell, which was holding Nate Walker and Asa Blackman.

"Well, well, well, if it isn't my old friend, Ded Axton," Nate said sarcastically. "Come to tell us goodbye, did you?"

"You might say that."

"Ded, I never had a better friend in the world than you. I never thought you would do anything like this to me. You not only betrayed me, you betrayed every man who had been under your command."

"Not every man," Ded said. "Over the course of the war, we had as many as thirty men in the group. Only six of you went bad. I tried to talk you out of it, but you wouldn't listen. Now you are going to have twenty years to think about it."

"I've got news for you," Nate said. "That's not what I'm going to be thinking about for twenty years."

"If you have any idea of revenge, just remember what I said. You brought this on yourself."

"Twenty years isn't forever," Nate said. "You'll go on to make your own life, and you'll forget. But I won't. And in twenty years, I'm going to come looking for you."

"Good-bye, Nate. I can't tell you how sorry I am that it had to end like this."

"I'll be seeing you," Nate replied, his mouth spreading into a sardonic grin.

CHAPTER FIVE

★

During and shortly after the war, Ded had been viewed as a hero of the South. But now he had achieved a different kind of fame. Nearly everyone knew that he had played a role in bringing to justice several members of his old army unit, but for a significant number of Texans, what Ded did wasn't a civic duty but a betrayal.

It wasn't just a betrayal. Many were convinced that he had been on the outlaw trail with them, and that he had avoided prison only by turning on the very men who had once trusted him. As time passed, that story gained more and more credence. "Pulling an Axton" became synonymous with "betrayal," even appearing in a couple of newspaper articles.

In addition to the scorn that was now almost universally directed at him, Ded was also besieged by demons, often encountering the ghosts of the men he had killed during the war. And if the ghosts weren't real, they were real in his mind, and that was real enough. Only when he was drunk could he put aside the ostracism and make the ghosts go away. As his drinking became heavier, he became more and more of a misanthrope, unfit for civilized society. He bounced from pillar to post, working just until he had enough money to get drunk, often leaving town, not by choice, but under the escort of a sheriff's deputy.

One cold day in February, Ded drank until he passed out, coming to only when a couple of sheriff's deputies were putting him on a horse.

"What is it?" he mumbled. "What are you doing?"

"We're running you out of town," one of the deputies said. "Next time you come to this town, you damn well better be sober. Now get!"

The deputy slapped his horse and it bolted ahead, with Ded hanging on to the saddle horn for dear life. The horse galloped for about half a mile before Ded got it under control. Then, with the horse proceeding at a leisurely walk, Ded pulled a full bottle of whiskey from his saddlebag and began drinking.

Ahead lay the Davis Mountains, and because Ded was drunk and not thinking very clearly, he started through the pass too late in the day. When it grew dark he stopped and made camp. It had turned much colder, so Ded wrapped himself up in a blanket and his slicker. The sky was clear and filled with bright stars when he bedded down, and he went to sleep quickly, aided by the quantity of whiskey he had consumed.

During the night, though he was unaware of it, his slumber was visited by an unusually heavy fall of snow.

The snow came down softly, silently, from the night sky, so that it was quite a surprise when he awoke the next morning, hungover but sober, to find himself buried in snow.

For a moment he panicked, thinking that perhaps he had been caught in an avalanche, and quickly he tried to get to his feet, finding to his relief that he had not been buried. The snow was very deep though, halfway between his knees and his waist. To make matters worse, his horse had wandered off sometime during the night and there was no sign of him. The pass was blocked solid and piled high with snow, and it was nearly impossible for him to move.

Ded couldn't remember if he had taken his saddle off the horse the night before. Normally he did, but he had been very drunk and could only barely remember riding into the pass, so he didn't know if he had removed the saddle or not. The saddle was critical, because he had some jerky in one of the saddlebags and he had a feeling that he was going to be stuck here for a while. Without the jerky, he was likely to get very hungry.

Because the snow was so deep, Ded knew that even if he had removed the saddle, it would be completely covered by now. If he was going to find it, he would have to work out a very complicated search grid, stomping through the snow and feeling with his feet. Fortunately, as he tramped through the snow, it left a clear path indicating where he had been, so he was able to establish a grid that he could follow.

He found nothing the first day, and during the night it snowed again, so that when he awoke the next morning, it was to another unblemished and pristine field of white. This was his second day without food, and he was getting very hungry, so he had no choice but to continue searching using a grid. Unfortunately, he was no more successful than he had been the day before.

Ded's third day without food was also his third day without any liquor. He didn't know which he needed most.

"All right, Ded. You've got two choices. You can just stay right here and die, or you can try and work your way down out of the pass, where you still might die, but at least you'll die trying."

He had spoken the words aloud because he wanted to hear a human voice, even if it was his own. His words sounded so small and weak against the blows of nature that it seemed to just highlight the hopelessness of his situation.

"I choose to try and get out!" he said, yelling this time, hoping at least for an echo. But because the snow had blocked the pass and piled up against the sides of the mountains, there was no echo.

Ded had no idea where he was, other than that he was somewhere in the Davis Mountains in West Texas. He also didn't know if there was a town that he would be able to walk to, or even a farm or ranch house, but he believed it would be better to die trying to save himself than to just give up.

As he trudged down the pass through snow, with

drifts that reached as high as his chest, he was leaving behind him a long, black scar to trace his path. Ded had never been a praying man, not even in the midst of the most intense battles. But at some point on his way down he began to pray:

"Lord, I know that you haven't heard much from me since I was a kid. But I need some help now. Though I'll be truthful with you, Lord, not praying is a long way from being my only sin. I've done more things that I'm not proud of than I can count, so I don't deserve any help. But I'm just asking you for it, hoping you'll have mercy on this sinner. Amen."

It was mid-afternoon when Ded saw a horse and rider coming toward him. He yelled and waved, then tried to run, but the snow was still too deep. It was all he could do to trudge forward slowly, awkwardly, hoping to reach the rider before he turned away.

It took at least five more minutes before he reached the rider, who was an older man with white hair and a long white beard.

"Mister," the man said, "you seem to have gotten yourself in quite a fix here."

"Yes," Ded said. "Can you help me? My horse is gone, and I haven't eaten in three days. Do you have anything to eat?"

"I don't have anything with me," the man said. "But my house is only a mile or so on down the trail, and the missus has got some hot soup on. Climb up behind me, I'll have you there in no time at all."

"Oh, thank God," Ded said as he swung into the saddle behind the old man.

"Thank God is right," the man said. "How do you think I happened to come up this way?"

"I don't know."

"God sent me up."

"What do you mean?"

"Look behind you, mister," the rider said.

Looking back up the pass, Ded saw the long black trail he had left in the snow. But three quarters of the way up, there was a depression in the pass that ran at right angles to Ded's trail, and in that depression the sun had melted the snow, leaving a swath as dark as the trail Ded had cut coming down from the mountain.

The result was a geometrically perfect black cross laid out in the pristine white snow.

"I saw that cross," the man said. "And I knew I had to come up here to get a closer look. So when you say 'Thank God,' then you need to mean it. There's no doubt in my mind that God made a cross out of your path as a call for help."

"And you answered it," Ded said.

"I couldn't not answer it," the man replied. He clucked at his horse and it started back down, finding the going a bit easier, as it was following the same trail it had broken coming up.

There was smoke pouring from the chimney of the small log house as they approached it, and Ded didn't think he had ever seen a more welcome sight in his life.

His rescuer helped him down from the horse, then led him inside. The room was both illuminated and warmed by the golden glow of flames that were snapping in the fireplace.

"Woman of the house, look what I've brought home with me," the man said.

An older woman, seeing Ded's condition, came to him.

"Oh, you poor thing," she said. "Please get out of those cold, wet things. Paul, get something for him to wear."

A few minutes later, warm and in dry clothes, Ded was sitting at the table, eating his third bowl of a rich, hearty soup.

"You are lifesavers, literally," Ded said.

"We haven't even had the opportunity to introduce ourselves," the man said. "My name is Paul Malcolm. This is my wife, Marjane."

"Mr. Malcolm, I'm Ded Axton. And believe me, I was never so glad to see anyone in my life."

"If you don't mind my asking, Mr. Axton, what were you doing up in Wild Rose Pass at this time of the year?"

"I'm embarrassed and ashamed to tell you that I don't have any idea what I was doing there," Ded said. "I had been drinking. In fact, I wonder . . . I'm almost reluctant to ask, but I wonder if you might have something to drink?"

"Oh, I'm afraid not," Malcolm said. "We're both teetotalers here."

"I see. Well, it was most ungrateful of me to ask anyway, considering everything you have already done for me. I'll just get a drink when I go into town."

"Oh, that might not be as easy as you think," Malcolm said. "The nearest town is twenty miles from here. And at this time of year the road is quite impassable for a wagon, and nearly so for a horse. Of course, Marjane and I will hitch up the wagon and go into town come spring. You will be quite welcome to ride in with us then, of course."

"When will you be going into town?" Ded asked in a concerned voice.

"Oh, I'd say in about two more months. Around the end of April."

"Two months," Ded said.

"Don't worry," Malcolm said brightly. "We have plenty of food and plenty of coffee. We'll get along just fine."

"I hate to be an imposition for that long."

"Nonsense, it'll be good to have someone to visit with. We do get a little lonely up here, being isolated for so long."

Within twenty-four hours after that first meal, Ded was undergoing full-scale withdrawal symptoms. He lost all appetite, his hands began shaking, and he became nauseous, running outside to throw up until he no longer could. Then he had to deal with dry heaves.

On the third night Ded woke up screaming. Grabbing one of his boots he began beating on the bedroll that had been spread out for him.

"Ded, Ded, what is it?" Malcolm asked.

"Rats!" Ded said. "Can't you see them? They are all over my bed! They've been biting me! There's one!" Ded slammed his boot down onto the floor.

By now Marjane had come into the room wearing a flannel housecoat.

"What is it?" she asked in a frightened voice.

"You know what it is," Malcolm said. "He's got the horrors."

Ded quit beating the bed and floor with his boot, then sat down and pulled his knees up in front of him. He wrapped his arms around his legs and began shaking.

Marjane sat down beside him, put her arms around him, pulling him to her, holding him until he quit shaking.

"Ded, you haven't eaten a bite in two days," Malcolm said. "Why don't you let Marjane warm up some broth for you? I think you should try and get some kind of food in you."

"All right," Ded said. "Thanks, I'll try."

Half an hour later the shakes were gone, and Ded was sipping a cup of chicken broth.

"Thanks, this is very good," hc said. He looked around and saw that it was dark outside. "What time is it?"

"I think it's about two o'clock," Malcolm said.

"Two o'clock in the morning? Oh, I can't believe what a problem I've been for you. I'm so sorry."

"Don't be," Malcolm said. "I'm just glad we've been here for you."

"I've read about delirium tremens before," Ded said. "I've never seen them, and I've never before experienced them."

"Delirium tremens? Is that the real name for the horrors?"

"Horrors? Yes, that is an even better name for it," Ded said. "It's what someone who has been drinking too much has when he stops drinking."

"It's been five days since the horrors first started. Like as not, you won't be havin' no more of it."

"I hope you're right."

"They never have come back on me," Malcolm said easily.

"You've been through this?"

"Yes."

"Then I couldn't have picked a better place to have come."

"You didn't pick it, Ded. Remember the cross?"

"I remember."

"What are you going to do about it?"

"What are you saying?"

"Seems to me like maybe that cross was sort of a callin', if you know what I mean."

"Yes," Ded said, nodding. "Maybe I do know what you mean."

CHAPTER SIX

★

Ded Axton went to seminary at the University of the South in Sewanee, Tennessee, where he studied to become an Episcopal priest. Seminary wasn't easy for him. For one thing, he was at least ten years older than any of the other seminarians, and it wasn't just chronological age. Ded had already seen more, and done more, in his life than any other student or any member of the faculty. He believed there was no sin that he hadn't committed, nor was there any terror he hadn't faced.

But he did have two things going for him. He already had a college degree earned at West Point, and he was an exceptionally smart man with a mind that was a sponge for learning. He read voraciously, not just the theological tomes and treatises that were required reading, but books of history, philosophy, poetry, and literature.

He exhibited leadership and maturity that was far beyond anyone else in the school and, being exceptionally perceptive, could relate quickly to others. Ded could see through any defensive subterfuge they might erect, which would let him get to the core of what might be bothering them. And because of this, Ded became somewhat of a father confessor and counselor for the other seminarians and for the faculty as well.

Then, on the very day before his class was to graduate, Ded, who was now three years sober, was asked by Bishop Chris Coats, the dean of studies, to come meet with him. Unlike the small and cramped faculty offices, the bishop's office was roomy and pleasant, with polished wooden floors and a huge, mahogany desk. Large oval photographs of bishops and previous heads of the college were hanging by suspension wires from a picture rail that was just under the ceiling. The most prominent photograph was one of Bishop Leonidas Polk, who was one of the original founders of the school.

Bishop Coats poured two cups of coffee and handed one cup to Ded. He saw Ded looking at the bishop-general's photograph.

"You knew Bishop Polk, didn't you, Mr. Axton?"

"I didn't know him as a bishop, but I did know him as a general," Ded said. "I served with the general, very early in the war."

He could have added, but didn't, that Axton's Texas Raiders was the direct result of an idea proposed by Bishop-General Polk.

Bishop Coats took a swallow of his coffee and studied Ded over the rim of his cup.

"You were quite . . . active . . . in the war, weren't you?"

"Yes."

"And even after the war. I understand that the . . . Axton Raiders . . . continued to operate."

"Yes, but without me," Ded said.

"You are the one who stopped them?"

"Yes."

"Did you betray the others to save yourself from prison?"

"No, Bishop. I stopped the others to save my soul from eternal damnation."

Bishop Coats nodded. "Very good answer," he said. "I have to tell you, Mr. Axton, that the staff and faculty are split right down the middle as to whether or not you should be ordained. Half of them are adamantly in favor of your ordination. But the other half—because of your, shall we say, rather colorful background—are just as adamantly opposed. Tell me, Mr. Axton, how many men did you kill during the war?"

"I don't know, I didn't keep count."

"But you have killed."

"Yes."

"And you have stolen?"

"Only as part of a military mission, but yes, I have stolen."

"Have you been with women? And by this I mean in a carnal way."

This conversation was getting very difficult, and

Ded considered just getting up and leaving. Then he decided that he would stay and follow this to the end.

"Yes, Bishop, I have."

"So you have killed, you have robbed, and you have committed the sin of fornication."

"I have also lied, taken the Lord's name in vain, and worked on Sunday," Ded said. "I think I'm all right with the other four. I was a drunk, too, but that one isn't in there."

Ded's response was perhaps a bit sharper than he had intended, but he had to admit that the bishop's inquisition was beginning to get to him.

"You can see, can you not, why some might have reservations about you becoming an Episcopal priest?"

"Bishop, from the moment I arrived, I've never tried to hide my background," Ded said.

"No, you haven't. But this has put me in quite a dilemma. You see, with the faculty split right down the middle, that means that the final decision as to whether or not you shall be ordained is mine."

Ded didn't say anything. He drank his coffee and looked directly at the bishop without blinking.

"What do you think I should do, Mr. Axton?"

"As you said, Bishop, the decision is yours to make, not mine," Ded said.

The bishop chuckled. "I must say, you aren't helping me that much."

Ded didn't respond.

"Would you not feel it a waste of your time having come here if, at the end of your studies, you weren't ordained?"

"No."

"No? Are you saying that, after having completed your studies, that if you are not ordained, you wouldn't consider your being here a waste of time? That seems like a strange thing to say."

"Not at all. Whether I am ordained or not has nothing to do with the reason for my coming here."

The bishop looked genuinely surprised. "Then why did you come here?"

"I believe I was called. It was in my power to answer that call and I did. Whether I am ordained or not is not in my power."

"You believe you were called."

"Yes, Bishop."

"You are familiar with our Lord's words in Matthew 22:14, are you not?"

"'Many are called but few are chosen,'" Ded replied.

"Yes," Bishop Coats said. He set his cup down on the desk. "I must tell you, Mr. Axton, I haven't made up my mind yet, and nothing you have said here today has helped me form an opinion one way or the other. I'm going to have to sleep on it and pray on it. If you are indeed chosen, you will know by graduation tomorrow."

"All right," Ded said, without exhibiting the slightest bit of anxiety or concern.

★　★　★

The next morning Ded went to the graduation ceremony, where he and forty-seven other graduates were to be given their diplomas and degrees. Then the head of the theology department, himself a priest, stood, facing Bishop Coats.

"Reverend Father in God, I present unto you these persons present, to be admitted to the Order of Priesthood. I have inquired concerning them, and also examined them, and think them so to be qualified."

"Then these are those whom we purpose, God willing, to receive this day into the holy office of priesthood," the bishop replied.

"Reverend Father, the first to be presented is Ded Axton."

Ded was the first in his class not only alphabetically but academically. When his name was called he looked toward Bishop Coats, who, with a slight smile and a small dip of his head, acknowledged that he had made his decision.

Ded moved down to the altar rail and knelt before the bishop, who put his hands on the head of the priest-to-be.

"Take thou authority to preach the Word of God, and to minister the holy Sacraments in the Congregation, where thou shall be lawfully appointed thereunto."

After leaving Sewanee, Ded returned to Texas, where, for the first two years of his ministry, he was a supply priest. It was now almost five years since he had nearly died in the snowstorm in the Davis Mountains, and he had been stone-cold sober since that time. After two years of wandering around from parish to parish, he was called by the Holy Spirit Episcopal Church in Estacado, Texas.

Because Ded had been a supply priest, he was used to traveling by horse, so he rode into Estacado, arriving the day before he was expected. Part of the "package" offered by the church was the rectory, a two-story, three-bedroom house that was next door to the church. He considered the house much too large and too extravagant for a bachelor priest, but, he reasoned, he had to live somewhere, and since the church already owned the rectory, it would be foolish to turn it down.

When he stopped in front of the house, he saw that the front door was ajar; so, tying his horse to the hitching rail, he took down his bag, walked up to the house, pushed the door open, and stepped inside.

There was a woman on her hands and knees. Beside her was a bucket of water, and she was scrubbing the brick hearth. She was wearing clothes that were obviously to be worn only for such labor, and her cap served no other purpose than to help keep her hair back. Despite her disheveled appearance, Ded could easily see that she was an exceptionally pretty woman. Because of the scraping sound the brush was making on the bricks, she hadn't heard Ded come in.

Ded set his bag down on the floor beside him and,

crossing his arms across his chest, leaned back against the wall to watch her work.

The woman on the floor turned to dip her brush in the bucket again and, on seeing Ded, emitted a little startled cry.

"I'm sorry, I should have said something, but I didn't want to startle you. Evidently I did anyway," Ded said.

Noting Ded's clerical collar, the woman smiled and pushed back an errant string of blond hair.

"Father, we weren't expecting you until tomorrow. I wanted to have this all cleaned up for you."

Ded looked around the house. "You've done a good job. It already looks spotless to me."

"Miss Pendrake, do you know whose horse that is tied up out front?" a man coming in through the front door at that moment asked. When he saw Ded, he paused. "Father Axton?"

"Yes. I know I wasn't due until tomorrow, but I'm anxious to get started."

The man smiled and stuck out his hand. "I'm Carl Byrd, the senior warden."

"And this young lady?" Ded asked.

"This is Mary Pendrake. She is the local schoolteacher and, I'm glad to say, a very active member of our parish. As long as you are here, would you like to step next door with me and see the church?"

"Yes, thank you, I would."

"I'll hurry up and try to be gone before you return," Mary said.

Ded held his hand out. "Please, Miss Pendrake, don't hurry on my account."

For the next half hour Byrd showed Ded the church, explaining the idiosyncrasies of the furnace, which windows could be raised, and which ones couldn't because they were stuck.

"As you can see, we are absolutely going to have to replace some of the windows." He opened a door and held his hand out. "Here is the sacristy, and on the other side"—Byrd led Ded through the little room where there were stored vestments, hangings, and altar linens—"is the priest's office."

Ded went inside and, at Byrd's invitation, sat behind his desk.

"You don't recognize me, do you, Father?" Byrd said.

Ded felt a sudden sense of apprehension. Had he caused this man some harm in his past?

"I'm afraid I don't," Ded said cautiously.

"I was one of the soldiers with you the morning we stopped Nate Walker and his raiders from robbing the bank in Allenton."

"Oh," Ded said. He smiled. "Forgive me for not recognizing you, but it's good to see you again."

Byrd chuckled, and patted his stomach. "No reason why you *should* recognize me. I've put on quite a bit of weight since then. By the way, I'm glad all those stories about you betraying Nate and the others have died out. I want you to know that I have done my best to kill them."

"I appreciate that very much, Mr. Byrd."

Byrd smiled. "I have to tell you though, Father, I know about your war record, and you may be about the last person in the world I ever thought would become a priest."

Ded returned his smile. "You know what, Mr. Byrd? I agree with you. Now, let me ask you something. The young lady I just met. I did hear you call her *Miss* Pendrake, didn't I?"

Now Byrd laughed out loud. "Funny you asked me that. When she learned that we were getting a new priest, she asked the same thing about you. Yes, she is unmarried."

HOLY SPIRIT EPISCOPAL CHURCH MAKES CHRISTMAS PLANS

Father Ded Axton, pastor of Holy Spirit, has announced special Christmas plans. At 11:00 o'clock on Christmas Eve, there will be given a cantata of Christmas music and recitations, under the direction of Miss Mary Pendrake. Miss Pendrake and her young grammar-school-age pupils have been working faithfully for the last three weeks and an interesting entertainment is promised. It is hoped there will be a large crowd for the exercises.

All the children of the church are asked to bring their gifts for the poor at this time. Each class in each department has been asked to bring a certain article. These donations that are brought will be used in making up baskets that evening to be distributed among the needy families on Christmas Day.

After the service, which was one of lessons and carols, Mary waited outside the church as the congregation filed out. Ded was standing in the doorway, greeting the parishioners individually as they departed, wishing them a Merry Christmas and offering complimentary comments to the parents and grandparents of the children who took part in the service. When he was congratulated for the program, he was quick in every instance to credit Mary, who not only came up with the idea of the participation of the children but who had worked with them to get them ready.

When the last parishioner had left, Ded closed the door and smiled at Mary, who had been standing on the bottom step, receiving and giving compliments as well.

"It is such a beautiful night . . . would you like to take a walk?"

"I would love to," Mary said.

"You don't think it's too cold tonight?"

"No, it's Christmas Eve. It's against the law to be too cold on Christmas Eve."

Ded chuckled. "I'm not aware of any such law, but I'll take your word for it." He offered his arm, and Mary took it as they began strolling down the street.

"Well, maybe it's not really a law. It's more of a city ordinance," Mary teased.

"Look," Ded said, pointing to several houses. "See how a light has been placed in the middle window? That's an old European custom. The candles are supposed to light the way for the Christ Child."

They continued to walk until they reached downtown, where streetlamps made golden puddles of light at each corner. All the stores were closed except for the apothecary, where the druggist was preparing a potion for someone who had become ill.

"It's such a lovely night," Mary said. "It's a shame more folks aren't out to enjoy it."

"No doubt everyone is inside stoking their stoves," Ded said.

"And looking out at us, wondering why we are so foolish as to be out in the cold," Mary replied.

"Well, I have a perfectly good reason for being out," Ded said.

"I know. You are walking me home."

"No, I have a better reason than that."

"And just what would that reason be?" Mary asked with a little laugh.

"Well, my reason for being out here is to ask you to marry me," Ded said, speaking the words so routinely that Mary wasn't even sure she had heard them.

"What?" she asked, barely able to respond.

Ded was already holding Mary's hand, and he lifted it to his lips and kissed it.

"Miss Pendrake, would you do me the honor of becoming Mrs. Axton?"

"Yes," Mary replied with a huge smile. "Yes, I will."

One month later, Ded and Mary Pendrake were married. Eleven months later, Mary presented Ded with a son.

CHAPTER SEVEN

★

The Huntsville Penitentiary was the only prison in the eleven Confederate states still standing at the end of the Civil War, and the increase in lawlessness that accompanied the end of the war resulted in more people than ever before being sent to prison. That also caused the prisons to be overcrowded, so on this day, fifteen years after they were incarcerated and five years before the completion of their twenty-year sentences, prisoners Walker, Petrie, Filbert, Blackman, Colby, and Loomis were released from prison.

The men were issued civilian clothes, given a twenty-dollar bill apiece, and escorted to the front gate.

"Now, you men try to stay out of trouble," the guard who had escorted them to the gate said. "I don't want to see you back here again."

"You aren't likely to," Nate said.

"Open the gate," the guard said.

"What do we do now?" Petrie asked.

"After we get a beer, you mean?" Colby asked.

"Yeah, after we get a beer."

"We take care of some business," Nate said.

MAY 15, 1881
DOUBLETREE RANCH,
VAL VERDE COUNTY, TEXAS

"You're sure they let you out, now. I mean, you didn't escape or anything, did you?" Dagan Walker asked.

"What's the matter, Dagan? After all these years, are you trying to tell me you aren't happy to see your big brother again?" Nate Walker asked.

"Well, yes, of course I'm happy," Dagan said. "It's just that I don't want to see you in any more trouble by breaking the law, is all."

"You needn't concern yourself. We were legally discharged. Besides, who are you to question me about breaking the law? Where do you think the money came from to pay the taxes on this place after the war? How do you think Pa held on to Doubletree, while the Axtons weren't able to hang on to Twin Hills?"

"Well, I . . . I don't know. Pa never said."

"It came from me, that's where it came from. Money that I managed to divert from Yankee coffers. So legally, or perhaps illegally," he added with a grin, "this ranch is mine."

"I . . ." Dagan started to say something, but he was so stunned by the unexpected comment that he couldn't speak.

Nate laughed and put his hand out to touch his brother on his shoulder. "Don't worry, little brother. I'm not about to throw you, my sister-in-law, and my nephews out. In fact, I am willing to sign a quitclaim deed transferring any interest I have in this place over to you. All I want for it is six horses and tack."

Dagan smiled. "That's all you want? That's easy, I've got plenty of horses!"

"That's all I want."

JUNE 5, 1881
ESTACADO, TEXAS

Nate Walker, Logan Petrie, Moe Filbert, Asa Blackman, Carl Colby, and Todd Loomis had spent the previous night just outside Estacado and, at the moment, gathered around the campfire. Nate Walker held a branch in the fire until it flamed, then he held the flame to the end of the cigarette he had just rolled.

"Fifteen years," he said. "Fifteen years in the stinking pen because of that son of a bitch. And to think that he was once my closest friend."

"Hell, he was a friend to all of us," one of the others said. "Leastwise, I had always thought he was a friend.

But now, thinking about this day is the only thing that's kept me going for the whole fifteen years."

"When are we going to do it?" another asked.

"As soon as I take a leak," Nate said, unbuttoning his pants.

"Ha! I wonder if the son of a bitch knows he's just one piss away from perdition," someone said, and the others laughed.

Buttoning up his pants, Nate Walker pulled his pistol, opened the cylinder gate, and checked his loads.

"Everyone be sure and check your guns, make absolutely certain they are loaded," Nate said.

"Hell, you act like there ain't none of us ever held a gun before," Petrie said.

"It's been a while," Nate said.

"Yeah, fifteen years," Blackman said.

"If I hadn't held a gun in fifty years, I could do what we're goin' to do today," Colby said. "I've been lookin' forward to this from the time they put us in the pen."

"All right," Nate said, picking up his saddle and carrying it over to his horse. "Saddle up and let's go."

Fifteen minutes later, the six men rode up to the front of the Holy Spirit Episcopal Church. There were horses, wagons, buckboards, surreys, and buggies parked out front, the horses all waiting stoically.

"You sure this is the right one?" Petrie asked.

"Yeah, I'm sure," Nate said. He pointed. "Take a look at the damn sign. What does it say?"

HOLY SPIRIT EPISCOPAL CHURCH
Services at 9:00 o'clock Every Sunday Morning
Fr. Ded Axton, Rector

Dismounting, the six men started toward the red front doors of the church. Through the open windows they could hear a hymn being sung.

And make within our souls thy home;
Supply thy grace and heavenly aid
To fill the heart which . . .

Nate pulled his pistol, then looked at the others.

"We'll go in shooting," he said.

The others pulled their pistols as well, and when all were ready, Nate kicked open the door and the six men rushed in with their six guns blazing. Men shouted and women screamed, and Nate saw people going down under the onslaught.

Nate saw the look of shock on Ded's face at the totally unexpected intrusion. Logan Petrie rushed down to the front of the church, and just as Nate drew a bead on Ded, he leaped over the altar rail onto Petrie. Both went down, and Nate saw Ded grab Petrie's gun and shoot him. Next he shot Filbert and then Blackman. It wasn't until then that Nate was able to get another bead on Ded and, taking his shot, had the satisfaction of seeing Nate go down.

Of the six who had burst into the church, only Nate, Carl Colby, and Ted Loomis were still standing.

"Colby, Loomis, let's go!" he shouted.

Nate stood at the door as Colby and Loomis bolted by to get outside. He took one last look at the carnage they had caused. Men and women were on their knees around their dead and wounded. With Ded down, nobody else in the church represented a threat.

Once outside, Nate, Colby, and Loomis started splashing kerosene on the front porch. Nate struck a match and held it to the kerosene-soaked wood. Flames erupted. The men hurried back to their horses, then spurred them into a gallop. Nate could still hear the screams of the women and the angry shouts of the men as they rode away.

JUNE 22, 1881
DOUBLETREE RANCH, VAL VERDE COUNTY, TEXAS

After leaving the jail, with Asa Blackman trussed up on his bunk and an empty shotgun pointed at him, Ded rode out of town to begin his quest to find Nate Walker. Blackman had begged, pleaded, and cried, telling him he didn't know where Nate Walker was. Eventually Ded believed him, because Asa wet and soiled his pants. But Asa was able to tell him where Loomis, Colby, and the other two men who attacked the church could be found.

"Colby is from Belknap," Asa said, "so I know that's where he went back to. And Loomis, he goes ever'where Colby goes."

For the moment, but just for the moment, Loomis and Colby could keep. Right now he was most interested in finding Nate Walker, and the only place he knew to look was at Nate's old home.

Ded rode along an old and familiar trail. He came to a Y in the road. One arm of the Y went toward what had been the Twin Hills Ranch. The arched gateway that had once been over the road to Twin Hills was gone, but he rode up the road anyway. The cluster of buildings that had once made up his old homestead, the house, the barn, the granary, the machine shed, even the outdoor toilet, were all gone. The only thing remaining to show that there had ever been anyone living there was the circle of stones that showed where the well had once been. Dismounting, Ded looked down into the well, but it had caved in.

He walked over to the little family burial plot. There were three graves there: his mother's, his father's, and that of a sister who had died in infancy, even before Ded was born. The grave of his dog Rex was there as well. This was the first time Ded had been back since right after the war, and he felt a sense of guilt because of it.

"Ma, Pa, I'm sorry I haven't been here to see you before now," he said aloud. "But my life hasn't exactly gone as I had planned. And the land doesn't belong to me anymore anyway, so I . . . well . . . I'm sorry," he said again. He took another look around, then he saw a tree and remembered that he had carved something in it. Walking over to it, he saw that, despite the growth of the bark, the two sets of initials that had been carved there long ago were still there. "DA" and, a little farther down on the tree, "NW."

"Your initials are easier to carve than mine," Ded had told Nate. They were ten years old at the time.

"Huh-uh."

"Yes they are. All you have to do is carve a lot of straight lines. I have to make a curve to make the *D*."

"You could make it square," Nate proposed.

"No, then it would look like a box."

Remounting, Ded rode back up this side of the Y, then passed under the arch that stretched over the other arm of the Y:

DOUBLETREE, Dagan Walker, Proprietor.

When Ded rode up to the ranch house, he saw a woman hanging up clothes. Two young boys were playing nearby. The woman shielded her eyes against the sun as Ded arrived.

"Can I help you, sir?" she asked.

"I thought maybe I could water my horse and speak with Dagan if he is around."

"You know my husband?"

"Yes, ma'am, I've known him since he was born."

"Water your horse, then, get on out of here," a man

called from the porch. He stepped down from the porch and started toward Ded, holding a rifle pointed toward him.

"That's not a very friendly welcome for an old neighbor," Ded said, dismounting and leading his horse over to the watering trough.

"What do you want here?"

"I'm looking for Nate."

"I haven't seen him but once since he got out of prison," Dagan said. "Prison that you put him in."

"I suppose I did," Ded said. "At the time, it seemed the thing to do. I figured it would stop him from getting into any more serious trouble than he was already in."

"Yeah? Well, fifteen years in prison seems pretty serious to me. What do you want with him, anyway? I'm pretty sure he doesn't want to see you."

"Oh, I'm pretty sure he doesn't want to see me, either," Ded said. "Especially since he killed my wife and child."

Ded was looking directly at Dagan when he said that, and by the shocked expression on Dagan's face he knew that Dagan was unaware of what Nate had done.

Dagan lowered the rifle and pinched the bridge of his nose. "Oh, my God," he said. "Nate did that?"

"I'm sorry to say that he did."

"But how? Where? Why?"

"I don't know if you were aware, but I had become an Episcopal priest. I had a nice little church in Estacado. I had a wife and a son. On Pentecostal Sunday, Nate and five others broke into my church and started shooting. They killed Mary, Davy, and seven of my parishioners as well. Nine in all."

"Oh, Ded, oh, I'm . . . I'm so sorry," Dagan said. "I had no idea."

"Now perhaps you know why I'm looking for him."

"Yes, I can understand why. But I have no idea where he is. I truly don't know. And I doubt, seriously, if he will ever come back here again."

"Won't you stay and take dinner with us?" Dagan's wife asked.

"Thank you, no," Ded replied. He reached out to put his hand on Dagan's shoulder. Dagan's head was still lowered, and now his hand covered his eyes. "I think my staying would be too awkward and uncomfortable for all of us. I thank you kindly for the water."

Remounting, Ded rode away.

CHAPTER EIGHT

★

If anyone from Estacado had seen Ded today, they likely would not have recognized him. He still had the same chiseled face, the gray eyes, and that lightning streak of a scar. But the clerical collar was gone. So, too, was the black shirtfront, jacket, and low crowned hat. He was wearing denim trousers and a white cotton shirt. He was also wearing a Colt .44 pistol in a tooled holster, hanging low on his right side.

The first place Ded went to when he arrived in Belknap was the mortuary. There he dismounted and went inside to talk to the undertaker.

"Yes, sir, what can I do for you?" the undertaker asked in well-practiced dulcet tones.

"I shall require two coffins," Ded said.

"Oh, my, I am so sorry for your bereavement. Would these be for adults or children?"

"Adults."

"How soon will you need them?"

"As quickly as possible," Ded said.

"Yes, sir. And the interment, sir, will I be handling that as well?"

"Yes."

"Very good, sir. Well, you are in luck, because I already have two coffins ready. They are quite beautiful, black wood, trimmed in silver, with red felt lining. They are called the Eternal Cloud, and they are guaranteed to preserve the body for five hundred years."

"Is that so? Tell me, if I find that the bodies have deteriorated five hundred years from now, who do I see to get my money back?"

"Oh, heavens, sir, I . . ." The undertaker blinked a few times. "I understand, sir, you are teasing."

"All I want are two simple pine boxes. Can you do that for me?"

"Yes, sir. I'll have them ready by four o'clock this afternoon."

"Thank you."

Leaving the undertaker's office, Ded arranged to have a sign painted. The painter was a little hesitant at first, but Ded paid in advance.

Then, at four o'clock that afternoon, Ded picked up the two empty pine coffins and placed them in the middle of the town plaza, along with the sign.

THESE COFFINS ARE RESERVED FOR CARL COLBY AND TODD LOOMIS

As Ded knew it would, the coffins and signs drew a crowd. They also drew the two men Ded was looking for.

"What the hell . . . Who did this?" Colby shouted

in anger. "I want to know who the hell put these coffins and this sign here!"

"I put them there, Colby," Ded said, stepping out into the open from a narrow passageway that separated two of the buildings that fronted the street.

The others in the crowd, realizing that a showdown was about to take place, scattered away from the two coffins but stayed close enough to be able to watch the drama play out before them.

"Ded Axton! We thought you was dead!"

"Did you, now?"

"Look, Cap'n, we didn't find out until later that your wife and boy was kilt," Loomis said.

"Whether or not you knew that my wife and child were among those you killed doesn't matter. You killed nine people that day. The sin is no less."

"Sin? Ha!" Colby said. "What do you mean sin? What are you going to do, preacher man? Save our souls?"

"No," Ded answered. "I'm about to lose my soul, so why should I give a damn about yours?"

"You know, Loomis, I believe the cap'n wants to fight," Colby said with a broad grin.

"We don't have to fight," Ded said. "You can come with me down to the marshal's office, confess your sins, and I'll donate these coffins to the county so they'll have them available for you after you both hang."

"That ain't really what you want, though, is it?" Loomis asked. He pointed to the two coffins. "I mean, if that's really what you wanted, you wouldn'ta put them two coffins out here in the first place. You're wantin' to kill us your own self, ain't you?"

"You are a most perceptive man, Loomis. Yes. What I really want is for the two of you to draw on me so I can legally kill you."

"They's two of us agin' you, Cap'n," Colby said. "And bein' as you've been preachin' for some seven years or so, you like as not ain't as good with a gun as you oncet was."

"That might be true," Ded said. "I mean, a gunman priest? That sounds rather like an oxymoron, doesn't it?"

Colby grinned. "Yeah, it does sort of make you out to be a moron at that. Let me ask you a question, Cap'n. What are we to do with the extra coffin once we kill you?"

"Oh, I don't think there will be an extra coffin. Even if you get me, I'm pretty sure I'll get one of you." Ded stretched his lips into what could be called a smile. "Of course, the question is, which one of you will I kill?"

"Enough talkin'!" Loomis shouted, and he and Colby went for their guns.

The three pistols fired as one. Four shots were fired, two missed, and two found their marks.

As the smoke drifted away, it left Ded standing and Loomis and Colby sprawled out in the street. Still holding his pistol, Ded walked over to look down at the two men. He pointed his pistol at Colby and cocked it, but, seeing that he was dead, he eased the hammer back down and put the pistol back in his holster.

The gunfight had been witnessed by at least one hundred people, and for a long moment afterward there was nothing but stunned silence. Then someone broke the quiet.

"That's the damnedest thing I ever seen!"

That opened the floodgate as everyone ran back into the street from the safe places they had found to observe the gunfight from.

"What's your name, mister?" someone asked.

Ded didn't answer.

"His name is Axton. Ded Axton," one of the others said. "Leastwise, that's what Colby called 'im. That right, mister?"

"Make way! Make way! Let me through!" The loud, and authoritative voice could be heard above all others, and the crowd, responding to the orders, parted.

A middle-aged man with white hair, a hooked nose, and a star on his chest came up to look down at the two bodies.

"What happened here?"

Several started talking at once, until finally the lawman had the full story.

"Are you Father Axton?" the lawman said, walking over to talk to Ded, who hadn't left the scene but had been standing apart from the others.

"I'm Ded Axton."

"I'm Marshal Kincaid. I heard what happened to your wife and son, and to some of the others in your church."

"Are there going to be any charges?"

"Charges? No. Everyone here is willing to swear that they drew first. But even if they didn't, there's already a reward out for 'em, dead or alive. Fact is, if you'll stick around town for a couple of days, you've got a reward comin' to you."

Ded had been unaware of any reward; he had hunted Colby and Loomis down for his own satisfaction. But he no longer had a church, and he had to make a living, so he decided it would be foolish to turn it down.

"I'll wait," Ded said.

Later that same day, Ded walked down to the mortuary. The bodies of Colby and Loomis were lying in the two coffins he had bought. They were still wearing the clothes they had been wearing when they died, but the mortician had washed their faces and combed their hair. Both men were lying with their arms folded across their chests.

The mortician looked up when Ded came in.

"Yes, sir, what can I do for you?"

"I wonder if I could have a moment alone with Mr. Colby and Mr. Loomis."

"I don't know," the mortician said, the expression on his face showing both surprise that the man who had killed them showed up, and some concern as to what he might do.

"Don't worry, I have no intention of doing anything untoward with the bodies."

"You have no intention of doing what?"

"Please, allow me just a moment," Ded said.

The mortician looked at him for a moment longer, then he nodded and left the room. Ded stepped up to the foot of the two coffins, took his stole from his pocket, draped it around his neck, and held out his hand to make the sign of the cross.

"'To us who are alive, may He grant forgiveness, and to all who have died, a place of light and peace. Amen.'"

Two days later, Ded was in the marshal's office, receiving his reward money. The reward was five hundred dollars for each of the two men, and as Ded accepted the one thousand dollars, he was aware that it was almost as much as an entire year's salary had been from the church he had just left.

"What are you going to do now?" Kincaid asked. "I mean, from what I've heard, you don't have a church to go back to, seein' as they burnt it to the ground."

Ded glanced over toward the wall, where he saw at least a dozen wanted posters prominently displayed. He walked over to look at them and note the reward on each of them. Looking back toward Marshal Kincaid, he pointed to the posters.

"Am I to understand that anyone can bring these men in? That you don't have to be an officer of the law? And if they are brought in, that these rewards will be paid?"

"That's true," Marshal Kincaid said. "That's what bounty hunters do."

Ded looked at them a bit longer. The rewards ranged from five hundred to five thousand dollars.

"Are there people who actually do this for a living? Hunt down wanted men, I mean."

"Oh, yes," the marshal replied. "Some folks call them regulators. They are people who hunt down wanted outlaws and bring them in for the reward, dead or alive. At least, the ones for whom the rewards will be paid, dead or alive."

"It seems to me like you wouldn't have to bring in very many to earn a living," Ded suggested.

"Father, are you sure you want to get yourself involved with something like that? I have to tell you that most of the people on the wanted posters are brought in dead. Whether they resisted the bounty hunters or the bounty hunters just decided it would be easier to bring them in that way, we never know. If the reward poster says 'Dead or Alive,' then it really doesn't matter."

"Marshal Kincaid, that's the second time you've called me 'Father.' Please don't do so again," he said.

Kincaid studied Ded for a moment, then nodded.

"Decided to go into the bounty-hunting business, have you?"

"Are you saying I shouldn't?"

"It ain't my place to say. Does seem a little strange to me, though—I mean, for a man to go from saving souls to doin' somethin' like this."

"Marshal, if I were to preach today, I fear I wouldn't be saving souls, I would be putting them in jeopardy."

"All right, Axton, if you say so," Kincaid said. "I've got some extra dodgers over here in my desk if you want 'em."

"Yes, thank you."

CHAPTER NINE

★

Ded dismounted in front of the Brown Dirt Cowboy Saloon, made a halfhearted attempt to brush away some of the trail dust, then stepped up onto the porch and pushed through the batwing doors. After two years of bounty hunting, Ded had developed a certain routine when entering a saloon, and he followed that routine now. As soon as he pushed through the swinging doors, he would step to one side so that his back was against the wall, then he would peruse the room.

What he saw was a long bar on the left, with dirty towels hanging on hooks about every five feet along its front. A large mirror was behind the bar, but like everything else about the saloon it was so dirty that it was hard to see anything in it, and what he could see was distorted by imperfections in the glass. Over against the back wall, near the foot of the stairs, a cigar-scarred, beer-stained upright piano was being played by a cigar-chomping musician with one of the bar girls standing alongside, swaying to the music.

Out on the floor of the saloon, nearly all the tables were filled. A few card games were in progress, but most of the patrons were just drinking and talking.

"Yes, sir, what will it be?" the bartender asked.

"Seltzer water."

"What do you want with it?"

"I don't want anything with it. Just seltzer water."

"Mister, it'll cost you the same thing without whiskey or gin as it will with whiskey or gin."

"I know."

The bartender shrugged his shoulders, poured a glass of seltzer water, and slid it across the bar to him. Ded had taken an oath never to drink again, and though he had broken just about every other oath he had ever taken, he was determined not to break this one. In this case, the oath wasn't a moral issue; it was an issue with consequences far beyond any of the oaths he had broken.

Even though Ded no longer drank, he still frequented saloons, because a saloon was always the repository of information about the local scene. He often picked up information on someone he was looking for either by involving the patrons in casual conversation—he never asked a direct question—or sometimes by actually finding the subject in the bar, trying to stay out of sight.

Suddenly a knife flashed by in front of him, burying itself about half an inch into the bar with a *thock* sound. The impact of the knife left the handle vibrating back and forth.

Instantly, Ded drew his pistol and turned toward the direction from which the knife had come. He saw a man getting up from a table with a gun in his hand, but when that man saw how quickly Ded had drawn, he held his hands up, letting the pistol dangle from its trigger guard.

"No, no, don't shoot, Axton! Don't shoot!"

"Why not? You tried to kill me, didn't you?"

"How did you find me? I know damn well I covered my trail, how the hell did you find me?"

Ded didn't answer the man's question, because he had no idea who this man was.

The man turned the pistol around so that the butt was pointing toward Ded. "All right, I'm givin' up."

"That's a smart move," Ded said. "Who are you, anyway?" he asked.

"What? You mean you don't even know who I am? How did you track me here if you don't even know who I am?"

Ded chuckled. "I didn't track you. I just came in here, and here you were."

"The name is Sparrow, Clem Sparrow. Have you ever heard of me?"

"Yes, I've heard of you."

Sparrow smiled. "Damn, Death's Acolyte has heard of me. I must be doin' pretty good."

"I don't like that name," Ded said.

Until now, everyone in the bar had been looking on in fascinated silence. They had assumed that this was an ordinary lawman who had just found his quarry. But when Sparrow said the name "Death's Acolyte," they realized they were in the presence of a bounty hunter who had, within the last two years, blazed a deadly reputation across the entire state of Texas.

"Death's Acolyte," someone in the bar said. "Did you hear that? This here is Death's Acolyte." That was followed by a buzz of excitement as everyone strained to get a close look at the man who had earned such a reputation.

"All right, Sparrow," Ded said. "Come with me to the sheriff's office. I can get a receipt for you, and you can get a free meal."

"That'll be somethin' new for you, won't it? Turnin' in one of your prisoners while he's still alive?"

"They've all had their choice," Ded said.

"Yeah? Well, how about comin' over to take my gun. I don't want you shootin' me and usin' the excuse that I was still holdin' my gun."

Ded started toward Sparrow, but when he was halfway there, Sparrow executed a border roll, bringing the business end of the gun to bear on him. Ded, who had relaxed his own position to the point where he had actually let the hammer down on his pistol, and even lowered the gun, was caught by surprise. Now he had to raise the gun back into line while cocking it. And he was slowed by the fact that he first had to react to Sparrow's action.

The quiet room was suddenly shattered with the roar of two pistols snapping firing caps and exploding powder almost simultaneously. The bar patrons yelled and dived or scrambled for cover. White gun smoke billowed out in a cloud that filled the center of the room, momentarily obscuring everything.

As the smoke began to clear, Sparrow stared through the white cloud, smiling broadly at Ded. He opened his mouth as if to speak, but the only sound he could make was a gagging rattle way back in his throat. The smile left his face, his eyes glazed over, and he pitched forward, his gun clattering to the floor.

Ded stood ready to fire a second shot if needed, but a second shot wasn't necessary. He looked down at Sparrow for a moment, then holstered his pistol.

There were calls from outside, then the sound of people running. Several came into the saloon and stood under the rising cloud of smoke to stare in wonderment at the dead man on the floor. One of the new arrivals was a deputy sheriff.

"What happened here?" the deputy asked.

"That's Clem Sparrow," Ded said, pointing to the body, now lying facedown on the floor. "I think you'll find that he is a wanted man."

"I see," the deputy said. "And you'll be putting in a claim for the reward, no doubt." It wasn't a question, it was a matter-of-fact statement.

"No doubt."

"What's your name?"

"Axton. Ded Axton."

The deputy stroked his chin and studied Ded.

"I've heard of you," he said. "Folks seem to have a habit of dyin' around you, don't they?" He pointed to Sparrow's body. "How many does that make?"

"I offered him the opportunity of coming to see you. Apparently that wasn't the choice he wanted to make."

"Axton's right, Deputy, this here fella shot first. And before he shot at him, he threw that knife," the bartender said, pointing to the knife that was still protruding from the bar.

"How much is he worth?" the deputy asked.

"I'm not sure. I wasn't after him."

"You weren't after him?"

"No, I just happened to drop in to the saloon, and he introduced himself to me."

By now Tom Nunlee, the town mortician, had arrived. "Is this another county burial?" he asked.

"As far as I know, it will be," the deputy answered. He looked around the saloon. "Unless any of you know if Sparrow has kin here."

"He ain't got no kin that I know about," one of the patrons said.

"There you go, Tom. He'll be one of your twenty-dollar specials, I reckon."

"I reckon."

"Mr. Axton, I'll send a wire off to get what money you got comin' to you," the deputy said.

"I'm obliged," Ded said.

"Would a couple of you men help me load him onto my wagon out front?" Nunlee asked.

"I'll set up a free drink for anyone that does," the bartender said, and two men moved quickly to pick up Sparrow's body.

An hour later, Ded walked into the mortuary. Nunlee was sitting at his desk writing something and looked up when Ded came in.

"Every time it's a county buryin', I have to fill out half a dozen papers," Nunlee said. "What can I do for . . . wait a minute. You're the one that killed Sparrow, aren't you?"

"Yes."

"What are you doing down here? Come to make sure he's dead?"

"No. But I would like a moment alone with the decedent, if you wouldn't mind."

"You want a moment *alone* with the body?"

"Yes, if you don't mind."

Nunlee squinted his eyes. "I don't know about that," he said. "I'm responsible for the body now. I mean, not just to the county, I have an ethical responsibility."

"Indeed you do," Ded said. "And I assure you, I will do nothing that would cause you to be in violation of those ethics."

Nunlee drummed his fingers on his desk for a moment, then nodded. "All right. I trust you. I don't know why I trust you, but I do."

"Thank you."

Ded waited until Nunlee had left the mortuary, then

he walked over to the embalming table to look down at Sparrow. Taking his stole from his pocket, he draped it around his neck, raised his hand, and made the sign of the cross as he quietly intoned a blessing.

"'To us who are alive, may He grant forgiveness, and to all who have died, a place of light and peace.'"

Putting his stole back in his pocket he stood there for a moment longer, then turned and left the mortuary. Nunlee was standing out front. The way he was pointedly looking away from the building told Ded that Nunlee had been watching.

"Mr. Nunlee, I would appreciate it if we could just keep this between us," he said.

"Yes, sir," Nunlee agreed, making no effort to deny what he had seen.

MARCH 12, 1884

FORT WORTH

From the *Fort Worth Democrat*:

DEATH'S ACOLYTE

There are some names the mere mention of which will strike fear into the heart of the ordinary citizen. The gunmen Clay Allison, Luke Draco, John Wesley Hardin, and Ben Thompson are such names. But when it comes to the terrible effect with which one uses a pistol, no name surpasses that of Ded Axton.

Some of our readers who have a sense of history may remember that during the late War Between the States, Ded Axton commanded a band of raiders who, like the infamous Quantrill Raiders, operated outside the rules of conventional warfare. He is also known to have, at one time, been a man of the cloth, and because of that ecclesiastical background, coupled with the large number of men he is known to have killed, Axton has earned the sobriquet of Death's Acolyte.

Axton started on the gun trail three years previous, when six outlaws burst into his church in Estacado during a Sunday morning service. The outlaws began shooting, killing nine, including Axton's wife and child. It is said that Axton, using one of the outlaws' own guns, killed two that very morning. Soon after, he located and killed two more in the town of Belknap.

But it is what has happened since that time that has earned the reputation which now plagues this one-time Episcopal priest. He is known to have bested at least eight men in witnessed gunfights. In addition, he has brought in the bodies of six more wanted outlaws, the exact facts of their demise not known.

"Mister, do you really want to read that newspaper? Or would you rather talk to me?"

Nate Walker looked up at the woman who had

asked the question. She had put both hands on the table and was leaning forward, giving him a good look at her generous bosom.

"You don't really want to talk to me. You want me to drink with you, and that means that I buy the drinks."

The woman smiled. "That's how it works, honey."

"All right, get us a drink."

The woman ran her hand through Nate's hair, smiled, then walked over to the bar to get the two drinks. When she came back, he was looking at the newspaper again.

"Here's your drink," she said. "Tell me, what do you find so interesting in that newspaper?"

"I'm reading about an old friend of mine," Nate said.

"Really? Who?"

"Ded Axton."

The woman shuddered. "He's a killer. How can anyone be friends with a killer?"

"That's a good question."

"Let's not talk about him anymore," the woman said. "Let's talk about me." She flashed a big smile.

CHAPTER TEN

★

When the horse stepped into the prairie dog hole, his right foreleg gave way and Ded actually heard the bone snap. The horse went down and Ded had to jump clear from the saddle to keep from being trapped under the horse. That was an hour ago, and Ded was still sitting on the ground beside his horse, holding its head in his lap, rubbing the horse behind its ears.

"I'm sorry, old boy," Ded said. "You've been with me a long time, and you're the closest thing to a friend I have."

Ded leaned forward and put his forehead to the horse's head. He could hear the horse's labored breathing, and he could feel the horse shaking in fear.

Finally, with a sad sigh, Ded pulled his pistol and put the barrel against its forehead.

The horse looked up at him with its big, brown eyes, and it seemed to Ded that the horse knew what was about to happen. Was the horse telling him he understood? Or was he asking Ded not to do it? Ded pulled the trigger, and the horse shuddered once, then was still. He was thankful that it had been a quick kill.

Ded picked up his saddle and tack, threw it over his shoulder, and looked south. He knew he was north of the Southern Pacific Railroad, though he wasn't sure exactly how far north he was.

He started walking.

Four hours later he reached the railroad and dropped his saddle and gear alongside the tracks with a sigh of relief. Ded walked up the small grade to stand between the rails. Squinting his gray eyes and scratching at his scraggly beard, he peered eastward down the track. The Southern Pacific stretched from northeast to southwest, and the twin ribbons of iron were shining brightly in the late afternoon sun. He dropped to his knees and placed an ear to one of the rails, then smiled, for he could hear a faint humming that told him that a train was approaching. His timing had been almost perfect.

It was several moments more before the train appeared in the distance, and although it was approaching at better than thirty miles an hour, from where Ded stood the train appeared to be crawling. That distance also made the silhouette of the train look no larger than that of a caterpillar crawling on a stick. Even the smoke that poured from its stack was but a tiny wisp against the sky.

Ded continued to watch as the train drew nearer, close enough now that he could easily hear the puffing engine and see the steam escaping from around the drive wheels. Ded took a red shirt from his saddlebag, then stepped up to the track and started waving.

At first he thought perhaps the train wasn't going to stop, but then he heard the sound of the engine braking, so he picked up his saddle and gear. The train ground to a reluctant halt, puffing black smoke and emitting tendrils of white steam that shined orange in the light of what was now a setting sun. The engineer's face appeared in the window, while the fireman stepped out onto the platform between the locomotive and the tender. The door of the mail car slid open slightly, and Ded saw someone sneak a quick look through the narrow gap.

"What'd you stop us for?" the engineer asked.

"I lost my horse," Ded replied. "I need a ride into Sloan. I've got money to pay the fare."

"What the hell? You think this is a depot out here?" the fireman, who was a younger man, asked. "With what we're carryin', we can't go pickin' up every saddle bum we see."

"Jim Bob, don't be spoutin' off 'bout what we're carryin'," the older man said.

"Sorry," Jim Bob said contritely.

The older man stroked his beard. "Jim Bob's right about we got no business stoppin'," he said. "But I ain't one for leavin' a man stranded out in the middle of nowhere when I can help. Climb onto the first car behind the baggage car."

"Thanks," Ded said. He started toward the rear of the train, then climbed onto the first car behind the mail car. He was met, immediately, by the conductor.

"Mister, you think there's a depot here?"

"No," Ded said. "And I didn't think that when the fireman asked me, either."

"All right, if the engineer let you on, I'm not going to argue with him. But stoppin' out here in the middle of nowhere like he done wasn't very smart."

"Not smart, maybe, but it was a decent, humane gesture, and I'm grateful for it."

"Yeah, well, you never can tell when you stop like that, there could be a band of robbers waitin' just down off the berm," the conductor said.

"Especially if you're carrying a lot of money," Ded added.

The train started forward with a series of jerks, and Ded, who was standing on the vestibule with the conductor, had to spread his legs to keep his balance.

The conductor's eyes narrowed. "How'd you know about the money?"

Ded chuckled. "The fireman sort of dropped a hint."

"I may as well tell you since you've guessed anyhow. We're carrying ten thousand dollars to the bank in Sloan, and I'll sure feel better when we get shed of the money." He sighed. "All right, you're on now, so you may as well stay on. How far are you goin'?"

"I'm going to Sloan. And as I told the engineer, I'm willing to pay my fare."

"Yeah, well, like I said, there's no depot here, so I don't have any idea how much to charge you."

"What was the last town you went through?"

"Irwin."

"How much is it from Irwin to Sloan?"

"Two dollars."

"Then why don't we say that I got on in Irwin?" Ded suggested, giving the conductor two dollars.

"That'll work," the conductor replied. "You can leave your saddle and tack here on the vestibule if you like."

"Thanks," Ded said. He set his saddle down but picked up the saddlebags.

"You can leave your saddlebags too."

"Thanks, but my clothes and toilet articles are in here and I prefer to keep up with them."

Ded could have said, but didn't, that he also had over seven thousand in cash in his saddlebags, reward money for nearly three years of bounty hunting.

As Ded stepped into the car, the passengers looked up at him. He had been on the trail for two weeks, and he had walked for four hours this afternoon, so he was sweaty and dirty. His unkempt beard and the visible scar on his face gave him a menacing appearance. The glances he received from the other passengers weren't exactly welcoming, and Ded could see them leaning away from him as he walked down the aisle toward the rear of the car.

"Mamma, that man smells bad," one little girl said as Ded walked past.

"Carol, hush!" the little girl's mother said. The tone of her voice was more that of a frightened woman than of someone correcting an ill-mannered child.

Ded chose the last seat in the car. Those who were closest to him stood and pointedly moved farther up in the car, making the separation even more pronounced. Ded sat down, then pulled his legs up so that his knees were resting on the back of the seat in front of him. He draped his saddlebags across his lap, pulled his hat down over his eyes, and crossed his arms. The exhaustion of his long walk, coupled with the rhythmic motion and sounds of the train, soon put him to sleep.

Some distance ahead of the train was a water tower known as Tank No. 10. Some railroad maps also referred to it as "400 Mile Tank," because the railroad had water tanks located every forty miles. Marv Jensen was sitting on a rock next to Tank No. 10, eating cold beans from a can. Jensen was a man of medium height and size, with a pockmarked face and a drooping eye. He and three others were camped near Tank No. 10, and a few minutes earlier Bledsoe had climbed to the top of the tower and was now looking to the east.

"Them beans woulda been better if we heated 'em up," Ed Branchfield said.

"It's nighttime," Jensen said.

"What's that got to do with it?"

"You can see fire for a long way in the nighttime. If the train crew sees a fire, they're likely to get suspicious."

"So what? They got to stop for water anyway, don't they?"

"Hey, Jensen, I can see a light comin' way down the track," Bledsoe called down from the tank. "The train's a-comin'."

Jensen stuck the spoon down in his pocket and tossed the can of beans aside.

"All right, Bledsoe, come on down. Branchfield, McCoy, come over here. Let's go over again what we're goin' to do."

"Hell, Jensen, we done been over it a dozen times or more," McCoy said.

"We're goin' over it again," Jensen said. "When the train stops for water, we wait till the fireman comes out and pulls down the spout. Once he does that, they're stuck and the engineer can't do nothin'. We'll keep the fireman and the engineer covered while Branchfield puts a stick of dynamite on the door of the mail car. When it goes, me 'n' Johnston will be standin' here on the bottom part of the water tank. That will put us even with the open door and we'll jump into the mail car, get the money from the mail clerk, then clear out."

"The train's gettin' a lot closer," McCoy said. "We'd better get hid."

Ded didn't wake up when the train stopped for water, but he did wake up when he heard a heavy, stomach-jarring noise from the front of the train.

"What was that?" someone asked.

"Sounded like an explosion!"

One of the passengers went forward, stepped out onto the platform, then returned a moment later, his eyes open wide and shining in the light of the car lanterns.

"The train is being robbed!" he said excitedly. "They just blew the door off the mail car, and there are men on horses, holding guns."

"Will they come in here, do you suppose?" a woman asked in a frightened voice.

"I don't know whether they aim to or not, but I'm goin' to be hidin' my money," a man said.

The other passengers, following the speaker's example, began hiding their valuables. They were so distracted by what they were doing that none of them noticed Ded.

Ded got up, slowly and quietly, then eased out the back door. Once outside, he stayed in the dark shadows of the train and, ducking below the lighted windows, moved up to the rear of the baggage car. He stepped into the space between the two cars.

Pulling his pistol, he looked around the back corner of the baggage car to see what was going on.

"Bring the horses up!" someone shouted from inside the car. "We've got the money!"

Ded saw someone toss a money bag out from inside the car. He aimed at the robber who was waiting for it, then squeezed off a shot just as the money pouch hit the robber's hands.

The bullet plowed into the robber's chest and he was

knocked from his horse. He lay flat on his back with his arms flung out to either side. The money pouch lay on the ground beside him.

"Branchfield, get the money!" a voice shouted from inside the car. "Get the money pouch!"

There was only one rider outside the train now, and when he dismounted to pick up the money pouch, Ded fired again. He went down to join the first robber.

With the two outside men lying dead on the ground, Ded ran out from behind the car so he could look into the baggage car.

"Who's out there? Who's doin' the shootin'?" a voice called from inside the car. Ded stuck his pistol in his waistband at the small of his back. Then he picked up a pistol from one of the two men on the ground.

"You men in the car, come on out!" Ded called. "You're trapped in there. You have no place to go."

Two armed men stepped into the door. They were holding a third man with them.

"Throw your gun down, mister, and put your hands up," one of the two armed men said. "If you don't drop that gun now, I'll kill this man!"

Ded dropped his pistol.

"Bledsoe, hop down there and get the money, I'll keep you covered."

"All right," Bledsoe said. Jumping down, he picked up the money pouch, then mounted one of the horses and led a second one over to the open door of the baggage car.

"Jensen, come on, let's get out of here," Bledsoe said.

Jensen pushed the messenger back into the car, then got on his horse. While their attention was distracted, Ded reached behind his back and retrieved his pistol.

"Now let's shoot that son of a bitch!" Jensen said, and both he and Bledsoe pointed their pistols toward Ded.

They were shocked to see that he was holding a gun in his hand, pointing it toward them.

"Drop the guns!" Ded shouted.

"The hell we will!"

One of the men fired, and Ded could hear the bullet fly past his ear. He fired back twice, and both men fell from their horses.

Suddenly the messenger reappeared in the doorway, carrying a shotgun.

"Hold it! You won't be needing that!" Ded called. He walked over, picked up the money pouch, and threw it back into the open car.

"I think this belongs to you," he said.

CHAPTER ELEVEN

★

Sloan was like most towns along the network of railroads that covered the West in that the lifeline of the community was the railroad, its heartbeat the daily arrival and departure of the trains. Trains brought newspapers and goods from distant places, providing the small town with a real and visible link to the rest of the country. The arrival of a train always caused a large and enthusiastic gathering of the townspeople.

The Pacific Flyer was due to arrive at 11:30 p.m., and even at that late hour several of the town's citizens were beginning to gather at the depot, arriving half an hour before the train was due. The size of the crowd grew with each passing minute until there were two score and more on hand. Then came the high point of the evening, the arrival of the train. The whistle could be heard first, far off and mournful.

"Here she comes!" someone would shout, though no such announcement was ever necessary. The laughter and talking would stop as if everyone were consciously giving the approaching train the respect it was due for being the star attraction of the evening.

The first thing that came into view was the light, a huge, wavering yellow disk, the gas flame and mirror reflector shining brightly in the distance. That sighting was followed closely by the hollow sounds of puffing steam, then the glowing sparks whipped away in the black smoke clouds that billowed up into the night sky. Finally the engine came rushing by with white wisps of steam escaping from the thrusting piston rods, sparks flying from the pounding drive wheels, and glowing hot embers dripping from the firebox.

The yellow squares of light that were the windows of the passenger cars paraded by, slowing as the train finally ground to a halt with a shower of sparks, a hissing of air from the Westinghouse air brakes, and the sound of steel on steel.

Even after the train came to a complete halt, it wasn't quiet because the opening and closing of the relief valve vented steam with loud, gushing sighs, as if the train were a living thing. In addition, the overheated journals and bearings popped and snapped as the locomotive sat stationary but not silently in front of the depot.

"Look!" someone shouted, suddenly noticing. "Look at the door on the mail car! It looks like it's been blowed off!"

"What do you think happened?" another asked.

The express man came to stand in the open door of the mail car, his hand up on the twisted doorframe. There was a bandage wrapped around the top of his head.

"What happened, mister? What happened to you and your door?" someone from the depot platform yelled up at him.

The messenger didn't answer but instead turned and disappeared back inside the car.

The arriving passengers began to disembark and were met by family and friends. Very quickly after that, the stories they carried were repeated throughout the crowd, even among those who weren't meeting anyone.

"Did you hear? Someone tried to hold up the train!"

"Tried? You mean they didn't get away with it?"

"Nope. They was all four kilt."

"The messenger kilt them?"

"Nope. It was one of the passengers that shot 'em."

Sheriff Lindsay Duncan and his deputy, Harley Barnes, were pushing their way through the crowd toward the mail car.

"Get back," Harley was saying. "Get back, ever'body. Make way! Let me an' the sheriff through here!"

The mail clerk, hearing that the sheriff had arrived, climbed down from the train and walked over to him.

"What happened to you?" Sheriff Duncan asked, seeing the bandage.

"Someone tried to rob us, Sheriff," the mail clerk said.

"Did they get the money?" an overweight, middle-aged man asked, pushing through the crowd. This was Drew Clark, the banker.

"No sir, Mr. Clark," the messenger said, proudly. "The money pouch is safe."

"We got four bodies on board, Sheriff," the conductor said. "What do you want to do with 'em?"

"Four bodies?"

"It's the men who tried to rob the train."

"All right, get 'em out here and lay 'em on the platform," he said. "Let me take a look at 'em."

Soliciting help from a couple of men in the crowd, Harley soon had the four bodies taken from the express car and laid out on the wooden platform. Sheriff Duncan, leaning down and holding a lantern over their faces, examined each of them carefully. The crowd moved in for a closer look.

The sheriff straightened up, then looked up and down the platform. Most of those who had come to meet the train—as well as the passengers who had arrived and those who were still on the train—were now gathered around for a closer view of the grisly sight. The women were holding handkerchiefs over their noses, though it was more of a natural inclination than a necessity. The men were somewhat bolder, although Sheriff Duncan noticed that the expressions on the faces of more than a few of them showed that, like the women, they were a little put off by viewing bodies so recently killed.

"Hey, Sheriff, this here is Marv Jensen," Harley said.

"Yeah, but it's not just Jensen, it's his whole gang," Sheriff Duncan said. "That's McCoy there, Bledsoe, and Branchfield.

"You know what we're looking at here, Harley?" the sheriff asked.

"What?"

"We're lookin' at eight thousand dollars. Five for Jensen and a thousand apiece for the other three." Sheriff Duncan looked up at the conductor. "Did someone say one of the passengers shot these men?"

"Yes. *He* shot them," the conductor said, pointing toward Ded, who was standing off to one side, his saddle on the ground beside him.

"I'll be damned," Sheriff Duncan said. "Harley, you know who that is?"

"Who?"

"That's Ded Axton. He's about the best bounty hunter there is. That's why they call him Death's Acolyte."

The conductor pulled his watch from his pocket and checked the time.

"Sheriff, are you goin' to need me for anything? We're already runnin' behind."

"I reckon not. There were enough passengers got off that I can get what I need from them."

The conductor hurried back to the train, then shouted out: "'Board!"

There was a flurry of activity as passengers who were boarding here, as well as several of the through passengers who had left the train to check out the excitement, now hurried back to the train.

The conductor gave a wave toward the front of the train, then climbed into his vestibule. The engineer gave three short toots of the whistle, then opened the throttle bar. A gush of steam hissed from the actuating cylinder, and the connector rod grabbed the driver wheels, causing them to spin before they gained purchase, allowing the train to start forward. The conductor was still standing in the vestibule, looking out toward the sheriff as his car passed him. By the time the last car cleared the depot, the train was moving faster than a man could run, and within another quarter mile it was up to a full speed of thirty miles per hour.

Sheriff Duncan walked over to Ded. "I reckon you'll be puttin' in for the reward on these men," he said.

"Yes," Ded said. "It's eight thousand dollars, if they are who I think they are."

"You have all the rewards memorized, do you?"

"That's my job."

"Yeah," Sheriff Duncan replied, using a tone of voice that clearly indicated he didn't approve of what Ded considered his profession. "Well, that's the right amount all right, so I imagine they are who you think they are. But I'm curious, Axton: How did you know they planned to rob the train?"

"I didn't. I had to put my horse down, so I managed to catch a ride on the train. I just happened to be on board when they tried."

Sheriff Duncan stroked his cheek, then turned and looked back at the four dead outlaws. "That was unlucky for them, but lucky for you. Eight thousand dollars is a pretty good haul."

"Yes, it is."

"Let me ask you something, Axton. Do you ever feel unsettled about killin' men for a livin'?"

Ded didn't answer the question, but his eyes narrowed in disapproval. "How long before I can collect the money?"

"A couple of days."

"I'll wait."

"Yeah, I thought you might. Oh, Axton," Sheriff Duncan called as Ded turned to walk away.

Ded stopped, but he didn't turn around.

"Here's a little information that might interest you."

Ded turned toward him.

"Maybe you know, maybe you don't know, but there's a seventy-five-hundred-dollar reward out for you now."

"Why? I haven't violated any laws."

Sheriff Duncan chuckled. "I didn't *think* you knew about it. You don't understand: the reward on you hasn't been put out by the law. It's outlaws who have put out the reward. I thought I'd tell you that so you'd know to be on your toes."

After making arrangements to store his saddle at the depot, Ded walked down the street to the Del Ray Hotel. Because it was now after midnight all the buildings along both sides of the street, including the saloons, were dark. When he went into the lobby of the hotel, it was illuminated by an overhead chandelier.

Ded stepped up to the front desk and saw the clerk

sitting in a chair that was tipped back against the wall. The clerk's eyes were closed and his mouth was slightly open, his lips whistling each time he exhaled.

"Clerk?"

The clerk opened his eyes; then, on seeing Ded, he got up quickly and moved up to the desk.

"I was just restin' a bit," he said. "You need a room?"

"And a bath."

"Yes, sir, we can handle that. We got two bathing rooms down at the end of the hall up on the second floor. All you got to do is start the fire in the water heater, give it a few minutes to heat up, then turn the spigot. Before you know it, you'll have a whole tub full of hot water."

"Thanks," Ded said as he signed the register.

"The room will cost you a dollar a night, Mr."—he turned the register around to look at it, then his eyes opened wide—"Axton? Ded Axton?"

"Yes."

"Well, Mr. Axton, here is the key to your room. And may I say that the Del Ray Hotel is honored to be your host?"

"Thanks," Ded said again. He took the key, then went upstairs. Before he went to his room, he walked down to the end of the hall to one of the bathing rooms. He opened the unlocked door, went inside, and started a fire in the water heater, then walked back down the hall to check out his room while he gave the water time to get warm enough for his bath.

It wasn't a very large room, but he knew that it was considerably better than the frequent nights he spent out on the trail. On the other hand, the room couldn't compare with the rectory that he had shared with Mary and Davy. It was three years now, and the memory of his wife and child was still green. But he couldn't think of them without mixed emotions: the remembrance of them was sweet, but recalling what happened to them was bitter. He did exact his revenge, partly. Of the six men who had broken into his church and killed his wife, his child, and several of his parishioners, five were now dead. Ded had killed four of them, Asa Blackman had been hanged. Only Nate Walker had escaped both the law and Ded's vengeance. But the satisfaction of that bloodlust did nothing to fill the vast emptiness that was left in his heart. And while he still wanted Nate to pay for what he had done, his life was no longer dominated by searching for him.

Now Ded was always looking down the road or over the next hill, searching for something he couldn't put a name to. But no matter how much he wandered, no matter how much he searched, the pain of his loss was always just a thought away.

Ded pinched the bridge of his nose to force back those terrible memories. He knew he could never make them completely go away: they were always there, just beneath the surface of his consciousness. And that had left him so detached from life that he was absolutely without fear. He literally didn't care whether he lived or died.

Certain that his water was now warm, Ded took a razor, his shaving cup and brush, and a fresh change of clothes from his bag, then walked back down to the bathing room. A woman was just getting into the tub when Ded opened the door. She stood there, totally nude, so surprised by his unexpected appearance that she made no effort to cover herself.

"Sir, as you can readily see, this room is occupied," the woman said calmly. She still made no effort to shield herself from his gaze; not only that, but the small smile that played across her lips indicated that she didn't find the intrusion that disagreeable.

Ded smiled as well. "Yes, ma'am, I do see that it is occupied. I had built the fire for my own bath, and I didn't expect to see anyone here."

"You should have knocked," she said.

"You should have locked," he replied.

"I thought I had."

"There's another bathing room next door. I'll use it."

"Yes, thank you, I believe that would be most appropriate."

CHAPTER TWELVE

★

When Ded went down to breakfast the next morning, the waiter, a young man that Ded believed to be about seventeen or eighteen, came over to his table and, without being asked, poured him a cup of coffee.

"Order whatever you want for breakfast, Mr. Axton," the waiter said. "Your breakfast is free this morning."

"Oh? Why is that?"

"Because Mr. Clark, the banker, is paying for it."

"Well, that's very nice of Mr. Clark."

"He says it's because you saved the bank's money. So, what will you have?"

"What's your name?" Ded asked.

"Caldwell, sir. Billy Caldwell."

"Well, Billy, you know this place better than I do. Why don't you just bring the kind of breakfast you would order if it didn't cost you anything?"

Caldwell smiled. "Yes, sir!" he said.

Forty-five minutes later, after a breakfast of ham, eggs, and pancakes, Ded left a tip on the table for his young waiter, then walked down to the mortuary. The undertaker had one of the bodies on the embalming table and the other three lying on another large table.

"Good morning," Ded said.

"I've been waiting for you," the mortician said.

"Oh?"

"Yeah, I've heard that you like to come take a last look at the folks you've killed, so I figured you would be droppin' by."

"Have you also heard that I like a moment alone?"

"Yes. But don't take long, please, I've got four of 'em to get ready."

"I'll be but a moment," Ded said.

Ded waited until the undertaker left; then, as was his routine, he draped the ecclesiastical stole around his neck, raised his hand, and, as he made the sign of the cross, gave his blessing.

"'To we who are alive, may He grant forgiveness, and to all who have died a place of light and peace.'"

That afternoon, while waiting for the reward to be approved, Ded went into the Lone Star Saloon, ordered a seltzer, then found an empty table. He saw a woman wearing a figure-clinging red dress with a neck that was scooped low enough to show the tops of her breasts. Such dresses, Ded knew, were designed to tease by showing just a little of what the wearer had to offer. In this case, however, no tease was needed, because Ded had already seen everything that was there. This was the same woman he had seen stepping into the bathtub last night.

The woman walked over to his table and smiled at him. "May I join you?" she asked.

"Yes, please do," Ded replied, standing up quickly and pulling out a chair for her.

"Oh, my, I'm not used to such gentlemanly behavior," she said.

"May I buy you a drink?"

"If you wish."

"What would you like?"

"Sam will know."

Ded stepped back over to the bar. "The lady said you will know what drink she likes."

"I'd better know," the bartender replied. "The lady is my boss. She owns the place."

"Really? What's the lady's name?"

"Boyce. Jo Ann Boyce."

Sam reached under the bar for the bottle, poured a shot, then replaced the bottle.

"That'll be a quarter," he said.

Ded smiled. "Miss Boyce has expensive taste."

"She can afford it."

Ded brought the drink back to the table and set it in front of the woman. "So, you own this place," he said.

"Yes."

"I'm impressed."

"I was on the line for two years, Mr. Axton, and unlike many of the other girls, I managed to save my money. When I had enough, I bought this saloon."

"How do you know my name?"

"Who doesn't know Death's Acolyte?"

Ded shook his head. "Please don't call me that."

"I'm sorry, I meant no offense. It was just a name I heard, that's all."

Ded's smile returned. "If you meant no offense, none is taken."

"How long will you be staying in Sloan?" Jo Ann asked.

"A couple of days, just until I have some business cleared up. I saw you in the hotel last night, and I . . ."

A huge smile spread across Jo Ann's face. "Oh, yes," she said. "I would say that you did, indeed, *see* me last night."

"I'm sorry, I didn't mean it that way. I was just wondering if you lived in the hotel."

"I do. I like having my room cleaned for me, and I like leaving my laundry out to be done. I find hotel living very convenient."

Ded nodded. "I can see that."

Jo Ann pointed to Ded's glass. "You don't drink, but you come into a saloon?"

"I enjoy the ambiance of a saloon," Ded said easily. He held up the glass. "And I've made an odd discovery. I enjoy the ambiance even more when I'm sober."

Jo Ann ran the tip of her finger around the rim of her glass and, leaning forward, smiled seductively. "What else do you enjoy, Mr. Axton?"

In his hotel room that night, Ded opened his eyes. Something had awakened him and he lay very still. The doorknob turned and, sitting up, Ded pulled his pistol from the holster that hung at the head of his bed. He got up and moved quickly and quietly to the wall on the side of the door where he would be hidden when the door was pushed open. Naked except for a pair of underdrawers, he felt the night air on his skin. His senses alert and his body alive with readiness, he cocked his pistol and waited.

As the door came open, a triangular wedge of light spilled into the room from the lighted hall. Outside the hotel he heard a tinkling piano and a burst of laughter. From one of the Mexican cantinas on the other side of the track came the high-pitched bleat of a trumpet. Ded took a deep breath and smelled lilacs. He smiled. He had smelled this same perfume earlier.

"We seem to have a habit going into each other's space without knocking, don't we?"

Jo Ann gasped, then she chuckled. "I can't very well say I've made a mistake, can I?"

Ded eased the hammer down on the pistol, then pulled the door open wider, changing the golden puddle of light that spilled into the room from a triangle to a large square. Jo Ann was standing in the doorway, her thin cotton wrap backlit by the hall light so he could see her body in shadow behind the cloth.

"Come on in," Ded invited, moving back to let her step inside. He closed the door, then crossed over to light the lantern on his table.

"Oh, my. You aren't wearing much, are you?" Jo Ann said, seeing Ded in his drawers.

"If you want, I'll get dressed."

"Why bother? You'll just have to get undressed again."

Afterward, as they lay side by side in the bed, quiet now and breathing easy once more, Jo Ann spoke.

"Mr. Axton . . ."

Ded interrupted her with a laugh. "Don't you think we've gone a bit beyond the 'Mr. Axton' stage?"

Jo Ann chuckled as well. "Very well, Ded," she said. "Ded, I wouldn't want anyone to see me coming out of your room tomorrow. I don't want to give anyone the wrong idea."

"The wrong idea?"

"I am a woman alone, and I own a saloon. That is not something many women do. And I'm afraid that if someone saw me coming from your room in the morning, it would be easy for them to misunderstand . . . for them to think that I was supplementing my income by going back on the line again.

"I am no longer a whore and there are very few here who knew that I ever was. As far as the men around here are concerned, I am unapproachable. That's what they think and that's what I want them to think."

"All right," Ded said.

"Of course, you may think my coming to your room tonight belies my claim to being unapproachable. It must seem like a bold thing to do, perhaps even a slatternly thing to do. But it's all a part of my plan, you see, because once I left the line, I made up my mind that I would decide when—and I would decide with whom—I would ever make love again. That way, I am in control. Do you understand that?"

Ded chuckled, softly. "I not only understand it, I appreciate it."

"And you'll keep this our little secret?"

"Would you say that what you just told me was in the form of a confession?"

"A confession? Well, I don't know that I would put it quite that way, but yes, I suppose in a way it was a confession."

"Then you may rest assured that your secret is safe with me," Ded said.

Jo Ann laughed. "You are a strange one, Ded Axton."

"I suppose I am," Ded agreed.

"Here's your eight thousand dollars," Sheriff Duncan said the next day, after counting the money out. "That's an awful lot of money."

"Yes, it is."

"What are you going to do with it?"

Ded stared at the sheriff, a hard, unblinking stare that caused the lawman to look away.

"Of course," the sheriff said, clearing his throat, "whatever you do with it, it isn't any of my business."

"Of course," Ded said.

The first thing Ded did was buy a horse to replace the one he had had to put down. He looked at several until he found one that he wanted. He was a sorrel standing around fifteen hands high, leggy, and well muscled. He looked at the horse's teeth, then into his eyes.

"How old is he?"

"He's three years old," the dealer said.

Ded reached up to wrap his fingers around the horse's ear, and it dipped its head in appreciation.

"You want to get out of here, don't you, boy?" he said. "How much?"

"Eighty-five dollars."

"I'll give you seventy."

"Eighty?"

"Seventy-five," Ded said.

"Mister, you just bought yourself a horse."

The next thing he bought was a saddle satchel, a strap that stretched across the horse with two large pouches that would allow him to carry a lot more than normal saddlebags. He wanted the larger pouches because it would allow him to carry more personal things. His next stop after leaving the tack shop was the bookstore. There he bought two new books, *Ben-Hur* by Lew Wallace and *The Trumpet Major* by Thomas Hardy. When he was on the trail, he always stopped while there was still enough light to read for a while.

With all his purchases made, Ded stopped by the Lone Star to tell Jo Ann good-bye, gracefully declining her invitation to "stay just awhile longer." He left town, heading west, with no particular place to go and no particular time to be there.

CHAPTER THIRTEEN

★

Nate Walker waited on top of a fifteen-foot precipice alongside the road that provided stagecoach service between Kerrville and Boerne. His horse was tied to a small tree on the ground behind the rock. A moment earlier he had placed his rifle in a crevice with the barrel pointing out toward the road.

Looking north, he saw the stagecoach approaching and lay down on the rock so as not to be seen against the skyline. As the coach drew closer, he could hear it, the drumming of the hoofbeats from the six-horse team, the jangle of bits, bridles, and harness, the rumble of the rolling wheels, the rattle and squeak of the coach's chassis, and the calls and whistles of the driver. He pulled a cloth sack with holes cut for his eyes down over his head.

He watched the coach approach; then, just as it passed under him, he dropped down onto the top. The attention of the driver and the guard riding shotgun was still directed toward the road in front of them, so neither noticed him until he brought the butt of his gun down, hard, on the guard's head. The guard dropped his weapon and slumped forward.

"What the hell . . ." the driver said. He hauled back on the reins and put his foot on the brake, bringing the coach to a halt, still not having seen Nate.

"Order your passengers out of the coach," Nate said.

"Where'd you come from?" the driver asked, startled by Nate's sudden and unexpected appearance.

"Look up on that rock behind you. Do you see the rifle that's pointed at you?"

The driver looked around and saw the rifle Nate was referring to, pointing in their direction from the crevice in the rocks.

"Yeah, I see it."

"Order the passengers out."

"You folks in the coach, everyone out!" the driver shouted.

"What's going on here?" an elderly man said as he climbed down from the coach.

"All of you," Nate said. "Get over there on the side of the road and put your hands up."

There were five passengers: the old man; a younger man wearing a suit who had the look of a drummer; a woman and her two children, a small boy and a younger girl. None of them represented a danger to him.

"Reach down into the boot and hand me up the money pouch."

"What makes you think we're carrying money?" the driver asked.

"You have a guard, that's why I know you are carrying money. Now, are you going to hand it to me, or do I have to kill you and get it myself."

"No, no, I'll give it to you," the driver said. Reaching down into the boot, he brought up a leather pouch. "I don't know how much money is in it, though."

"I'm sure it will be enough," Nate said. "Now, hand me your pistol, the guard's pistol, and the shotgun."

The driver complied, and Nate unloaded all three weapons, then tossed them onto the ground. After that, he jumped down on the same side as the passengers standing near the stagecoach.

"You folks may return to the coach now," he said.

"Mister, are you a real stagecoach robber?" the young boy asked excitedly.

"Yes, I am, young man. And now you can tell all your friends that you were robbed by a real stagecoach robber."

"You should be ashamed of yourself," the woman scolded.

"Yes, ma'am, sometimes I am," Nate said. "Now, please, all of you, climb back into the coach."

Nate watched until the passengers had boarded, then pointed his pistol into the air and fired.

"Heyah!" he shouted, and the team bolted forward.

It was now one month since he had robbed the stagecoach, the holdup netting him two hundred and eighteen dollars. Nate was pleased with the amount: it was enough to see him through two or three months, and yet it wasn't enough to arouse a great deal of interest in finding the "solo highwayman," as the newspapers had referred to him. Nate had managed to keep a low profile as an outlaw, doing his jobs few and far between. He also kept the jobs small, so that his name had never turned up on a wanted poster somewhere.

Even if his name had shown up on wanted posters, it wouldn't bother him now. The man who had been Nate Walker was no more. Shortly after that holdup, he had changed his name to Angus Pugh. The name had no particular meaning to him, he just liked the sound of it. It hadn't been hard to shed himself of his former name: he knew that he would never see his brother again, and nearly all of his friends were dead, except for Ded Axton.

Could he still call Ded a friend? Well, perhaps "erstwhile friend" would be a better description. In point of fact, Ded Axton was one of the reasons Nate had changed his name. He didn't want to encounter Axton now. He no longer felt a desire for revenge for having spent fifteen years in prison. He had already exacted his revenge, much more terribly than he had originally intended. He didn't know until after the fact that when he and the others had burst into the church that day, they had killed Ded's wife and child.

Now the shoe was on the other foot: Ded Axton was the one who would be looking for revenge. And while there had been a time when Nate Walker thought he would be a match for Ded Axton if it ever came to a shoot-out between them, he wasn't sure of that anymore, especially if all the stories about Death's Acolyte could be believed. The best tactic, he decided, would be just to avoid ever encountering him.

Avoiding Axton would be much easier as Angus Pugh. Nobody had ever heard of Angus Pugh, but everyone, by now, had heard of Death's Acolyte. Ded's exploits were often written up in the newspapers, and even when not reported in the press, word of mouth kept Pugh apprised of where Ded was. It was almost like belling a cat, and Pugh smiled at the concept.

The clouds that had been building up in the west were about to deliver on their threat, so Pugh reached around behind his saddle, pulled out his slicker, and put it on. Soon the rain started coming down so heavily, he could almost believe he was under a waterfall. There was nothing he could do about it but hunker down in the saddle and keep riding. When he saw the little town of Pipe Creek appearing through the gray curtain of falling rain, it was a welcome sight.

After he reached town, the first thing Pugh did was go to the livery to get his horse out of the weather. That taken care of, he picked his way across the muddy, horse-apple-strewn street and stepped up onto the porch of a saloon bearing the unlikely name of the Slaughter House.

Just inside the saloon, there was a long board of

wooden pegs nailed to the wall about six feet above the floor. Pugh dumped the water from the crown of his hat, then hung it and his slicker on one of the pegs to let them drip-dry. A careful scrutiny of the saloon disclosed a card game in progress in the back. At one of the front tables, there was some earnest conversation. Three men stood at the bar, concentrating only on their drinks and private thoughts. A soiled dove, near the end of her professional effectiveness, overweight, with bad teeth and wild, unkempt hair, stood at the far end. She smiled at Pugh but, getting no encouragement, stayed put.

"What'll it be, mister?" the bartender asked, making a swipe across the bar with a sour-smelling cloth.

"Whiskey, then a beer," Pugh said. He figured to drink the whiskey to warm him from the chill of the rain, then drink the beer for his thirst.

The whiskey was set before him and he raised it to his lips, then tossed it down. He could feel its raw burn all the way to his stomach. When the beer was served, he picked it up, then turned his back to the bar for a more leisurely perusal of the room. He saw one of the players leave the card game, so he took his beer with him and walked back to the table.

"I see you have an open seat. May I join you?"

"Sure. It's always good to have new blood in a game," one of the players said.

"Adam ain't teasin'," another player said. "Forget about your money. We go for blood."

Pugh joined the others in laughter as he sat down. He was a very intelligent man, with a good memory and mathematical acumen, which could be used to great advantage in card games. He was able to remember cards played and he could determine, quickly and with amazing accuracy, the odds of the appearance of needed cards. In addition to the intelligence required to play well, Pugh had developed a manual dexterity that allowed him to deal the cards he wanted.

One hour later he left the game a thirty-dollar winner, though he had spread some winning hands around to other players as well so that nobody suspected him of cheating.

AUGUST 11, 1884

Ded was tired. It wasn't just a saddle-sore tiredness. It was a tiredness that went straight to the bone, a weariness of constant wandering, with one dusty town behind his back and another just ahead. This anchorless drifting had become a part of him. He was now defined by the saloons, cow towns, stables, dusty streets, and open prairies he encountered. He was both a long way from home and as close to home as the nearest hotel or back room in a saloon. More often than not, his home was a bedroll.

It was mid-afternoon when he rode into the town, the name of which he hadn't even noticed. The boardwalks along each side of the street were filled with men, women, and children.

"Honey, come here, look at this," a young woman said, calling her husband's attention to a display in a store window.

"Mama, I want a penny candy!" a small boy said, his voice carrying above the ambient sounds of the town.

"Not now. It will ruin your dinner," the boy's mother replied.

Ded had learned to keep such sounds at bay. He could still remember a world of husbands and wives, children and homes, schools, churches and socials, but he no longer wanted to.

For some time now, Ded had earned his living by hunting wanted men for the bounties the government paid for them. He had done well enough that, if he wanted to, he could buy a small ranch somewhere and settle down.

But he didn't want to.

By now Ded had been in scores of gunfights. And though he was always on the side of law and order, he had earned such a fearsome reputation with a gun that there were very few names in the West that evoked as much dread as did his. There were other skilled gunmen, to be sure, but there was only one Ded Axton.

Ded tied his horse off in front of the Ace High Saloon, then went inside. Because it was out of the sun, the shadowed interior gave the appearance of coolness, but it was an illusion only. The air was hot, still, and redolent of the sour smells of beer and whiskey, and the stench of sweating, unwashed bodies.

Ded Axton put a nickel down on the bar and ordered a seltzer water.

"Ha! You want a seltzer wat—" the bartender started to say; then, taking a closer look at his customer, he nodded. "Yes, sir, one seltzer water coming up."

As he was waiting for his seltzer, Ded turned to survey the saloon. A cloud of tobacco smoke hovered overhead, and two scantily-clad bar girls moved among the half dozen tables, laughing, flirting, and teasing the dozen or more men into buying more drinks.

The bartender put a beer in front of him. "Here you go, sir, seltzer water. Nothing's too good for Death's Acolyte."

"That's not a name I care for," Ded replied.

The bartender smiled broadly. "But it is you, ain't it? I *knew* it. I seen you back in Sweet Water when Toby Mathis called you out. He drawed first, but you still beat him, and you plugged him dead center."

Ded didn't respond, instead he took his seltzer water to a table that was near the black iron stove. Because it was summer the stove was cold, but the smell of last winter's fires still hung around it.

A man who was standing at the far end of the bar had heard the exchange between Ded and the bartender, and he hurried out of the saloon, leaving his beer half-finished. There was something familiar about the man, but Ded couldn't place it. He also noticed that the man hadn't finished his beer, which he thought was a little odd.

The man who had left the bar was named Lon Otis, and he hurried from the Ace High Saloon down to the far end of the street to Nunsinger's Corral.

"Hello, Otis," Nunsinger asked. "Comin' to ask me for your job back, are you?"

"No, I come to see Slayton and Ingersoll."

"It's a good thing you ain't comin' to get your job back, 'cause I wouldn't give it to you. Hell, you were drunk more'n you was sober. What do you want to see Slayton and Ingersoll about?"

"It's private."

"All right, go on back there. But don't keep 'em away from their work too long."

Otis hurried into the back where the two men were working. Slayton was mucking out one stall and Ingersoll another, right across from him.

"Lon," Slayton said, looking up. "Nunsinger give you your job back?"

"No, I don't need to work for him no more. And neither do you two."

"What do you mean?" Ingersoll asked, leaning on his rake.

Otis smiled. "I mean I know where we can get twenty-five hunnert dollars apiece. That's more'n two years' wages, workin' for Nunsinger."

"Where?" Slayton asked.

"Guess who just come into the Ace High?"

"Who?"

"Ded Axton. They's a seventy-five-hunnert-dollar reward to anyone that kills him."

"I got two things that's wrong with that," Slayton said. "First of all, we can't collect the money if we're dead. And the second thing is, it ain't the law that's got the reward out, so since he ain't really wanted, if we kill 'im, it'll be murder."

"Not if we draw him out into a fair fight."

"Ha! From what I've heard, if you get into a fair fight with Axton, you'll be dead."

"No we won't. I've got it all figured out," Otis said. "He kilt my brother, remember? I'll start ridin' him about that."

CHAPTER FOURTEEN

★

Ded had been sitting at the table for about fifteen minutes, when he saw two men come into the saloon together. They were talking to each other as they came through the swinging doors, but once they were inside, they separated. One, a big bearded man, went to one end of the bar, while the other, who had a handlebar mustache but no beard, went to the opposite end. Both of them appeared to take no notice of Ded, but he did notice that they were studying him in the mirror.

By now Ded Axton had become a man who lived on the edge, surviving on instinct and the ability to perceive danger long before it was apparent. To most, the fact that these two men had come in together talking as if they were old friends, then taken up positions far apart from each other, would mean nothing. But for Ded it activated a little signal of alarm. Then, when he saw that they were looking at him in the mirror, he knew that something was up. Slowly and without being seen, Ded slid his pistol out of his holster, then held it on his lap under the table.

A moment after the two men came in, the man that Ded had seen leave a few minutes earlier came back in.

This man walked right to the center of the bar, then turned to face Ded with a pistol in his hand.

"Would you be the fella they call Death's Acolyte?" he asked.

"My name is Ded Axton."

"Is that a fact? Well, Mr. Ded Axton, do you recall killin' someone named Otis? Lee Otis?"

"I do."

"I'm Lon Otis. Fact is, Mr. Ded Axton, Lee was my twin brother, and there ain't no one any closer than twins. You shot him down in the street, so I'm calling you out. Draw."

With that announcement, there was a sudden repositioning of all the other patrons in the saloon as everyone moved to get out of the line of fire should shooting begin, especially those who had been standing at the bar. Ded noticed, however, that neither of the other two men who came in just before Lon Otis had moved. In fact, they seemed totally uninterested in the conversation that was going on between Ded and his adversary, which was in itself a dead giveaway.

"You're asking me to draw, but you are already holding a gun in your hand."

Otis smiled broadly and looked down at the pistol he was holding. "I do, don't I?"

"Mr. Otis, are you going to give me the opportunity to stand up so I can face you in a fair fight? I mean, here you are with a pistol already in your hand, while I am sitting down. Don't you think that puts me at an unfair disadvantage trying to draw my pistol from a seated position?"

Otis laughed a gruff and very unpleasant laugh. "Yeah, I reckon you are at a disadvantage. But you know what they say: Sometimes chickens, sometimes feathers."

"You're not being fair."

"Fair? You think this is some kind of a sportin' match, Axton? Fair don't have nothin' to do with it."

"So, then, what you are saying is, I don't have to be fair, either, do I?"

"Ha! I reckon you can say that."

"Good, I'm glad you understand. You can walk away, now, Mr. Otis, and you can live. Or you can stay here and you'll die. Which will it be?"

"Let me get this straight. You're sayin' *you* are goin' to kill *me*?"

"Oh, not just you," Ded said. "I'm also going to kill your two friends that are standing at either end of the bar."

"Damn you, Otis! Quit your jabberin'! Shoot the son of a bitch and be done!" the bearded man shouted.

As Otis smiled and cocked his pistol, Ded squeezed the trigger. His gun blazed from under the table and Otis's smile changed to an expression of shock as he felt the bullet tear into his stomach.

"How the hell . . . ?"

Even as blood was pooling in his hands as Otis clasped them over his wound, Ded was turning over the table to use it and the adjacent potbellied stove as cover. The two men who were standing at opposite ends of the bar fired at him. One of those bullets hit the stove, ringing loudly and sending up an aromatic puff of coal dust. The other bullet burned into Ded's left side, feeling exactly as if someone had held a red-hot poker against his flesh.

Rolling over to his right side, Ded fired at the big, bearded man, choosing him because he had proven to be the more accurate of the two remaining assailants. Ded saw a black hole appear in the bearded man's forehead and knew that he was dead before he even hit the floor. The remaining shooter fired a second time, again missing but getting close enough to Ded that he could feel hot shards of lead from the bullet as it was shredded on impact with the stove. Ded's final shot crashed into the shooter's heart, soaking his shirt with a sudden gush of blood.

The bearded man had gotten one shot off; the one with the mustache had fired three times, firing the last shot as he was twisting around and going down. That bullet crashed through the front window of the saloon.

Ded also pulled the trigger three times, but each of his bullets had found its mark. The acrid smoke resulting from seven discharges was now curling into a dark gray cloud to push away the tobacco smoke gathered just beneath the ceiling of the saloon.

After the final crash of gunfire, there was a long,

pregnant moment of absolute silence, broken only by a measured tick-tock, tick-tock from the swinging pendulum of the Regulator clock that hung on the back wall by the scarred piano.

Then, from outside, came a woman's loud scream.

"He's dead! My son is dead! Someone shot my little boy!"

The bartender hurried over to the door and looked out over the batwings.

"Holy shit," he said quietly. "A wild bullet just kilt the Martin boy."

With a grunt and a groan, Ded pulled himself up from the floor and settled into the chair. He was holding his hand over the wound in his side.

"Did you say there's a boy outside that was hit by a bullet?" Ded asked.

"Yeah, but you didn't do it. You wasn't even shootin' in that direction," the bartender said. "More'n like it was that feller there," he said, pointing at the shooter with the handlebar mustache.

Ded looked at the three men he had killed.

"'Let the sinners be consumed out of the earth, and let the wicked be no more,'" Ded said, holding his hand up in front of him.

"Mister, I ain't never seen nothin' like that," the barkeep said in awe. "You took on three of them."

"Bring me a bottle of whiskey and a clean towel," Ded ordered through gritted teeth.

"Yes, sir, you got it," the barkeep said. "It's on the

house too. You got 'ny idea what you just did for business? Folks'll be comin' from all over to see where Death's Acolyte took on three men. I'm goin' to get me a sign made."

The barkeep hurried to the bar, got a bottle of whiskey and a clean towel, then brought the items back to Ded. Ded poured whiskey onto his wound, tore off a piece of the towel, and poured whiskey on it as well. He stuck the whiskey-soaked towel into the bullet hole, grimacing as he did so.

"It probably would be good if you would take a couple of drinks of that as well as pouring it on your wound," the bartender said.

Ded raised the bottle halfway to his lips, then stopped, put the bottle back down, and shook his head.

"No," he said.

"You ought to let a doc see that," one of the men said.

Ded looked up. "Is there a doctor in this town?"

"Not here, but there's one in the next town over. It's only about ten miles. We could send for him."

"Never mind," Ded said. "I'll take care of it myself."

Ded got up from the chair and, still holding his hand over his side, staggered toward the door.

Once outside, he looked toward a group of several people who had now gathered around the body of a young boy lying on the boardwalk right in front of the saloon. This was the same boy Ded had heard ask for a piece of penny candy.

A woman—Ded was certain it was the boy's mother—was kneeling beside her dead child, crying uncontrollably. Ded made the sign of the cross, and breathed a quick prayer.

"O almighty God, with whom do live the spirits of just men made perfect after they are delivered from their earthly prisons, I humbly commend the soul of this child into thy hands."

Then, with crying and cursing filling the street behind him, he climbed onto his horse and rode away.

Ded rode out of the town intending to ride to the next town to find a doctor. About ten miles out of town, though, he felt his head spinning and he grabbed hold of the saddle horn.

When Ded came to, he had no idea where he was or how he had gotten there. He was lying on the ground in blankets. Near him was a campfire, the smoke from which was curling up through a hole at the top. As he looked around, he saw that he appeared to be inside an Indian teepee.

An old Indian man was singing and waving a feather through the smoke of the fire. Ded and the old man were the only two in the teepee.

"Where am I?" Ded asked.

"You are with me," the old man said.

"Who are you?"

"I am Two Bears."

"You brought me here?"

"You fell from your horse. At first I thought it was because you could not ride. But then I saw that you had this in you."

Two Bears held up a bullet.

"You took that from me?" He put his hand on his wound and felt, not a bandage, but some sort of vegetation.

"If you wish to be healed, I will heal you," Two Bears said.

"How are you going to do that?"

"I am going to pray for you."

Ded shook his head. "I'm afraid that prayers will do no good for me. I am beyond prayer. I have a dead soul."

"What is your name?" Two Bears asked.

Ded hesitated for a moment before he answered. Over the last few years his name had become quite well-known . . . and feared.

"My name is Ded Axton."

"If the spirit of the man named Ded Axton is dead, then you must take a new name and a new spirit," Two Bears said.

"How do you take a new soul?"

"There is spirit inside and outside the body. Spirit is life and energy, and you will learn to know, live, breathe, walk, and speak with a new spirit."

"That sounds like a pretty big order," Ded said.

Two Bears lit a pipe, then handed it to Ded.

"You must smoke this pipe," he said.

"Why?"

"Tobacco is the herb of prayer, given to us by the Great Spirit so we can speak with him and with nature. With your first puff, you must think a good thought and make a prayer. With your second, quiet your mind and rest in stillness. With your third puff, you will receive knowledge, and with knowledge comes healing."

Ded followed the old Indian's instructions, and he learned from the Indian how to sing a song in Comanche and in English:

> *Yani'tsini'hawa'na!*
> *Yani'tsini'hawa'na!*
> *Hi'niswa'vita'ki'ni*
> *Hi'niswa'vita'ki'ni*
>
> *Yani'tsini'hawa'na!*
> *Yani'tsini'hawa'na!*
> *We shall live again!*
> *We shall live again!*

At first, Ded thought that the translation "We shall live again" was similar to the Christian concept of being "born again," or being resurrected.

But Two Bears told him that was not the case.

"I know who you are, Ded Axton. I know that you have killed many men, and that is why your soul is dead.

"So you must also kill Ded Axton. You must become

a new man, with a new soul. Only then will you be healed in body and in spirit."

"Yes, there may be something to what you say," Ded said.

"There is much in what I say," Two Bears said. "You must listen, and you will learn."

For the next two weeks, Ded remained with Two Bears. The old Indian taught him a song, and insisted that he sing it:

The voice I hear in the winds
The breath that gives life to the world
Give strength and wisdom
To one who is hurt in body and spirit.
Teach me the lessons
That I will see what cannot be seen
And I will hear what cannot be heard.
Make my ears hear your voice
Make my eyes see what is hidden in every leaf and
rock

One day, in Ded's third week under Two Bears's care, the old Indian came into the teepee carrying two shovels. He gave one shovel to Ded.

"Come," he said.

"What are we going to do?"

"We are going to bury Ded Axton."

For just a second Ded was startled by Two Bears's statement, then he knew exactly what he was saying.

"All right," Ded replied.

"We must find something of yours into which we can put your spirit. It is that spirit that we will bury."

Ded nodded. "Let me look through my saddlebags."

Ded opened his saddlebags, and the first thing he did was check the false leather lining, behind which he kept all his reward money. The lining had not been disturbed, the money was still there, and for a moment he felt guilty for suspecting Two Bears.

He emptied the contents of his saddle pouches—except for the money—on the blankets that had been his bed for the last three weeks. There were six wanted posters for outlaws he had not yet caught up with, and there was a silver communion cup from the first Eucharist he had conducted after his ordination. Somehow, those two extremes seemed to sum up the life of Ded Axton. Two Bears added the bullet that he had taken from Ded's side, and the feathers he had used in the healing ceremony.

"They must be wrapped in something that you wear," Two Bears explained.

"The shirt I was wearing when I was shot," Ded said.

"Yes, that will be good, for it has the blood of the man we are burying," Two Bears said.

Two Bears put the wanted posters, the communion cup, the bullet, and the feathers on the shirt, then rolled the shirt up around the items.

"Come," he said. "We will find a fine grave for the spirit of Ded Axton."

Ded followed Two Bears up a small hill. From the top of the hill, there was a good view of a stream shining gold in the late afternoon sun, limned on either side by green so that the course of the stream could be tracked by following its green borders far into the distance, even when the water could no longer be seen.

"This is a good place to bury a soul," Two Bears said.

"It is at that," Ded agreed.

The two men dug for about half an hour. At first Ded thought they would just dig a hole deep enough for the shirt, but Two Bears insisted that it must be a full-size grave in length, width, and depth.

When the grave was finished, Two Bears lay the shirt and the other items in the bottom, then raised his arms over his head and looked up.

> *Raven, take this spirit*
> *Wind, take this spirit*
> *Rain, take this spirit*
> *When it is clean*
> *Give it back.*

Ded said his own silent prayer.

> *Bless me, Father,*
> *That my unrighteousness shall be forgiven,*
> *And my soul be restored.*

CHAPTER FIFTEEN

★

One week later, when Two Bears returned with fish he had caught, he saw that Ded was sitting on the ground just outside the teepee. Ded was fully dressed, and for the first time since the day he left Estacado in pursuit of the men who had attacked his church, he was not wearing his pistol, having packed it away in a saddle pouch.

"You are continuing your journey," Two Bears said. It wasn't a question, it was a statement.

"Yes. Thanks to you, Two Bears, I am healed."

"You are not healed, you are reborn. The old spirit of the man called Ded Axton is gone. You have a new spirit now, and the new spirit was not wounded."

Ded smiled and nodded. "I must say, Two Bears, even during my time at the seminary, I don't know that I ever experienced anything more spiritual than I have in this last month."

"You will eat fish with me before you leave."

"Yes, I very much want to share a last supper with you."

"That will be good. But we have no wine."

Ded chuckled. He hadn't known whether or not Two Bears would catch the symbolism.

"What name will you take, my new friend?" Two Bears asked.

"Why, I don't know, I haven't thought about it."

"Your new spirit must have a new name. You buried your old name with your old spirit."

Ded thought of two of his friends from West Point who had been killed during the war, the two who he and Mike Lindell had spoken of. Ken Kirby, who fell for the South at Antietam, and Merlin Casey, who, while fighting for the North, was killed at Gettysburg. He would honor them.

"I shall take the name Ken Casey," he said.

"Ken Casey," Two Bears repeated. "Yes, it is a good name."

After supper, Ded told his new friend good-bye, then mounted his horse and rode off.

The setting sun, losing both heat and brilliance, seemed poised in the west above the desert floor. A dark gray haze was beginning to gather in the notches of the rugged escarpment, hanging there like drifting smoke. The sandy red loam was dotted with blue cedar and mesquite, limned in gold from the setting sun.

After the sunset, Ken Casey spread out his bedroll to go to bed.

Out on the prairie, a coyote howled.

An owl hooted.

A falling star flashed across the dark sky.

A soft evening breeze moaned through the mesquite.

And he slept.

★ ★ ★

He was standing on the bank of a swiftly flowing stream of water, and he could see it sparkling in the sun.

He heard someone approaching and, looking around, recognizing himself not as Ken Casey but as Ded Axton.

"What are you doing here, Axton?" he asked.

"Why have you buried me, Ken Casey?"

"Because I want to forget Ded Axton. I don't want to be troubled by your past."

"Do you want to forget your wife, Mary? Do you want to forget your child, Davy?"

"No. But how can I remember them without remembering the other things . . . the men I have killed . . . the sins I have committed?"

"I will take unto myself the memories of the men I have killed," Ded said. "I will take unto myself the sins that I have committed. I will give you this tranquillity, but you must promise me, Ken Casey, that, even in your new self, you will remember the good things."

"What good things?"

"Your love of God. Your love of Mary and Davy. Your love of literature, poetry, history. You must promise me that you will remember those things."

"I cannot love God—not now, not after all I have done."

"But you, Ken Casey, have done nothing. You are free to love God as He loves you."

"I will try."

"Then go, Ken Casey, and be no more troubled by your sins. Let this be your moment of transfiguration."

★ ★ ★

Casey poked a stick into the small mesquite campfire he had built that morning, stirring the coals. This was his favorite time of day. The sun was barely one full disk up above the eastern horizon, and the air was soft and cool. Sitting cross-legged before the fire he watched as a doe came out of a stand of cottonwood trees, looked around for a moment, then looked back. She was joined by a fawn. The two of them went down to the stream to drink, and Ken watched them until their thirst was satisfied. With a final look around, they disappeared back into the trees.

Casey was vaguely aware that he had dreamed something during the night that had just passed, but he couldn't remember it. There were, however, disconnected images and scattered memories drifting through his mind.

Tranquillity . . . good things . . . transfiguration . . .

He had no idea what that meant, or how those words had been a part of his dream, but he this morning did have a sense of "the peace of God, which passeth all understanding," and realized that it had been many years since he felt such a personal calm.

From the *Fort Worth Democrat*, Monday, August 11, 1886:

WHERE IS DED AXTON?
Some Believe the Famous Gunman Is Dead

The noted Regulator and onetime clergyman, Ded Axton, whose exploits with the pistol earned him the sobriquet of "Death's Acolyte," has apparently dropped off the face of the earth. It was two years ago on this day, August 11th, 1884, that Axton was last seen, riding away from the town of Soda Springs, having put his pistol to deadly effect in besting three men who sought to kill him.

That they may have succeeded is now the thought of many, because since the renowned gunman rode away, clutching his hand over a grievous wound in his side, no one has seen him.

Some say that he died on the trail, his body not found because it was either consumed by wild animals or buried by some responsible citizen who did the humane thing, not knowing the celebrity of the decedent. But there are others who think that, tormented by the fact that an innocent child was killed in the shoot-out, though not by Axton, he is still alive, but has withdrawn himself from the public eye.

Whether alive or dead, Axton won't soon be forgotten, for he left a trail of bloody justice by sending many a desperado to perdition.

It wasn't just Buckley Burton Paddock, editor of the *Fort Worth Democrat*, who was wondering what had happened to Ded Axton. His disappearance was the subject of speculation and discussions all across Texas and throughout the West. The mystery of what hap-

pened to Ded Axton rivaled that of the strange disappearance of the crew of the *Mary Celeste*, which had
mystified the world for some thirteen years now, ever
since the ship had been discovered six hundred miles
east of the Straits of Gibraltar, abandoned, with no sign
of foul play, and not one of the crew, its captain, or the
captain's wife and baby daughter accounted for.

Just as there were theories about what happened to
the crew of the ghost ship, there were theories about
what had happened to Ded Axton. Some said he had
left Texas, taking all his bounty money back east, where
he was living like a king. Others said that he was in a
monastery, living a life of deprivation in atonement for
his sins. This was plausible, they explained, because he
had once been a man of the cloth, and where better to
lose oneself than in a monastery?

Most, however, thought he was dead, having died
from the bullet wound he received in what was now
being called the "Shoot-out at Soda Springs."

Although he was no longer in the public view, he
was very much in the public memory, and the legend
grew. But that legend concerned Ded Axton, and Ded
Axton was no more.

PIPE CREEK, TEXAS

"I wonder if the son of a bitch really is dead," Angus
Pugh said as he laid the paper down.

"Who, honey? Who are you talking about?"

Pugh was in what was now referred to as "his" table in the saloon. The woman who had asked the question was Annabelle Clayton, the "queen" of the girls who worked the saloon.

"Ded Axton," Pugh said. "According to the newspaper, he hasn't been seen in over a year."

"Is he the one you are always looking for?" Annabelle asked.

Pugh looked at her with a surprised expression on his face. "What do you mean? What are you talking about?"

"Ever since I've known you, you've been sort of lookin' over your shoulder like someone is after you. I thought at first it was because maybe you are a wanted man, but the sheriff and his deputies come in here all the time and none of them ever bother you. Besides which, Pearlie Goodman told me there isn't any paper out on you."

Pugh chuckled. "What were you trying to do, Annabelle, set me up so you could turn me in for the reward?"

"Oh, no, honey, nothing like that!" Annabelle said. "It's just that you act like you're lookin' for someone all the time."

"Well, don't worry your pretty head about it," Pugh said. "Because if I had been looking over my shoulder—and I'm not saying that I was, but if I had been—I won't be looking anymore."

BOOK TWO

★

KEN CASEY

CHAPTER SIXTEEN

★

The rider approached a small town from the east, watching it rise before him, small and flyblown, its weathered buildings barely discernible from the rocks and hillocks that made up the terrain. The lone horseman could not be described as handsome, though from time to time there had been women who were attracted to him by what they called his intriguing appearance.

Others, though, were drawn by his eyes. They were gunmetal gray, but it wasn't the color that the observers found absorbing; it was what they saw in his eyes, depending upon the way the light played on them. Sometimes, in a pale light, there was so much pain in those eyes that just looking at them could bring someone to tears. At other times they were soft and compassionate. There had been times, however, when they were hard and deadly.

Ken Casey had been riding through West Texas with no particular destination in mind when he ran across a set of railroad tracks. He followed the tracks, which led him to the town that now lay just ahead.

Stopping about a quarter of a mile away from the town, he stood in the stirrups to get the blood circulating again. He looked around at the sagebrush and through the shimmering heat waves that rose from the prairie surrounding the little town. A rabbit popped up in front of him, ran for several feet along the trail, then darted under a low-lying, dusty mesquite tree. The thick musk of cattle drifted to his nostrils, carried on a breeze that felt as if it had been blown directly from hell.

Casey reached around to massage the cheeks of his butt; then, sitting back in his saddle, he urged his horse forward with the barest suggestion of a squeeze from his knees. Entering the depot grounds, he saw a sign that read:

BRAKEMEN BEWARE
NO SIDE CLEARANCE FOR RIDERS

There was a brick platform that ran from the depot building out to the track, and on that brick platform sat a green luggage cart with red iron wheels. The depot itself was a redbrick building that had a small sign, black letters on white, attached to the east side of the building:

WARDELL, TEXAS
ELEVATION, 2,586 FT.

Moving on beyond the depot, Casey turned right to ride down what he figured to be the main street. A sign on the street corner declared this street to be Broad Avenue.

The hoofbeats of his horse sounded hollow on the sunbaked earth, and little puffs of dust drifted up to hang suspended behind him, as if reluctant to return to the hot, hard ground. As he continued riding down the street, he examined the ripsawed clapboard buildings. There were several houses; a tannery, a tack store, a smithy's shop, and a general store that had its name, "Sessions," displayed on a high false front. Across the street from the general store was a smaller building, a café called Little Man Lambert's, and a few doors down from the café was a saloon with red letters, outlined in black, spelling out the words "Red Bull Saloon."

From the blacksmith shop came the ring of steel on steel as the smithy pounded his hammer against a red-hot horseshoe, shaping it to his needs. The smithy straightened up from his anvil to wipe the sweat from his brow and fix Casey with a long, curious, but not antagonistic stare.

A sign, shaped like a man's hand with a pointing finger, hung from an arm that protruded from the front of the tack store it advertised. The sign squeaked as it moved back and forth in answer to a hot breath of wind.

Across the street from the Red Bull was the Wardell Livery Stable. Casey headed for the livery, then dismounted just as a young boy of about fourteen came out to meet him. The boy had an unruly shock of sun-bleached hair and a face full of freckles.

"You want to board your horse, mister?" the boy asked.

"I do."

"Puttin' him up is five cents a night, hay is another nickel, or if you want oats that'll cost you ten cents," the boy said.

Casey gave the boy a dollar. "Give him oats and a rubdown," he said.

"That'll be a quarter. I'll get your change."

"You can just keep the money for now," Casey said. "I don't know how long I'll be here and I don't want to keep having to come back every day to pay for board. Will you look after my tack?"

"Yes, sir, it'll be safe here. You got my personal guarantee on that."

Casey smiled. "Your personal guarantee, huh?"

"Yes, sir."

"I don't suppose I can ask for anything more than that."

From across the street came a woman's high-pitched scream, then a burst of laughter. As the woman's laughter followed, Casey figured that whatever had caused the scream was all in fun. Taking his saddle pouch and draping it over his shoulders, he walked over to the saloon, paused on the front porch for just a moment, then stepped inside.

There were several young men in the back corner, along with a young woman whose dress was cut so low that it looked as if her breasts were in danger of spilling out. One of the young men said something that Casey didn't hear, and there was another burst of laughter.

Casey stepped up to the bar, where he was greeted by the bartender, a heavyset man who wore neatly trimmed chin whiskers, although the face above and below his mouth was clean-shaven. He had on a blue-striped shirt and a red bolo tie. He welcomed Casey with a smile.

"What can I get you, mister?" he asked.

"I don't suppose you have any sarsaparilla, do you?"

"Sure do," the bartender said.

More laughter from the table of young men, and the bartender chuckled.

"Ol' Quince is on a roll today," the bartender said as he walked back to draw a glass of the caramel-colored soft drink from a wooden barrel.

"Quince?" Casey asked as he paid for the drink.

"You see the young feller there with the fancy gun and holster?"

The man the bartender pointed out was smooth-faced, about five feet ten, with dark hair that hung to his shoulders.

"That's Quince Anders. He works for Murdock Felton, who owns the Tumbling F Ranch. Well, the fact is, all them boys work for Mr. Felton."

"That's quite a holster set he's wearing," Casey said as he took the beer.

"Yes, sir, well, Quince is really good with the gun, so I reckon the holster ain't out of place."

"What do you mean by 'good with a gun'?"

"Oh, don't get me wrong, he ain't what you would call a gunfighter or nothin' like that. I mean, he ain't never kilt nobody. But he's 'bout the fastest I've ever seen, and he always hits what he's shootin' at."

"The hell I can't!" Quince said loudly. "I know damn well I can do it."

"You willin' to put your money where your mouth is?"

"What do you mean?"

"I'll bet you a dollar you can't do it." The speaker was about the same size as Quince, with red hair and a red mustache.

Quince shook his head. "Huh-uh," he said. "A dollar ain't enough money. You want me to prove it to you, Stanley, it's goin' to cost more'n a dollar."

"How much more?" Stanley asked.

"Ten dollars. Five dollars for me, and I'll be givin' five dollars to Mindy for helpin' me out."

Stanley blanched. "Ten dollars? I ain't got ten dollars."

"We get paid Saturday," Quince said. "I'll hold your marker till then." Quince smiled. "Of course, you may be right. It could be that I can't do it at all; then you would be ten dollars richer."

"Yeah, I would, wouldn't I?"

Stanley stroked his chin as he contemplated the offer. "Let's make certain what we're bettin' on," he said. "What you're tellin' me is that Mindy is goin' to hold two glasses, one out to either side. Then she's goin' to drop those glasses, and you're goin' to draw your pistol and shoot both of those glasses before they hit the floor. Is that what you're sayin'?"

"That's what I'm saying," Quince replied. "Oh, and I'm goin' to try not to hit Mindy."

"You're going to *try* not to hit me?" the bar girl said. "What do you mean, *try* not to?"

"Well, if I was to hit you, I'd lose ten dollars," Quince said. "So it seems to me only natural that I'm goin' to try hard not to hit you."

"Wait a minute, I don't know if I want to do this or not. You're talking about losing ten dollars; I could lose my life."

"Nah, the worst that would happen is you'll prob'ly just get hit in the leg or something. And if that happens, I'll pay for the doctor."

"What?"

"I'm teasing you, Mindy. You aren't going to be hit. I tell you what, all you have to do is stand there and drop the glasses, and I'll give you five dollars whether I win or not. So, what do you have to lose?"

"I want the five dollars now."

"All right," Quince said, giving her the money. "But I would think you would just be proud enough to take part in something like this that you wouldn't even be asking me for money. Why, this'll make you famous."

"Wait a minute," the man who was making the bet said. "Let's get this straight. We are talkin' about whiskey shot glasses and not a beer mug, right?"

"Damn, Stanley, you're sure makin' it hard on me," Quince said.

Laughing, Stanley looked at the others. "I didn't think he'd take me up on it."

"Oh, I didn't say I wasn't goin' to take you up on it. I just said you were making it hard on me. Is it a bet?"

Stanley nodded. "Yeah," he said. "It's a bet."

Quince picked up a couple of shot glasses and gave them to Mindy. "Now, hold them out to your sides like this." He demonstrated by putting his own arms out.

"Hey, hold on, wait a second!" the bartender shouted. "Quince, you ain't plannin' on doin' that in here, are you?"

"Sure. Why not?" Quince replied.

"Why not? 'Cause it's dangerous, that's why not. Mindy, you're crazy for going along with it. And even if you don't hit Mindy, at the very least you'll be breakin' a couple of good glasses. And you'll be puttin' a couple of bullet holes in my floor."

"I'll pay you for the glasses. And it ain't like you don't have about a dozen holes in your floor already, maybe even more if you took all the spit-out tobacco chaws," Quince said.

"Don't take up them chaws," Stanley said. "Hell, that's what's holdin' the floor together."

The others laughed.

"Besides, look at it this way, Walter," Quince continued. "Once I do this, why, folks will be wantin' to come here to have a drink in the saloon where the great

Quince Anders done the best shootin' that's ever been done."

Walter laughed out loud. "I'll say this for you, Quince, you sure have a high opinion of yourself. All right, go ahead, try it. If you can do it, you're right, it might be a good advertisement for my place. And if you can't do it, well, it'll be good to see you gettin' your comeuppance—that is, as long as Mindy don't get shot."

"Mindy ain't goin' to get shot, and there ain't goin' to be no comeuppance neither. You can count on that," Quince replied.

Casey watched with an interest that was equal to everyone else's in the room as the young woman extended her arms to either side of her body, holding a glass in each hand.

"Somebody need to count or somethin'?" Stanley asked.

"No need to count," Quince replied. "Mindy, just drop the glasses when you are ready, but be sure and drop 'em both at the same time."

"All right," Mindy said, the timbre of her voice showing her nervousness.

The saloon grew very quiet as the other patrons realized what was about to take place. All eyes were on the girl.

Mindy closed her eyes, then dropped the two whiskey glasses. As they started falling toward the floor, Quince drew his pistol and fired two shots, doing it so quickly that it sounded as if only one shot had been fired. But there had been two shots as evidenced by the fact that both glasses were shattered before they were halfway to the floor.

There were several shouts of approval and applause.

The acrid and all-too-familiar smell of gun smoke drifted by Casey as he lifted his sarsaparilla to take another swallow.

Still smiling and accepting the accolades heaped on him, Quince turned toward Casey.

"Did you see that, mister?" he asked.

"Yes, I saw it."

"You ever seen anything like that before?"

Casey finished his drink and set the glass on the bar. Wiping his hand across his mouth he asked, "Where can someone get a good supper in this town?"

"Mister, you didn't answer me," Quince challenged. "Have you ever seen anything like that before?"

"I can't say as I have," Casey replied.

"No, sir, I don't suppose you can. And you ain't never goin' to see nothin' like that again, neither. I reckon I'm about the fastest gun you ever seen."

"It was quite impressive," Casey said. He turned back to the bartender. "My supper?"

"You might try Little Man Lambert's," Walter said. He pointed. "It's just up the street about three or four doors. He's got good food, but you might have to wait a bit, seein' as he's shorthanded now."

"Shorthanded?"

"He needs him a good cook," Walter said. "The cook

he had left a couple of weeks ago and he ain't been able to hire another one since."

"Thank you," Casey said, starting toward the door.

"Hey, mister!" Quince called to him. "If you see a pretty girl down there, her name is Lucy. You tell her what you just seen. You tell her you just seen the fastest gun alive."

"I'm afraid I'll have to let you tell her that, Mr. Anders. I'm sure I couldn't do the tale justice," Casey said as he left the saloon.

CHAPTER SEVENTEEN

★

Little Man Lambert's café stood out along the row of buildings because it was one of the few that had been painted. In addition, there was a flower box in front of the windows, and the flower box was filled with well-tended and beautiful flowers. Just before he went in, Casey reached over and pulled a sign from the window. The sign read: COOK WANTED.

He was approached by a very pretty young woman, slender, with a firm, high-perched bosom and a serene oval face with high, exotic cheekbones. Her lips were full and rounded over very white, even teeth. She was nearly as tall as Casey.

"You must be Lucy."

The young woman's face registered surprise. "Yes, I am. Do we know each other?"

"No, but I heard that there was a very beautiful young woman here named Lucy. You are here, and you are very beautiful, so I put two and two together."

Lucy blushed. "I'm afraid you are embarrassing me, Mr. . . . ?"

"Casey. Ken Casey."

"Will you be wanting supper, Mr. Casey?"

"I will," Casey said. He held the sign out toward the girl. "And I would also like to apply for this job, if it isn't already taken."

"Can you cook?"

Casey nodded. "Yes, ma'am, I can cook."

"Let me call my father."

Casey waited for a moment until a short, rotund man stepped out of the kitchen. Clean-shaven and bald, he was wearing a stained white apron upon which he was wiping his hands as he approached.

"Papa, this is Mr. Ken Casey," Lucy said. "This is my father, Jake Lambert."

"Everyone calls me Little Man," Lambert said, extending his hand. "My daughter tells me you would like to apply for the cooking job."

"I would, yes."

"She also says you want supper."

"I do."

"I tell you what. Step back into the kitchen and cook your own supper. If it's any good, you are hired and your supper is free, seeing as room and board comes with the job. Actually, your supper will be free whether I hire you or not, seein' as you will have cooked it."

"That's most gracious of you, Mr. Lambert," Casey said.

"The kitchen is back here."

Casey began with an egg, flour, water, and salt; then, rolling that out flat, he cut it into strips for noodles and let them set as he started carving off narrow strips of beef. He followed that by cutting up an onion, then he dropped the beef and onion into a skillet of bubbling lard. After a few minutes, he added some beef broth and red wine, while in a separate pan he brought more beef broth to a boil and dropped in the noodles.

When the noodles were finished, he removed them from the pot and put the beef strips and onions over them. After grinding up some black pepper, he offered the plate to Little Man.

"Oh," Little Man said after his first taste. "Oh, my. This is the best thing I've ever tasted in my life! You are hired!"

"Thanks," Casey said. He got another plate and served Lucy, who had been watching in curiosity, then served himself.

He wasn't sure how long he would be there, but for the time being he was home.

As Little Man had promised, part of Casey's pay was a free room at the back of the café. Emptying his saddle pouches, Casey carefully packed everything in a trunk that stood at the foot of his bed. Prominent in the trunk, and quite noticeable because of their juxtaposition, he placed an ecclesiastical stole and vestments as well as a Colt .44 pistol that was tucked into an unadorned and well-worn leather holster.

Before going to bed that night, Casey moved the pistol to one side, picked up the stole, held it to his lips, and kissed it. Then he draped it around his neck. Kneeling at the side of his bunk, he began to pray. The prayer was one of contrition, the same prayer Casey had said every morning and every night for the last five years:

"Almighty God, judge of all men; I acknowledge and bewail my manifold sins and wickedness which I most grievously have committed, by thought, word and deed. Forgive me all that is past. Amen."

When he finished the prayer, Ken Casey returned the stole to the trunk, then took out a book, a copy of Ralph Waldo Emerson's *The Conduct of Life*. He was a man looking for answers. More than that, he was looking for absolution. Would Ken Casey find it in the writings of this onetime Unitarian minister turned transcendentalist?

After he finished reading, Casey put out the lantern, then lay on the bed with his hands linked behind his head as he stared up into the dark. Unbidden, and even unwanted, poignant memories filled his mind. He found, though, that he could not push them aside.

"Can't you hurry Davy along, Mary? How would it look for the priest to be late for church? This is Pentecost Sunday."

"I know it's Pentecost, Ded, that's why it's taking so long. Davy is looking for something red to wear."

"Do hurry, will you?"

Mary came over to kiss her husband. "Aren't you the one who always says that the Lord loves a patient man?"

Ded smiled. "It's not fair to use my own words against me."

"Look, Daddy, I'm wearing a red shirt!" Davy said, running into the room with his arms up.

"Indeed you are," Ded said. He picked Davy up and swung him around, rewarded with the little boy's giggles.

"Now we must go, or I believe Mr. Byrd will decide to start without us."

"He can't do that. You're the priest," Davy said.

"Your daddy isn't just the priest, Davy, he's the most handsome priest in the world," Mary said, smiling broadly at her husband.

"You're just trying to butter me up so I won't get on you for being late."

"Don't worry, we'll be there in plenty of time."

The next morning a barking dog just outside his window awakened Casey. His room was over the café, and the window looked down onto Broad Street. Right across the street was the McKnight & Keaton freight office, where already wagons were backed up to the dock to take on their loads. Next to the freight office was Sessions's grocery store, where a man wearing an apron was sweeping his porch. Next to the grocery store was an apothecary, the business advertised not by words but by a large cutout of a mortar and pestle. Just to the right of the apothecary, a striped pole advertised the barbershop, and next to that a big tooth led patients to the dentist.

The north end of Broad Street crossed the Texas and Pacific Railway, then continued on north stretching out into the wide, mostly empty prairie.

The south end of Broad crossed Fourth Street,

which, appropriately, was the last of the four cross streets. There were two more parallel streets with Broad: Sage was east of Broad, and Mesquite was west. Wardell's only church was at the corner of Sage and Fourth, and Casey could see the steeple from his room.

It was still relatively early, and the town was just beginning to awaken. From somewhere a rooster crowed, the crowing answered by a barking dog. An empty wagon rolled north on Broad, while a lone horseman rode south. Across the street the man who had a moment earlier been sweeping the front porch of the grocery store was now just standing there, looking out over the street. From Casey's elevated position, he could see a woman hanging out clothes over on Sage Street. Turning back into the room, he got dressed, then went downstairs to start his day on his new job.

The first thing Casey did was lay a good fire in the wood-burning cookstove, the efficiency of the fire clearly indicated by the heat it put out, making what was already a very warm day almost unbearably so. The stove was the centerpiece of the kitchen. It was a big stove, standing over five feet high and almost three and a half feet wide. It was a dark, metallic blue, with a baking oven, a warming oven, a solid copper water reservoir with a tap, and a large cooking surface with six lids.

The next thing he did after laying the fire was to roll out the dough; then, by using the open end of an empty can, Casey began cutting out rounds to be baked for biscuits. After that, he washed and sliced up a dozen or so potatoes; then, when he had his oversized skillet so hot that the bacon fat was popping and snapping, he dropped the potatoes into the fat and began frying them. Breakfast this morning would consist of potatoes and eggs . . . not potatoes as a side dish but eggs scrambled in with the potatoes, thickly carved bacon, biscuits and gravy.

Next he put on the coffee, then settled back in a chair to wait for Mr. Lambert and his daughter. By the time they arrived, he already had breakfast prepared for them.

"Well, good morning, Mr. Casey. I didn't expect you into the kitchen so early."

"I didn't want to be late on the first day of my new job."

As he did the night before, Casey served both Little Man and Lucy their breakfast.

"What is this?" Little Man asked, looking at the concoction. "Have you scrambled eggs in with the potatoes?"

"Yes."

"Why, I've never heard of such a thing." He took a bite.

"It's delicious!" Lucy said.

"Yes, it is," Little Man added.

"Thank you."

"Where did you come up with something like this?"

"It's just something that I thought I would try."

Casey filled his own plate and, after being invited, joined the other two at the table.

"Where did you come from, Mr. Casey? What I mean is, someone with your talent for cooking . . . why, I'm surprised you aren't cooking in some fancy restaurant somewhere," Little Man said.

"My food is good, but it isn't fancy," Casey said.

"I can't wait to see how the customers react to your cooking," Little Man said.

The customers' reaction was just as enthusiastic as Little Man's and Lucy's had been. It was very positive, and within two weeks after Casey had arrived, everyone in town was talking about "the new cook" at Little Man's Restaurant. It was considerably more than just talk, though, because every table was filled for every meal, and there were almost always people waiting to get a table.

Casey had been cooking for Little Man Lambert's café for about a month when Lucy came into the kitchen one morning as Casey was preparing breakfast.

"Good morning, Mr. Casey," she said.

"Good morning, Miss Lambert."

"You've been here for a whole month and you're still calling me Miss Lambert. Don't you think you could call me Lucy?"

"Well, I suppose I could," Casey said. "Though I confess to not feeling comfortable about calling the boss's daughter by her first name."

"But I am the boss's daughter, not the boss," Lucy insisted.

Casey chuckled. "You've got me there. Do you want some breakfast?"

"Your cooking is so good that it's going to make me fat. Then where will I be? No, I think I'll just have a biscuit and a cup of coffee," Lucy said. She sat on a stool, then lifted a book and began to read.

"What are you reading?" Casey asked as he put a biscuit on a small plate, then poured a cup of coffee.

"It's a book of poems by Walt Whitman."

"Very good choice. Walt Whitman is an excellent poet," Casey said.

"You have read Whitman?" Lucy asked, surprised and just a little skeptical that a cook had read anything but cookbooks and labels, let alone Whitman.

A broad smile spread across Lucy's face. She hesitated for a second before she spoke again.

"I think you might be pulling my leg, just a little," Lucy said. "I'll bet you don't even like poetry."

"Is that what you think?" Casey asked with a twinkle in his eye.

"I do indeed," Lucy replied.

"Poetry is the spontaneous overflow of powerful feelings; it takes its origin from emotion recollected in tranquillity," Casey said.

"Oh, my," Lucy said. "What an absolutely beautiful and delightfully poetic thing to say. Why, do you know you are using poetry to describe poetry? That's positively brilliant!"

"Yes, William Wordsworth is a brilliant man all right."

"William Wordsworth?"

"He is the one who first described poetry in a way that even the most uneducated among us would be able to understand, and appreciate. The phrase 'recollected in tranquillity' is his offering, not mine."

"I'd like to visit Mr. Wordsworth sometime, just so I can tell him how much I appreciate his comment."

"Alas, you won't be able to do that, dear girl. Unfortunately, Mr. Wordsworth died in 1850. But tell me, Lucy, what poem are you reading right now?"

"It is called 'To A Stranger,'" Lucy said. "I think it is one of Walt Whitman's most interesting poems."

"Yes, I like it too," Casey said. He was reflective for a moment. "You might even say that it resonates with my soul."

Casey cleared his throat, and began to recite:

> "Passing stranger! you do not know how longingly
>   I look upon you,
> You must be he I was seeking, or she I was seeking,
>   (it comes to me as of a dream,)
> I have somewhere surely lived a life of joy with you,
> All is recall'd as we flit by each other, fluid, affec-
>   tionate, chaste, matured,
> You grew up with me, were a boy with me or a girl
>   with me,
> I ate with you and slept with you, your body has
>   become not yours only nor left my body mine
>   only,

You give me the pleasure of your eyes, face, flesh, as
we pass, you take of my beard, breast, hands, in
return,
I am not to speak to you, I am to think of you when
I sit alone or wake at night alone,
I am to wait, I do not doubt I am to meet you again,
I am to see to it that I do not lose you."

"Oh, how marvelous!" Lucy said, clapping her hands. "You spoke the words so beautifully, why, it was much more enjoyable than just reading the poem."

"Once you get the meter and understand the tone and tint of the poem, you will get as much enjoyment from reading poetry as you can by hearing it read," Casey said, setting Lucy's breakfast on the small table by her stool.

CHAPTER EIGHTEEN

★

"Papa, who do you suppose Mr. Casey is?" Lucy asked.

"What do you mean, darlin'?" Little Man replied. "He's Ken Casey."

"I don't mean that," Lucy said. "I mean, why do you think he is a cook?"

Little Man laughed. "He's a cook because he is the best cook I've ever seen. Since he hired on, our business has nearly doubled."

"Oh, I know he is a good cook, but I think he is more than that. Did you know that he reads all the time?"

"Lots of folks read, I suppose."

"Yes, but they don't read the kind of books that Mr. Casey reads. He reads books on philosophy, religion, and poetry. This morning I mentioned a poem by Walt Whitman, and he was able to recite the entire thing."

"Maybe he just likes poetry," Little Man suggested.

"No, it's more than that," Lucy said. "He is a man of great mystery and, I think, sadness. I wonder about his past." She smiled. "I know: I'm going to investigate his past. I'm going to solve the mystery."

"Darlin', have you ever thought that he may not

want the mystery of his past solved? Some people don't want their past brought up," Little Man said. "If you value Mr. Casey's friendship, you'll leave this be."

"Oh, stuff and feathers," Lucy said. "You know there isn't anything in Mr. Casey's past that it would bother him for anyone to know."

"You don't know that," Little Man said. "I'm telling you, Lucy. Leave it be."

"All right, all right, I won't go digging around trying to find out anything. But I do wonder."

"Ha! He ain't nothin' but a scarred-up old man," Quince Anders said when Lucy shared with him her curiosity about Casey. "He's gotta be fifty or sixty years old. When it's somebody that old, you can't really tell how old he is. And what are you curious about? He's a cook, that's all. He ain't never been anything else."

"Yes, but why is he a cook?" Lucy asked. "Why, he could be a schoolteacher, a lawyer, or just about anything he wanted. He's the smartest man I've ever met."

"He can't be all that smart, else he wouldn't be cookin'," Quince said. He was taking his lunch in the café at the time, and he spooned some beans into his mouth. "But I'll say this for him: he sure can cook."

"Papa says he's the best cook he's ever seen."

"Listen, don't you go be gettin' all interested in him now, you are likely to make me jealous."

"Oh, pooh," Lucy said. "In the first place, it's like you said, he's much too old for me. And in the second place, what right do you have to be jealous, anyway? I don't belong to you."

"Not yet, you don't," Quince said. He smiled and ate another spoonful of the spicy beans. "But one of these days you will."

"Aren't you being just a little overconfident?" Lucy said flirtatiously.

"Nah, I'm just sure of myself is all," Quince replied with a broad smile. "And you know it, too, don't you?"

"You talk too much," Lucy said, but she ameliorated her charge with a demure smile.

Later that evening, when Casey went out behind the café to dispose of some trash, he saw Quince Anders and a couple of other cowboys out in the alley. Quince had painted a circle on a couple of boards and they were standing up about fifteen yards away.

"Now, here is what I'm goin' to do," he explained to the others. "I'm goin' to have my back to these two targets. I'm going to hold my hand out like this, with a rock on the back of it. Then I'm goin' to turn my hand and let the rock fall—pull my pistol, whirl around, and shoot a hole in the middle of the circle on both boards . . . and I'll do all that before the rock hits the pie pan."

"There can't nobody do that," Stanley Goff said.

"It's goin' to cost you a dollar to see me do it."

"What if I pay you a dollar and you can't do it?"

"I'll give you the dollar back," Quince explained.

"I'll pay a dollar," Dooley, one of the others, said, and soon all four came up with a dollar each.

"What about the cook?" Stanley asked, pointing to Casey, who was standing just outside the kitchen door. "He's standin' there at the back door of the café. Is he goin' to have to pay a dollar too?"

"No. We'll let him hold the money," Quince said. "If I can do it, he'll give all the money to me. If I can't do it, he'll give the money back to each of you. Is that all right with you, cook?" he called.

"That's fine with me, Mr. Anders," Casey answered.

The four young men gave their dollars to Casey, who leaned against the back wall of the café with his arms folded across his chest to watch Quince's shooting display.

Quince turned his back to the targets, put a pie pan on the ground, then held his right hand out in front of him and put a rock on the back of his hand. After a second of hesitation, he turned his hand and the rock fell. At the same time, his right hand snaked his pistol from its holster and he whirled and fired in one extremely fast and fluid motion. After the sound of the pistol, Casey heard the sound of the rock hitting the pie pan.

"Ha! You have to give the dollar back! You only shot once."

"I shot twice," Quince said.

"What do you mean, you shot twice? I was standin' right here, I heard it. You only shot once!"

"Look at the targets," Quince said.

"All right, I'll look at the targets, then you'll see that I'm . . ." Stanley paused in mid-sentence. "I'll be damned! How the hell did you do that?"

There was a bullet hole inside the white ring on each of the boards.

"Wow! You must be the fastest gun ever!" Dooley said, and the rest agreed with him.

"Yeah, I reckon I am," Quince said. He came over to Casey. "What do you think, cook?" he asked. "Am I the fastest you've ever seen?"

"You may be," Casey said.

"I'll bet he's not faster than Ded Axton, or Luke Draco," Dooley said.

"Ded Axton is dead," Quince said.

"Luke Draco ain't dead," Stanley said.

"Maybe *he* ain't dead, but Ded Axton is."

"I don't think Axton is dead, either," Dooley said.

"Sure he is. He was kilt in a gunfight back in Soda Springs, Texas, three or four years ago," Quince insisted.

"He wasn't kilt. He kilt three men in a shoot-out. Some say he was shot hisself, and some say he wasn't. But he rode out of town, and there ain't nobody seen him since then. And there didn't nobody ever find the body. There's some that say he's still alive," Dooley said.

"Then how come nobody has ever heard from him since then?" Quince asked. "It's been at least three or four years."

"No it ain't. It's only two years," Dooley said. "I still

got a copy of the newspaper with the article about him in it."

"All right, two years. You think somebody can just disappear for two years and don't nobody ever see 'im?"

"I don't know. Maybe he has his reasons."

"Anyway, if he was still alive, I could beat him. Why, he's got to be an old man now. I could beat him easy. Hell, I could beat anyone you name: Clay Allison, John Wesley Hardin, Luke Draco, or Ded Axton. You name 'em, I could beat 'em. Don't you think I could beat them, cook?"

"No, you wouldn't beat any of them," Casey replied.

The quiet response startled Quince and surprised everyone else.

"What do you mean I wouldn't beat them? You seen how fast I am. Do you think that any of them, even in their best day, is faster than I am?"

"No, I didn't say that. You may well be faster than any of them," Casey said. "But if it came down to a gunfight between you and any of those men you just named, you would lose."

"Ha!" Quince said. "How do you come by that conclusion? Didn't you just say I was probably faster?"

"Yes, I did."

"Well, then, there you go."

"You don't understand," Casey said, his tone condescending.

Quince was confused. "What is it I don't understand?"

"You don't understand what it takes to be a good gunfighter. A gunfighter isn't good because he is fast, or accurate. A gunfighter is good because he can kill a man without qualms."

"What does 'qualms' mean?" Quince asked.

"It means killing someone without so much as a second thought. Could you kill a man without even thinking about it?"

"Well, I . . ." Quince started, then he paused. "Killing a man—now, that's not something you'd do without even thinking about it. I mean, who could actually do that? But I suppose I could if I had to," he concluded.

Casey shook his head. "It's too late, Mr. Anders, you are already dead."

"What do you mean, I'm already dead?"

"I mean you're dead because you had to stop to think about it. While you were thinking, Allison, Hardin, Draco, or Axton would be shooting, and you would be dead."

"Yeah, but you was just askin' a question. If'n it was for real—" Quince started to say.

"If this had been real, you would already be dead," Casey interrupted. "Like you said, Mr. Anders, killing a man isn't something you do without even thinking about it. It is an awesome thing, and at that last moment, just before it's time to pull the trigger, most decent men will hesitate, just as you did when I asked you the question."

"Yeah, well, everyone would," Quince insisted.

"No, not everyone," Casey disputed. "There are some who don't care if they live or die. And since they have no regard for their own life, they have no regard for the life of another. Such a man can kill without qualms."

"Are you telling me that's why someone like Ded Axton was so good at killin' people? That he didn't care if he lived or died, and that he could kill a man like . . . like it wasn't no more'n squashin' a mosquito on his arm?"

"That's exactly what I'm telling you."

"And because of that, no matter how fast I am, you're saying that Ded Axton would beat me?"

"Yes."

"How do you do that? What I'm askin' is, what does a fella have to do to get to be like Axton is? Someone who could kill without . . . qualms?" Quince asked.

"One has to sell his soul to the devil," Casey answered. "And I don't think that is something you want to do."

Casey handed the money over to Quince, then went back into the kitchen, leaving Quince and the others staring at the back door.

"What do you suppose that was all about?" Dooley asked. "That business about selling your soul to the devil."

"I don't know," Quince answered. He pulled the cylinder from his pistol, removed the empty shell casings, then reloaded. "And what's more, I'm not sure I want to know."

"Yeah, well, I wouldn't worry about it. He's an old man. What the hell does he know about such things, anyway?"

"I've got a feeling that he knows a lot more than anyone might think," Quince said. "There's somethin' about him. It's like Lucy said . . . somethin' kinda mysterious, if you know what I mean."

"Ha!" Dooley said. "There ain't nothing mysterious about him. He ain't nothin' but an old cook. And all that talk about gunfightin' and the like. Hell, what does he know about it? He don't even wear a gun."

MONDAY, SEPTEMBER 12, 1887
FORT WORTH, TEXAS

Elliot Crabtree was a small man who was always meticulously dressed in a three-piece suit. He wore rimless glasses, and carried a gold watch in his vest pocket, the watch secured by a gold chain that stretched across his chest. Crabtree was a very practical man who earned his living as a telegrapher for the Texas and Pacific Railway. When, in the course of his duty, he came across some information that he realized could be profitable for him, he undertook a careful study of all angles to see how he might best take advantage of the information. Of course, there was never any question of him using it directly; Crabtree was much too cautious for that. But information like this had a price, and the best way to utilize this valuable knowledge would be to sell it.

The question was, of course, who would be his best customer? On the surface it might seem that the best customer would be the one who would pay him the most money, but for a thinking person like Crabtree, there was more than money involved. And because Crabtree was a careful man who planned every move, he made a list of things he must consider.

1. Who would pay him the most?
2. Who had the best chance of success?
3. Who would be least likely to involve him in anything beyond the initial exchange of information?

As he contemplated those questions, he also considered the people who would make up his customer base. He had to be very careful and choose the right one, because information like this couldn't be put out on a "highest-bid" program. The fewer people who knew about it, the better the chance of success. And the fewer who knew about it, the less chance there was that his own involvement would be discovered. Once he made the decision as to who to go to, he would have to let the buyer know that he was the *only* one with the information.

That evening, Crabtree had dinner with Buckley Paddock, the editor and publisher of the *Fort Worth Democrat*, the town's only newspaper.

"Tell me, Buckley," Crabtree asked as he was salting his meat, making the question as offhanded as possible, "you've reported on many outlaws. Who, in your opinion, is the smartest among them?"

"That's rather a trick question, Elliot. I suppose someone who is really smart wouldn't be engaged in criminal activity at all."

"That's probably true, but I'm sure you know some outlaw who is very smart."

"Well, I suppose that would be Angus Pugh."

"What makes him so smart?"

"First of all, he's a college graduate, and he is very book smart. But he is also smart in other ways. I know that he has been involved in a dozen different illegal activities, but he's never been caught, because he's never made a mistake that would let the law chase him down."

"That's very interesting," Crabtree said.

CHAPTER NINETEEN

★

The day after his lunch meeting with Buckley Paddock, Crabtree sent an unauthorized telegram to the head of the Texas Rangers, indicating that it was from the city marshal of Fort Worth:

> SEEK INFORMATION ON ANGUS PUGH STOP WHAT IS LAST KNOWN LOCATION STOP JIM COURTRIGHT CITY MARSHAL FT WORTH

Within half an hour, Crabtree received a reply:

> LAST KNOWN LOCATION OF ANGUS PUGH IS PIPE CREEK TEXAS STOP NO KNOWN PAPER OUT FOR HIM STOP ALLEN MARSH CAPTAIN TEXAS RANGERS

Elliot Crabtree took a stagecoach to Pipe Creek, then went to the Purple Pig, which was the first saloon he saw. Buying a beer, he found a table back in the corner where he could observe the other customers. He had been there less than half an hour when he overheard a conversation that he could use.

"Hey, Kelly, didn't I see you with Angus Pugh yesterday?"

"Yeah, so what?"

"I thought you 'n' Pugh had a fallin'-out."

"We got it all worked out."

"So now you 'n' Pugh's tight again?"

"Yeah, we're friends. Unless he wants to borrow money," Kelly added. "Real friends don't try to borrow money from friends."

"Well, where the hell are we supposed to borrow money if not from friends?"

The others laughed.

Crabtree observed the interplay in silence, then he stepped up to the bar.

"Yes, sir?" the bartender asked.

"Do you know that gentleman over there? I believe I heard the others call him Kelly."

"Yes, Roy Kelly, I know him."

"I should like to buy his next drink," Crabtree said.

"Why?"

"Because I want to meet him."

The bartender looked at him with a questioning expression on his face. "You ain't one of them *funny* men, are you? 'Cause if you are, I'm tellin' you right now, Roy Kelly ain't someone you're goin' to want to meet. He's likely to haul off and clean your plow good."

For a second, Crabtree wasn't sure what the bartender meant by "funny" man. Then it dawned on him.

"What? No, no! If you are asking if I am a pederast I most definitely am not. I want to make a business proposition to the gentleman, that's all."

"A business proposition?"

"Yes."

"What kind of business proposition?"

"That would be between me and Mr. Kelly."

"All right, what kind of drink do you want to buy him?"

"Oh, I have no idea. But when he comes over to buy another, give him whatever he wants, and if he questions you as to who paid for it, I would appreciate it if you point me out to him." Crabtree put a dollar on the table. "This should cover the cost of the drink."

"Oh, yeah, that'll more'n cover it, since the most expensive drink we have is a dime," the bartender said, taking the dollar. "The reason I ask what kind of business you're a-wantin' to do with Kelly, is 'cause he ain't exactly what you would call a businessman."

"As I explained, it is business that involves no one else, if you understand what I mean," Crabtree said pointedly. "Oh, and keep the change."

"Yes, sir," the bartender said, looking around first, then pocketing the dollar. "I understand exactly what you mean."

"Thank you."

Crabtree returned to his table and waited. About

ten minutes later Kelly stepped up to the bar to get another drink. Crabtree watched the bartender push Kelly's money back, then tell him that someone else had bought the drink for him. Crabtree even saw the surprised look on Kelly's face, then he saw Kelly turn to look in his direction. Picking up his drink, Kelly walked over to Crabtree's table.

"Why did you buy me the drink?" Kelly asked suspiciously.

"Because I want to do some business with you," Crabtree replied.

"What sort of business?"

"I understand that you are acquainted with Angus Pugh."

"Yeah, I know him. Mister, if you got it in mind you want me to kill 'im, you better get yourself another man."

"No, it's nothing like that. I would like for you to arrange a meeting between us, that's all."

Kelly looked at Crabtree with a surprised expression on his face, then he laughed. "*You* want to meet Angus Pugh?"

"Yes."

"Excuse me, mister, but why in hell would you want to meet Angus Pugh? I don't know what you want with him, but I can tell you right now that you 'n' Pugh ain't the kind that's likely to have a friendly drink together. Fact is, you look to me like the kind of person Pugh would just as soon shoot as talk to. I'm pretty sure you don't really want to talk to him."

"I have a business proposal for him."

"No you don't," Kelly said.

"Yes I do."

"Listen to me, mister. You bought me a drink, so I figure I owe you this much. I'm tellin' you, Pugh is not the kind of man somebody like you would want to have anything to do with. So if you're smart, you'll take my advice and drop this, right now."

"What do you mean, somebody like me?"

"You know what I mean. You got the look of proper about you. Pugh don't exactly run in what you would call proper circles."

"I have been told that Angus Pugh is a very intelligent man, that he is even a college graduate."

"Yeah, he's smart all right. Most of the time when he's talkin' I don't have an idea in hell what he's talkin' about. But just 'cause he's smart don't mean he'd be interested in becomin' your friend. Pugh don't make friends very easy."

"I've no interest in becoming friends with him. My interest is purely from a business point of view."

"What kind of business?"

"As my proposal is for Pugh, it is really none of your concern," Crabtree said.

"Well, if it's none of my concern, why the hell would I be interested in setting up a meeting for you?"

"Would twenty dollars be enough to get you interested?"

"Wait a minute, let me get this straight. You're willin' to give me twenty dollars, and all I have to do is just to set up a meetin' between you and Angus Pugh?"

"Yes."

"You're goin' to give me twenty dollars to set up a meetin', but you won't tell me what the meetin' is about."

"Part of the twenty dollars is to keep you from asking me any more questions."

Kelly stroked his chin as he stared at Crabtree.

"Where is the money?"

"You set up the meeting first. If he shows up, I'll give you the twenty dollars."

"I want half of it now."

"All right," Crabtree said. He took ten dollars from his billfold and handed it to Kelly.

"I'll be back in a few minutes."

After Kelly left, Crabtree remained at the table, nursing his beer and looking around at the other patrons of the saloon. Most were loud and unsavory, and he tried to make himself as invisible as possible, because he didn't want anyone to come speak to him. After about ten minutes, Kelly came back into the saloon, and Crabtree breathed a sigh of relief. He was ready to leave this place.

"Did you find Mr. Pugh?" Crabtree asked.

"Yes."

"Good. Where is he?"

"There's a saloon on the other side of town called the Slaughter House. You go there and wait. Pugh will meet you there."

"The Slaughter House?" Crabtree said, flinching at the name. "Good heavens! Do you mean to tell me there is actually a saloon in this town that is called the Slaughter House?"

"Yeah. It took its name from the fact that it's real close to the slaughterhouse where they kill beef and pork and such. But some say it's also 'cause they's so many folks that gets kilt in there. Seems like it's just 'bout ever' month or so."

Suddenly the saloon he was in right now didn't look all that bad to him. "Couldn't you ask Mr. Pugh to come here to meet me?"

"You want to meet him or not?"

"Yes, I do."

"Well, Pugh's kind of a particular man, you see. If folks want to talk to him, they have to go to *him*. He don't go to meet nobody."

"But to meet in a place called the Slaughter House? Perhaps we could meet somewhere else, and I could go to him."

"Look, it don't matter to me whether you meet him or not. I set up the meeting, which is all I was s'posed to do. You can give me the rest of my money now, or you can give the rest of the money to me over at the Slaughter House. It's up to you."

"All right, if this is the only way I can meet him, I'll go along with it. Take me over to the Slaughter House."

"What do you mean, take you over to it? Hell, can't you walk?"

"I would prefer not to go alone."

Kelly stared at Crabtree for a long moment, then he laughed.

"I tell you what, I'd damn near do this for free, just to see someone like you go into the Slaughter House."

When the two men reached the Slaughter House Saloon, Crabtree could tell just from the outside that this was a much more scandalous establishment than anything he had ever before visited. There were a couple of passed-out drunks on the wooden porch in front of the saloon, and the saloon itself—indeed the entire street—reeked of the smell of sour whiskey, stale beer, unwashed bodies, and even the unmistakable odor of urine, all this even over the smell of the nearby slaughterhouse.

"This is it," Kelly said. "Give me the rest of my money, then go on inside and wait for him."

"This place? You want me to go into a place like this?"

"What's the matter?" Kelly asked. "Are you scared?"

"I'm . . . a little uneasy, yes," Crabtree said.

Uneasy? He felt a sense of fear, bordering on terror, and for a moment he was ready to just give up his idea. But no, there was too much money involved, and in order for his plan to work, he would have to do business with someone like Angus Pugh. And if that meant he had to meet him here, then so be it. At least it was the middle of the day, and in a public place. He didn't think he would be in danger in a public place if he did nothing to provoke anyone. And he would be very careful not to provoke anyone.

"Would you . . . would you go in with me?" Crabtree asked.

"Look, I'll go in with you, but I ain't goin' to stay. There's a man hangs around here by the name Pecorino, and me 'n' him ain't exactly been gettin' along lately. So we've come to a understandin': I don't come in here, and he don't come into the Purple Pig."

"All right, thank you," Crabtree said.

Taking a deep breath—which, given the stench, he regretted instantly—and squaring his shoulders, Crabtree followed Kelly through the batwing doors and into the saloon.

"All right," Kelly said. "I got you in here. You just wait, Pugh will contact you."

"How will he recognize me?" Crabtree asked, and Kelly laughed.

Crabtree began looking around the room and realized at once why Kelly had laughed. Crabtree was not a very large man, his hair was blond and thinning, and he was wearing a suit and tie. He stood out among the other saloon patrons as a kitten would among a pack of wolves.

"Hey, Kelly!" the bartender yelled. "You better get on out of here. If Pecorino comes in here and sees you, he's liable to shoot you."

"Or I'll shoot him," Kelly said.

"Either way, I don't need any more shootin' in my place, and I thought you and Pecorino had a deal cooked up betwixt the two of you."

"I'm goin', I'm goin'," Kelly said. He glanced over at Crabtree. "You're on your own."

CHAPTER TWENTY

★

Crabtree watched Kelly leave, then felt frightened and exposed. It was funny: Kelly was not the kind of person Crabtree would choose to be around, but given the situation, he would rather have Kelly with him than to be in a place like this alone. He thought of the saying "Better the devil you know than the devil you don't."

Cautiously, quietly, and wishing he could slip by without anyone noticing him, he walked through the saloon and chose a table at the back corner, staying as far away from everyone else as he could. Men like the ones who frequented this saloon made him extremely uncomfortable, and the loud and boisterous talk did nothing to ease his apprehension.

The bartender called over to him. "Mister, we ain't got table service here. If you want a drink, you need to come here to get it."

"Thank you, but I shan't require anything for the moment. I'll just sit here quietly and out of the way," Crabtree replied.

"The hell you will. This here ain't no restin' place," the bartender said. "If you come in here, you have to drink."

The thought of consuming anything in this establishment was enough to make Crabtree gag, but he decided that the alcoholic content of a beer might be enough to keep it from poisoning him. He started to call it out, but remembered that the bartender said he would have to come up to get it, so he walked up to the bar, paid for a beer, then returned to the table.

Crabtree knew he was unlikely to meet any of his acquaintances in this place. At least that part of it was good, because it made it an extremely remote possibility that there would be anyone here who might recognize him. And for his plan to work, it was very important that he not be recognized.

Nervously, Crabtree checked his pocket watch as well as the clock that stood against the wall of the saloon, and he nursed his beer slowly as he waited. There had been no definite time established for him and Angus Pugh to meet. Kelly had only said, "Pugh ain't the kind of man that you can set a time to. But he'll be there, and he'll find you."

Maybe Pugh was the kind of man who didn't go by any sense of time, but Crabtree was. He made up his mind that he would give Pugh only fifteen minutes more, and if he didn't show up by then, Crabtree would leave.

"You've never been here before, have you, mister? I know you haven't, because I would remember a handsome fellow like you."

The speaker was one of the bar girls who had come

over to his table and was now running one of her hands through his hair. She leaned over him, and Crabtree thought that one or both of her breasts might spill out on him. He found the woman, by her dress and action, to be repugnant and yet strangely stimulating as well. She was attractive in a rather hard-looking way.

"No," Crabtree answered, "I haven't been here before."

"What brings you here now, honey? Did you just discover us?" Now she had taken a lock of her hair and was curling it around her finger.

"I . . . I'm not quite sure why I came here," he answered, and that was almost the truth, because he was beginning to have second thoughts about the entire operation.

"Would you like to have a good time, honey? It doesn't cost much," the girl said.

"I'm not sure what you mean by 'a good time.'"

"I mean go upstairs to my room with me. I think we can figure out something to do once we get there, don't you?"

"Oh, uh, no, thank you, I'd rather not. I'm waiting for someone."

She straddled his leg and pressed herself against his thigh. "Oh, honey, I can make certain that you finish in plenty of time," the girl said in a seductive voice.

"No, I . . . uh . . . am not a habitué of prostitutes. Please, I told you, I'm waiting for someone."

"You know what, Mabel, I think you've got a fella

that don't know what to do with a woman," one of the saloon patrons said.

"Maybe he don't even like women," another suggested, and to Crabtree's fear and chagrin he had not only been noticed by the others, he had suddenly become the butt of the jokes of the men in here. He was both embarrassed and frightened. This was not at all what he wanted. He wanted to come in here as unobtrusively as possible, get his business taken care of, then leave.

"Leave Mr. Crabtree alone," a cold, calm voice said. "We have business to discuss."

The girl, with a look that Crabtree could only describe as fear, hopped up from his leg and walked away quickly. The man, who Crabtree thought must be Angus Pugh, sat down across the table from him. He realized now that this man had been in the saloon for the entire time, because he had seen him standing at the bar when he first came in.

"You are Crabtree, aren't you?"

"Yes," Crabtree said.

Pugh pulled a long black cigar from his shirt pocket and held a match to the end. Not until his head was wreathed with cigar smoke did he speak again.

"Get up," Pugh said.

"I beg your pardon?"

"Get up and switch chairs with me. I don't sit with my back to the room."

"All right, if you insist." Crabtree got up from his chair and Pugh came around to take it.

"And while you're up, get me a whiskey," Pugh said.

"A whiskey. Yes, of course," Crabtree said. "I'll be right back."

Crabtree walked over to the bar, feeling the eyes of everyone on him, wishing he could have arranged this meeting anyplace else in the whole country. "Mr. Pugh wants—"

"I know what he wants," the bartender said, pouring a whiskey. He waited until Crabtree paid for it before he slid it across the counter. Crabtree took it back across the room and handed it to Pugh. Pugh removed the cigar from his mouth, tossed the whiskey down, then replaced the cigar.

"Kelly said you had a proposition," he said.

"Yes, I do."

"What is it?"

"It is one that could be most lucrative, for both of us."

Pugh squinted through the tobacco smoke. "How lucrative?"

"One hundred thousand dollars," Crabtree said. He studied Pugh's face to see if he could ascertain any reaction to the large sum of money, but the other man's expression didn't change.

"You must want someone killed awfully bad if you are willing to pay one hundred thousand dollars to have the job done."

"What?" Crabtree gasped. "Oh, my goodness, no! What are you talking about? What in heaven's name would make you think I want someone killed?"

"Believe me, with that much money involved, the chances are very good that someone is going to get killed," Pugh said easily.

"How would that . . . what I mean is . . . suppose that were true? Suppose in the course of this operation that it became necessary for someone to be killed? Not murdered, mind you, but killed in the carrying out of the operation. Would that deter you from getting involved?"

"This operation we are discussing—it would be a felony, would it?"

"A felony? Well, yes, I suppose it would be. But I have been led to believe, perhaps inaccurately, that . . . uh . . ."

"That I would be capable of committing a felonious act?" Pugh replied. "Yes, I am, I'm quite capable. But the point I am making is that if someone is killed during the perpetration of a felony, that killing is murder in the first degree."

"Oh."

"But to answer your question, I'm not concerned about someone getting killed, unless I'm the one dying," he said.

"Now you have made me curious," Crabtree said. "Suppose I had wanted you to kill someone. Are you telling me you would be willing to do something like that?"

"Mr. Crabtree, you are the one who wanted to meet me with some kind of business deal," Pugh said. "Did you perhaps assume that I was a choirboy?"

"What? No, uh, no, nothing like that. And please don't get me wrong: I'm not judging you. Far be it from me to judge you."

"I'm glad you feel that way. Because you need to understand that once you get involved with me, you are as guilty of anything I do with regard to this . . . proposition you have to offer, as if you had personally committed the act. You do understand that, don't you? *You* are no longer a choirboy."

"I—I guess not," Crabtree said. "But part of the reason I have chosen you is because I have been told, and I can see, that you are a very intelligent man. And it is my wish and expectation that my name be kept out of this."

"It's not merely a matter of keeping your name out of it," Pugh said. "The fact that you may never be connected to it in any legal way will not absolve your actual connection to the crime. Can your conscience accept that?"

"Yes," Crabtree said. "Yes, I'm quite sure I can."

"Good," Pugh said. "I wanted to get that established before we proceeded any further. I don't want to be dealing with someone who has a false image of moral superiority."

"I assure you, Mr. Pugh, I have no such image."

"Then let's discuss business, shall we, Mr. Crabtree? What, exactly, is this business deal you have?"

Crabtree paused for a long moment before he answered. What if Pugh agreed to do what he wanted but then decided to cut him completely out of the picture?

If he did that, what could Crabtree do about it? The truth was, he could do nothing about it.

Pugh stood up.

"What is it? Where are you going?" Crabtree asked.

"If you have something to discuss with me, tell me now," Pugh said. "Otherwise, I'm leaving. I simply don't have the time to waste."

"No, please, don't leave. It's just that . . ."

"You are afraid of me, aren't you, Mr. Crabtree?" Pugh said.

"I am a little, yes."

"What do you think I'm going to do to you?"

"I'm afraid that I'll tell you the plan and you'll cut me out."

"Are you?"

"Yes. I need your promise that you won't do anything like that."

Pugh laughed.

"What's so funny?"

"If you really think I might do something like that, what good would my promise be that I won't? I could just lie to you."

"Yes, I suppose you could."

"But you can't do this—whatever it is—without me, can you?"

"No."

"And since I don't even know what it is, it is equally certain that I can't do it without you," Pugh said. "So I guess we're just going to have to trust each other."

"Yes, I guess so."

"Let's talk about money," Pugh said. "Have you thought about how we're going to share the money?"

"Yes. Your share will come to forty thousand dollars."

"I thought you said this was a one-hundred-thousand-dollar deal?"

"Yes, it is."

"But my share is forty thousand?"

"Yes."

"No," Pugh said.

"Mr. Pugh, I would think you would be very pleased with that amount. As I'm sure you know, that is a great deal of money. That is more money than many people earn in a lifetime."

"But it isn't even half," Pugh said. "Why should you get more than half?"

"Because I am the one with the information. And I am the one who has come up with the plan."

"Information and planning are good," Pugh said. "But I assume whoever has this one hundred thousand dollars isn't going to give it to us just because we ask for it. Am I right?"

"Yes."

"Didn't you say a few minutes ago that you were concerned that I might just take all the money and leave you out of it?"

"Yes, I did say that."

"If I actually had that in mind, I wouldn't be arguing

with you about the amount, would I? I would agree with anything you say, then just keep the money anyway. But if you play fair with me, I'll hold up my end of the bargain."

"What would you consider to be a fair amount?"

"It comes down to what I said a moment ago. When it comes right down to it, you are going to need someone to actually persuade whoever has the money to give it to us. Is that right?"

"Yes, though if everything works as I have planned it, the persuasion will be more by trickery than armed robbery."

"Nevertheless, that possibility is there or you wouldn't need me," Pugh insisted. "And that means I'm going to have to have some men with me."

"Oh, yes indeed, you will need some armed men with you. That is a part of the ruse I'm constructing for you. The armed men will make the people of the town believe you are who you say you are."

"All right. If I have to have armed men, that means they'll have to be paid, and since they will be in on the operation, they will know how much money is involved. That means they'll have to be paid well. I tell you what. Let's make this sixty thousand for me and forty thousand for you."

"Wait a minute, now you have just reversed the numbers. This way, you'll be getting more than half," Crabtree said.

"Yes, I will."

"You said that the men you'll have with you will have to be paid well. Am I to take it that you will be responsible for paying them out of your share of the money?"

"If my share is sixty thousand dollars, yes, I'll be happy to pay them out of my share."

Crabtree stared at Pugh for a long moment. He was committed now, and in truth he had been willing to settle for twenty thousand dollars, just to make certain that there would be no way that the authorities could ever discover his involvement.

"These men you will get, they are trustworthy?"

"Trustworthy? They are trustworthy only so far as it suits their own purposes," he said. Pugh smiled, though it wasn't a smile of humor. "But then, Mr. Crabtree, we can say that same thing about either of us as well."

"What do you mean, either of us?" Crabtree asked.

"Tsk, tsk, tsk, Mr. Crabtree. I thought we had already dispensed with the moral superiority thing."

"Yes, yes, all right," Crabtree said. "But the men who are with you, they must not know of my involvement. No one must know. I'll provide you with the information, and I'll draw up the plan for you; but as far as anyone is concerned, this entire thing—from conception, to information, to planning, to the actual operation—is all your idea. Can we agree on that?"

"Yes, we can agree on that."

"Then I have no problem with you taking sixty thousand dollars as your share. And if this particular arrangement works as I have planned, and I'm sure it will, then I've no doubt but that we can find additional opportunities to work together."

"All right," Pugh said. "What is this plan you have?"

"Soon—I don't yet have the date, but will shortly—a Texas and Pacific train will be carrying a shipment of one hundred thousand dollars to a bank in San Diego, California. You and the men you will select to work with you, will go to Wardell, Texas, which is in Presidio County. That's where you will meet the train and take the money."

Pugh squinted at Crabtree. "Mister, there had better be more to your plan than that. What you're saying is that we are to rob the train when it gets to Wardell, and your end of the bargain is merely to tell me what train. That information is not worth forty thousand dollars. It's not even worth four thousand dollars."

Crabtree smiled and shook his head. "You misunderstand, Mr. Pugh. You won't rob the train: the messenger is going to turn the money over to you."

"Why would he do that?"

"Because I will provide you with six genuine Texas and Pacific Railway detective badges, a letter from the Texas and Pacific Railway, as well as a letter from the governor. The T&P letters, plus the one from the governor, will instruct the messenger to transfer the funds to you."

"How are you going to get those letters?"

"It's quite simple. I work for the Texas and Pacific, I will simply write out the letters on Texas and Pacific stationery."

"All right, but you also said something about a letter

of authorization from the governor that would have the money turned over to me. How are you going to get that letter?" Pugh asked.

"I'm not going to get it, Mr. Pugh. I already have it," Crabtree said with a smile as he removed an envelope from his jacket pocket and presented it.

Pugh opened the letter to read it:

Office of the Governor
State of Texas
Austin, Texas

September 5, 1887

To Whom It May Concern:
    Be it known that the carrier of this letter is authorized to act on my behalf with regard to the transfer of railroad funds.

                        L. S. Ross
                        Governor

P.S. The bearer is acting in accordance with guber-natorial directive and is hereby authorized to su-persede any and all local law officials until such time as the transfer of funds is made.

"How the hell did you get this from the governor?"

"It was simple," Crabtree said with a smile. "I simply asked him to authorize the transfer of railroad funds from the private account to the state account in payments for fees to the state. Then I added the P.S. to the letter he had already signed."

"Very smart," Pugh said with a smile. "I have to hand it to you, Crabtree. This is a good plan."

"Now, please, from this point on, I want no further contact with you," Crabtree said.

"How will you get your share of the money?"

"I have that figured out as well. Put the money in a box marked 'Books,' and send it by rail express to me at the Texas and Pacific Depot in Fort Worth."

Pugh stuck his hand across the table. "I suppose we can shake hands on this, for what it might be worth . . . that is, one immoral felon to another."

Hesitantly, Crabtree extended his hand.

"Mr. Pugh, I wonder if I might ask another favor of you?"

"What would that be?"

"I wonder if you would see me safely to the stagecoach depot. I find this particular area of the town rather disconcerting."

Pugh laughed out loud. "I'll be glad to," he said. "It won't do to have anything happen to you before this job is done. You said you don't yet have the date. When will I get the rest of the information?"

"I will know by next Friday. Come to the Texas and Pacific Depot in Fort Worth," Crabtree said. "I'll have all the information finalized by then. I will also have an additional letter that will help."

"Anytime on Friday?"

"Yes, anytime. I'm the telegrapher, and on Friday next I'll be working from eight in the morning until six that evening," Crabtree explained.

"All right. I'll be there," Pugh promised. He smiled. "Come on, I'll walk you to the stagecoach depot."

CHAPTER TWENTY-ONE

★

The town of Stapleton, Texas, was little more than a flyblown speck on the Texas and Pacific Railway. It had reached its peak when it was "end of track," a hell on wheels with enough cafés, saloons, and bawdy houses to take care of the men who were building the railroad. But as the railroad continued on its westward trek, it became less of a hell on wheels and was beginning to establish itself as a productive community.

Luke Draco was a bounty hunter who had been very successful at his trade. After tracking Muley Baxter to Stapleton, he paid someone ten dollars to deliver a message to Baxter. The message read:

I have a good-paying opportunity for you. I will meet you under the corner lantern at ten o'clock tonight.

Draco took up a position that was about fifty yards from the streetlamp. Standing between two buildings, he was far back in the shadows, unnoticed even by a couple of men who had walked by no more than ten feet from him.

"Hell, I told Danny he didn't have no more sense than a flea-bag hound dog if he actually thought he could ride that horse," one of them was saying as they passed by Draco.

"He shoulda listened to you. He wouldn't be all stoved up now with a broken arm if he had."

"He's lucky he didn't break his fool neck."

The two men moved on down the street, still talking, though now they were far enough away that Draco could no longer hear what they were saying.

He saw someone come out of the saloon and stand just in front of it for a moment, as if undecided what to do. He raised the rifle to his shoulder and waited. A woman came out to join the man, then the two started back along the side of the saloon, heading toward the woman's crib in the back alley.

Draco lowered the rifle.

Behind him his horse whickered and stamped its foot.

From a nearby house he heard the sharp, angry words of a woman berating her husband.

From the saloon he heard the tinkling sound of a piano being played, and then, over the music, a man's loud guffawing laughter.

A baby started crying.

Another patron came out of the saloon door and, like the first man, stood for a moment on the street, looking both ways. Draco watched him carefully, then saw him start toward the corner lantern. Again Draco raised his rifle.

The man stopped under the light of the lamppost, and Draco recognized Muley Baxter.

Draco aimed at the easy target the streetlamp provided for him, squeezed the trigger slowly, then was rocked back by the recoil. He watched as a spray of blood flew out from Baxter's wound, visible in the light of the streetlamp.

The heavy boom of the shot rolled all through the town, starting an immediate cacophony of barking dogs and screeching cats.

"What the hell was that?"

"Who's shooting?"

"Where'd that come from?"

Draco walked slowly across the street toward Baxter's body. By the time he got there, several people had poured out of the nearby saloon, and men, women, and even children had come from the nearby houses.

"Who did this?" someone was saying. "Did anybody see anything?"

Draco saw a glint of light on a star that was pinned to the questioner's chest. This was a lawman.

"I did it," Draco said, "and you're just the man I'll be needing to see." There was a quiet, hissing tone to his voice. He took a wanted poster from his pocket and showed it to the deputy.

Draco stepped under the light then, and his appearance startled everyone there, and frightened many.

He was wearing a black coat, black shirt, black trousers, and black boots. But what made his appearance startling, and even frightening, was the juxtaposition of his all-black attire with his chalk-white skin. The hair on his head was very short and very white—so white against the white skin that it was almost unnoticeable. It looked, at first, as if he didn't have any eyelashes or eyebrows, but they were there, blending, as did the hair, into his white skin.

There was no color at all to the eyes except for the pupils, which were bloodred.

"Mama, is that a ghost?" one little boy asked in awe.

"Hush, child," his mother said, the tone of her voice indicating that she was just as frightened.

The man with the badge looked at the wanted poster, then down at the dead man.

"Are you sure this is Muley Baxter?"

"Oh, I'm sure, Sheriff," Draco said. "I've been trailing him for three weeks."

"I'm not the sheriff, I'm a deputy. You'll have to have the sheriff verify this before you can be paid. That might take a few days."

"That's all right, I'll just enjoy your town while I wait."

"I've heard of you. You're Luke Draco, aren't you?"

"Now, what gave me away?" Draco asked, and as he gave a rather sinister-sounding laugh, he rubbed one of his white hands against his white face.

"All right, folks, there's nothing else to see here," the

deputy said. "Go on about your business. I'll get the undertaker down here to take care of the body."

"Don't let my body get away, Deputy. He's worth a thousand dollars to me," Draco said.

"I wouldn't worry about it, Mr. Draco. He isn't going anywhere," the deputy said.

Ellis McKenzie and Gordy Peters were former cowboys who, after being fired by their boss, rode away in anger. The problem was, they rode away on horses belonging to the ranch owner, and he filed a complaint against them with the local sheriff. As a result, wanted posters had been issued on the two young men for horse stealing.

Ellis and Gordy were unaware that they were wanted. They knew they had taken the horses, but they justified it in their minds by saying they had worked for the ranch owner for some time and had raised the horses from colts, broken, and trained them.

Since leaving the ranch, the two had been transients, making a living by taking on odd jobs, sometimes working at a stable, mucking out stalls; once they helped build a barn. They had even shorn sheep—though, as they considered themselves cattlemen, that wasn't a job they wanted anyone else to know about.

On the day after Muley Baxter was shot, the two young men arrived in Stapleton engaged in an intense conversation as they rode into town, their horses side by side.

"What are you tellin' me, Gordy? Are you tellin' me that you don't think a balloon could fly all the way to the moon? Why, what would keep it from goin' there? I mean, ain't you never seen what they call a balloon ascension? I seen me one oncet, back in Fort Worth, oh, some two years ago it was now. It was on the Fourth of July and it was the damnedest thing I ever seen. It had two men and a dog in it, and it went up so high all you could see of it was the big round top part."

"Ellis, if you think a balloon can go all the way up to the moon, then you're just dumb as dirt," Gordy said.

"Well, why couldn't it?" Ellis asked. "I mean, oncet they start a-goin' up, why, I reckon they'll just keep on goin' up if the feller in the balloon don't stop it."

"You ever looked how little the moon is and how big the sky is?" Gordy asked.

"Yeah, so, what about it?"

"Well, think about it, Ellis. Whenever a balloon goes up, the feller in the balloon can't steer it like you can a wagon. He can't make a balloon go anywhere other'n where the wind lets it go. What if you started up toward the moon but the wind was blowin' you away from it? You'd just sail right on by it."

"Yeah," Ellis said. "Yeah, I guess I hadn't thought about that. When you put it like that, maybe you would miss it. Unless," he said, brightening and holding up his finger with a new idea, "what if he had him a rope, and a hook on the end of the rope? If that was the case, maybe he could throw the rope out and hook onto the moon, then pull hisself over to it. You never thought about that, did you?"

Gordy chuckled, then pointed toward a saloon. "Yeah, that might work. What do you say we get us a couple of beers?"

"Sounds good to me," Ellis said. "Maybe someone in there will know where we can get work."

Pushing through the batwing doors, the two men entered the saloon and stepped up to the bar. The saloon was relatively quiet, with only four men playing cards at one table, three other men in conversation at another table, and someone standing down at the far end of the bar. The one at the end of the bar was nursing a drink, and he was one of the strangest-looking men either Ellis or Gordy had ever seen.

"Damn, mister, what's the matter with your eyes!" Ellis said. "I ain't never seen eyes like that."

"What'll it be, gents?" the bartender asked, coming down to them. He pulled a towel off his shoulder, swiped at the bar with it, then draped it over his shoulder again.

Ellis continued to stare back at the pale man, who had turned his gaze away and was now looking into his drink.

"Ellis?" Gordy said. "Give the man your order."

"What? Oh," Ellis replied. "Uh, two beers."

"Two beers it is," the bartender replied. He turned to draw the beers.

"And I'll have the same," Gordy said.

The bartender laughed. "You boys sound like you've got a thirst."

"I'll say. I don't reckon I've ever quite had a thirst like this," Gordy said.

"You boys must have been ridin' for a while," the bartender said as he put the beers out for them. "Where did you come from?"

"Oh, here and there," Ellis said. "We're lookin' for work."

"What kind of work?"

"We'd prefer somethin' on a ranch, but you name it and we've done near 'bout ever'thing."

"Everything, huh?" the bartender asked.

"Yes, sir, you just ask anyone about Ellis McKenzie and Gordy Peters, and they'll tell you that we are two hardworkin' men."

When Ellis said the names, Draco looked over at them, then stuck his hand in his pocket and pulled out a handful of wanted posters. He looked through them until he found the one he was looking for:

WANTED
For Horse Thievery
Ellis McKenzie and Gordy Peters
$250 Reward for Each

"There's no sense in you boys looking for work," Draco said.

"And just what would make you say somethin' like that?" Ellis asked.

The pale-faced man chuckled, but it was more an expression of derision than of humor. He looked toward them, and the red dots at the center of his eyes gave him a satanic appearance.

"You're wanted men, both of you. You're worth two hundred and fifty dollars apiece to me."

"We ain't worth nothin' to you," Ellis said.

"Oh, but you are. You are horse thieves, you see. And all I have to do to collect the money is take you down to the sheriff's office." Draco smiled.

"Yeah? Well, I'd like to see you do that, you pasty-faced son of a bitch."

The smile left Draco's face. "You don't understand, do you? I get paid whether you are dead or alive."

"Mister, I'm about to clean your plow," Ellis said angrily.

The bartender leaned across the bar and said very quietly, "Don't push this any further, boys. Don't you know who this is?"

"I don't give a damn who it is," Ellis said.

"You need to just let this pass. Listen to me, please. If you keep goin' with this, it's not goin' to end well," the bartender said.

"You damn right it ain't goin' to end well," Ellis said. " 'Cause what I'm goin' to do is, I'm goin' to mop up the floor with that red-eyed, pasty-faced son of a bitch."

"Mister, no, leave it be!" the bartender said to Ellis more desperately this time. "How can you not know who this is? I mean, my God, how many people do you know that looks like him?"

"Closest thing I've ever seen to anything that looks like him is a maggot," Ellis said. "And I'm tellin' you right now, if he says one more word to me, I'm goin' to knock 'im on his ass," Ellis said.

"Ellis, no, let's back off like the bartender says. I'm not feelin' good about this," Gordy said. "Come on, let's drink our beers and get on our way."

Ellis stared at the man for a moment longer; then, with a shrug he turned back toward the bar. "All right," he said reluctantly. "I'll let it go this time."

"I don't reckon your mama ever taught you any manners, did she?" the albino said. "But then, being as she worked in a whorehouse, I guess she just didn't have the time to deal with every bastard she whelped."

Ellis slammed his beer mug down on the bar so hard that some of it splashed out.

"That's it, mister!" Ellis shouted in almost uncontrolled anger. "I'm goin' to teach you a lesson you ain't never goin' to forget!" He put up his fists.

The albino drew his thin, colorless lips into a tight smile. "I tell you what, horse thief. Let's not waste our time. If we're goin' to fight, why not just make it permanent?"

He stepped away from the bar and flipped his jacket back, exposing a pistol that he wore low in the way of a gunfighter.

"Mr. Draco, I'm sure these boys will go to the sheriff with you," the bartender said. "There's no need to carry this any further. Boys, this is Luke Draco. Please, for your own good, apologize to him now."

"Luke Draco?" Ellis asked, the bravado leaving him.

"My God, how could you not know who this was?" the bartender asked.

"Ellis, come on, back off," Gordy said. "Please, back off. I've heard of Draco and I don't want to tangle with him."

Ellis realized then that he had gotten in much deeper than he ever intended, and he stopped, then opened his fists and held his hands, palms out in front of him.

"All right," Ellis said. "Maybe my friend is right. Maybe this is getting a little out of hand. There's no need to carry it any further. It isn't worth either one of us dying over."

"Oh, it won't be either of us, horse thief. It'll just be you," Draco said. He looked over at Gordy. "And you," he added.

Gordy shook his head. "No it ain't, 'cause there ain't neither one of us going to draw on you," he said. "So if you shoot us, it's goin' to have to be in cold blood, in front of these witnesses."

"What witnesses would that be?" Draco asked.

"What do you mean, what witnesses? Why, these men right . . ." Gordy looked out into the saloon and saw everyone heading toward the door, including the four men who had been playing cards. The card players were in such a hurry to depart that they had left their cards and their money on the table behind them.

"The bartender will see it," Gordy said.

The bartender shook his head. "I tried to warn you boys, but you wouldn't listen to me," he said. Then he moved quickly to the end of the bar, then stepped through the gate and hurried outside. The towel was still draped over his shoulder.

Now the saloon was completely empty, and except for the sound of muffled conversations from some people upstairs, it was quiet.

"Well, now," Draco said, his red eyes gleaming at them. "It looks like it's just us."

"Please, Mr. Draco, we'll go with you," Gordy said. "We give up. Take us down to the sheriff's office."

Draco shook his head. "It's too late. Everyone in here heard you resisting arrest."

"Resisting arrest? What do you mean, resisting arrest? You aren't a lawman. Who are you to arrest us?"

"It's called a citizen's arrest," Draco said. "I gave you the chance, you didn't take it. Now we'll do it my way."

Ellis and Gordy looked at each other; then, with an imperceptible signal, they made ragged, desperate grabs for their pistols.

Draco shot Ellis first, then Gordy, both men killed before they were able to get their pistols more than halfway out of their holsters.

Draco was just putting own his gun back in its holster when those who left the saloon a few moments earlier came back in.

The bartender looked down at the two young men who he had tried so desperately to warn, then he looked up at Draco, his face registering sorrow.

"You didn't have to do that, Mr. Draco."

"You heard them refuse to go to the sheriff's office with me, didn't you?" Draco glared at the bartender, who withered under the red-eyed stare.

"Yes, sir, I heard."

"I was sure that you did."

CHAPTER TWENTY-TWO

★

Harry Holder and Eric Durbin rode up to the front of the Slaughter House Saloon in response to an invitation to meet Angus Pugh. Securing their horses to the hitching rail in front of the building, they went inside, where they saw two men, one a smallish man with big ears, a nose so badly broken that it was flat, and dark, beady eyes. The other man had red hair and a bushy red beard. These were a couple of men they both knew.

"Abe Poindexter and Warren Canby," Holder said, calling out to them. "What are you two doin' here?"

The two men came over to meet them.

"Why, I'm doin' the same thing as you," Poindexter said. "I'm here to meet Angus Pugh."

"What do you say we get us a drink?" Durbin said. "My mouth is so dry, I can't even spit."

The saloon was already crowded with customers and the bar was full, but when Holder, Durbin, and Poindexter stepped up to the bar, they pushed others aside in order to make a place for themselves.

"Hey, what do you think you're doin'?" one of the customers who had been pushed out of the way complained.

"I think we're about to get us a drink. You got a problem with that?" Holder asked.

It did not escape the customer's notice that Holder had said "we" and that all three men were glaring at him. The men were also armed and wearing their holsters strapped low.

"No, I ain't got no problem with that," the customer said.

"I didn't think you would."

As the three men stood at the bar, they began pointing out other customers in the saloon. Occasionally one of them would get off a joke at someone else's expense, and the jokester and the other two would laugh uproariously at his cleverness, unaware or unconcerned that the rest of the people in the saloon were not laughing with them but instead taking it all in in embarrassed silence.

Then, as the three looked around the saloon, they saw one of the soiled doves sitting at a table with an older, gray-haired man. There were just the two of them, but the young woman was staying with the older man even though it would have been much more profitable for her to leave him and work the other customers.

"Look over there," Holder said, pointing to the girl and the older man. "Ain't that Roseanne?"

"It sure is," Durbin said.

"What the hell do you think she's sittin' there with

that old man for? I mean, look at him. He's a dried-up old fart."

"Ha! You don't know that, Holder," Poindexter said. "Just 'cause there's snow on the roof, that don't mean there ain't no fire below."

"You know what I think, Holder?" Durbin asked. "I think Roseanne don't love you no more."

"What do you mean, Roseanne don't love him no more?" Poindexter asked with a laugh. "Roseanne will love anyone that's got enough money."

"What time is Pugh s'posed to get here?" Holder asked.

"He didn't say what time. He just said he'd be in here sometime today," Poindexter said.

"Then that means I got time."

"You got time for what?" Durbin asked.

Holder smiled at the other two, then pointed to the young woman. "Time to prove that Roseanne still loves me. I plan to show her a trick or two."

Poindexter laughed. "Trust me, there ain't nothin' you can show Roseanne that she ain't never seen. I expect she's been rode more'n your horse."

Holder tossed down the rest of his drink, set the empty glass on the bar, wiped the back of his hand across his mouth, then hitched up his trousers.

"You just watch," he said. "Hey, Roseanne!" he called as he started toward her table.

Roseanne looked at him, then turned her attention back to the man sitting next to her.

"Roseanne, I'm talkin' to you."

"I believe that young man is trying to get your attention," the older man said.

Roseanne turned toward Holder. "Can't you see I'm busy with this gentleman? Come back when Mr. Taylor and I are finished with our conversation."

"Look here, you old fart," Holder said to the man Roseanne had identified as Taylor. "If you ain't got what it takes to show Roseanne a good time, then step aside and let her go with someone who can."

"It seems to me like that would be up to Roseanne," Taylor said.

"Yeah? Well, I say it's up to me," Holder said. He reached down to grab Roseanne's arm and started pulling on it.

"Ow, Harry, stop, that hurts."

"Leave her alone, sonny!" Taylor said angrily.

"Look here, you son of a bitch!" Holder said. "I've had about enough of you. Why don't you . . . uh! What the hell?"

Holder made a grab for his pistol, but it wasn't in his holster. He looked around quickly to see if it had fallen out and was lying on the floor.

"Would you be looking for this?" Taylor asked, holding Holder's pistol. He had snatched it from Holder's holster when he grabbed Roseanne.

"No!" Holder shouted, holding both hands out in front of him and stepping back away from the table. "What are you doing? How did you get my gun?"

"I tell you what, Harry. Why don't you go back over

there and have a drink with your friends while we wait for Angus Pugh?" Taylor said.

"Wait for Pugh. You mean, you're . . ."

"Yes, I am. You and I appear to have gotten off to a bad start, but if we are going to work together, I think we should get along together, don't you?"

"Yeah," Holder said. "Uh, that is, yes, sir."

Taylor emptied the shells from Holder's pistol and returned it to him.

Holder returned to the bar with the empty pistol. He started to reload it, but Durbin touched him on the shoulder.

"I wouldn't, if I were you," he said. Durbin pointed toward Taylor, who had his own pistol out now, lying on the table.

"Who the hell is that, anyway?" Holder said.

"His name is Mickey Taylor," Poindexter said. "He's been around awhile."

"Yeah, well, he ain't goin' to be around much longer if he don't watch hisself."

"Here's Pugh," Durbin said.

Holder and Durbin looked toward the front door.

"Who's that with him?" Holder asked. "Damn, I ain't never seen anyone that looks like that before."

"Don't you know who that is?" Poindexter asked. "That's Luke Draco."

"That's Luke Draco? Damn, I've heard of 'im, but I ain't never seen him before. He sure is an odd-lookin' duck, ain't he?"

"If I was you, I'd be just real particular about what I said in front of him."

Pugh and Draco started toward the bar. The others in the saloon, especially those who had heard of Draco, looked on in fascination and with some apprehension. As the two men reached the bar, the others who were standing there, with the exception of those who were there to meet Pugh, stepped away.

"Gentlemen," Pugh said. "It's good to see you are all here on time. Barkeep?"

"Yes, sir?"

"I am Angus Pugh. I believe I have made arrangements for a private room."

"Yes, sir," the bartender said. He pointed to a door beside the piano. "If you'll go through that door, you'll find a hallway. The private room will be the first door on the right."

"If you would please lead us there," Pugh said.

"It ain't hard to find, it's just . . ."

"I said lead us there," Pugh repeated, more forcefully this time.

"Oh, uh, yes, sir, of course, I'll be glad to," the bartender said.

Stepping out from behind the bar, he led the six men into the hallway and to the private room. As he reached for the doorknob, Pugh said, "Wait."

Pugh motioned for the others to step to either side of the door so they wouldn't be seen by anyone who might be inside the room when the door was opened. Pulling his pistol, he also stepped to one side.

"Open it," he said, motioning with his drawn pistol.

By now Pugh's caution had made the bartender somewhat nervous. With his eyes closed and his hands shaking, he opened the door.

Nothing happened, and the bartender opened his eyes, then let out a long sigh of relief, not realizing until that moment that he had been holding his breath. He smiled, then looked over at Pugh.

"Your room, sir."

"Thank you," Pugh said.

Pugh motioned for the others to go on inside and sit in the six chairs placed around a table in the middle of the room. Closing the door behind him, he came over to the table to join them. Then, smiling, he took a small cloth bag from his pocket and dumped it onto the table.

Six tin stars fell from the bag.

"What are these?" Poindexter asked.

Pugh picked one of them up. "These, gentlemen, are railroad detective badges."

"Are they real?" Durbin asked.

"Yes, they are real. As of today, we are detectives for the Texas and Pacific Railway. And if anyone should check on us, our positions are genuine."

"Is this the job you've got for us? Being railroad detectives?" Holder asked, the tone of his voice indicating that it wasn't a job that he found particularly appealing.

Pugh looked at Holder, but he made no direct response to the question.

"Gentlemen, on August twentieth, seventeen days from today, there will be a shipment of one hundred thousand dollars going by train to the bank in Wardell."

"You're wantin' us to rob a train?" Durbin said. "I don't know. . . . Robbin' trains ain't the easiest thing to do."

"Oh, I agree," Pugh said. "It's not an endeavor that should be undertaken lightly. That's why we aren't going to rob the train. We are going to go to Wardell as railroad detectives, with a letter from the governor of the state, authorizing the railroad to deliver the money directly to us."

"Do you actually have such a letter?" Taylor asked.

"Yes," Pugh said, showing Taylor and the others the letter.

Taylor read it, then handed it back. "Very good, that will help establish our credibility."

"What happens once we have the money?" Holder asked.

"You, Durbin, Poindexter, and Canby will get twenty-five hundred dollars each. Draco and Taylor will get five thousand each. I'll get twenty thousand."

"How come Draco and Taylor get more than we do?" Durbin asked.

"Draco for the obvious reason: we need his gun," Pugh said. "And Taylor because he has been a railroad detective, and we need his experience."

"Yeah, but still that only comes to forty thousand," Poindexter said.

"Yes, the remaining sixty thousand dollars is for the man who set this up for us," Pugh lied.

"Why is *he* getting so much?" Draco asked.

"He is the one who arranged the money shipment, he is the one who got us appointments as railroad detectives, and he is the one who got the letter from the governor."

"Still, that seems like an awful lot of money for someone who ain't even takin' a risk," Durbin said.

"You don't have to be a part of this," Pugh said. "I'm sure I can find someone who would be glad to have twenty-five hundred dollars."

"No, you don't have to do nothin' like that," Durbin said. "I was just commentin' is all."

"I have a question," Poindexter said. "Once we have the money, won't the city marshal be expecting us to hand it over to the bank?"

"By that time I expect to have the city marshal under control," Pugh said.

"What do you mean, 'under control'?"

Pugh smiled. "Well, if the city marshal and all his deputies are in jail, they will pretty much be under control, don't you think?"

"Yeah," Holder said.

"Holder, I want you and Durbin to go to Wardell now. Nobody is likely to recognize you. Look around the town, find out how much control the marshal has over things, see if there's likely to be any citizens of the town who could cause a problem."

"Mr. Pugh, neither me nor Durbin's got'ny money. I mean, best place to find out things would be at the saloon, wouldn't it? And we'll have to eat too."

"All right," Pugh said. "Here's two dollars apiece." He counted out the money. "But don't get into any kind of trouble. Don't make yourselves known. Do you understand that?"

"Yeah, we understand," Holder said.

"Should we wear them railroad badges?" Durbin asked.

Pugh picked a couple of them up, held them for a moment, then, shaking his head, put them back down.

"No," he said. "I think you had better not. If you go in there wearin' badges, you're sure to be noticed. I don't want anyone to notice you yet. All I want you to do now is just have a look around."

"All right," Durbin said.

"Want me to go with 'em, Pugh?" Canby asked.

"No. Two people can go unnoticed. Three can't."

"Yeah, but they might need my gun. I'm damn near as good as Draco," Canby said.

Canby was making a point, suggesting that, like Draco, he should be given more money because of his skill with a pistol. And although it was a belief he shared with no one, he was pretty sure that he was just as good.

"If there is any need for a gun at this point, it would wreck the whole plan. I think it's best just to send the two of them," Pugh said.

CHAPTER TWENTY-THREE

★

WARDELL, TEXAS

A big sign was posted at either end of Broad Street, seen by all who came into town:

Big Dance
7:00 P.M. Saturday, October 8
Sponsored by
Wardell Merchants and Cattlemen Association
Homestead Hotel
Come One—Come All

The band for the dance came by railroad all the way from Fort Worth, and when they stepped down from the train, they were surprised to be met by more than a hundred citizens of the town.

C. E. "Daddy" Felker, the mayor, and Harold Wallace, the city marshal, came out of the crowd to greet them.

"Gentlemen," Mayor Felker said. "On behalf of the citizens of Wardell, I welcome you to our fair city."

"My name is Keith Collins," one of the band members said. Collins wore a small, neatly trimmed mustache, which, like his hair, was flaked with gray. "I'm the band director. Have accommodations been made for our stay?"

"Indeed they have, Mr. Collins," Mayor Felker said. He turned to the city marshal, a very heavyset man. "This is Marshal Wallace."

"Mr. Collins, we have a wagon fixed up with seats to take you and the band to the hotel," Wallace said.

"Thank you, Marshal," Collins said. He turned to the rest of his band, consisting of four other men, and directed them to pick up their instruments and load them onto the wagon.

Quince Anders and Stanley Goff were in the bunkhouse at the Tumbling F Ranch, getting ready to go ride into town. Actually, Quince was ready, and he was standing at the open door of the bunkhouse looking up toward the Big House. Behind him, Stanley was still shaving.

"You reckon Mr. and Mrs. Felton will be a' goin' to the dance?" Stanley asked.

"I reckon they will. I heard Mrs. Felton say somethin' about it."

"That's funny," Stanley said.

Quince turned toward him. "What's funny?"

"A couple of old people like that a'-goin' to the dance."

"Ha! You better not let Mr. Felton hear you say

somethin' like that. You'll be lookin' for another outfit to get on with."

"Well, I don't mean *old* old, I just mean old," Stanley said.

"You better just hush up while you're ahead. How long does it take you to shave, anyhow? I would like to get to town before the dance is half over."

"Don't rush me," Stanley said. "I ain't a pretty boy like you. It takes me a while to make myself look good enough that I don't scare off the women."

"Ha, you couldn't make yourself look that good in a month of Sundays," Quince said.

"Quit your bitchin'," Stanley said as he wiped off the last of the lather. "I'm ready to go."

"Yeah, well, finally. It's about time you was ready, I was fixin' to just go into town without you." Quince reached for his gun belt.

"Damn, Quince, you ain't plannin' on takin' your gun, are you?"

Quince chuckled, then put the gun belt back down. "No, I reckon not," he said. "I'm not likely to be puttin' on a shootin' show at a dance, now, am I?"

Word of the dance had spread quickly, not only through town, but through much of El Paso County, and merchants with their wives and daughters; clerks; farmers and cattlemen with their wives and daughters; cowboys; railroad men; teamsters; and various ladies of the town began preparing for the evening's event. Crowds of people streamed along the boardwalks, the women in colorful ginghams, the men in clean blue denims and brightly decorated vests.

Many of them went into stores to shop, and the merchants beamed, for this was exactly the reason they had sponsored the dance. One establishment that was doing a booming business was Little Man Lambert's. In order to feed the exceptional number of customers, Casey made spaghetti with a tomato and meat sauce. The success of his effort spread through the town, so that he had to make an extra batch to accommodate everyone.

"Will you be going to the dance, Mr. Casey?" Lucy asked.

"Oh, I'm afraid dances are for young people," Casey replied. "I'd just be in the way."

"Don't be silly. The dance isn't just for young people, it's for everyone. Besides, I was counting on putting your name on my dance card."

Casey smiled. "Well, I certainly wouldn't want to disappoint a pretty young lady like you. But I'm sure it will upset some young man who would want his name there."

"A dance is for people to enjoy themselves," Lucy said. "And I would very much enjoy dancing with you."

"Then I shall look forward to it," Casey replied.

Both Quince and Stanley were in the restaurant when Little Man Lambert's closed that evening.

"Hey, cook, what do you call that stuff we ate? Those long skinny noodles," Quince asked.

"That is spaghetti *italienne*," Casey said.

"Yeah? Well, it's damn good, whatever it is."

"Thank you."

"Too bad you ain't goin' to the dance tonight. I'd let you have a dance with my girl," Quince said.

"It so happens that he *is* going," Lucy said. "And I have already asked him to dance with me."

"Ha! Is that old man going to use a cane?" Quince asked.

By dusk, the excitement which had been growing for the entire day was full blown. The sound of the practicing musicians could be heard all up and down Broad Street. A little before seven o'clock the people who had come for the dance started moving toward the hotel. Horses and buckboards began arriving, and soon every hitching rail was full from Broad Avenue south to the railroad and north to Fourth Street, and along Second Street, east to Sage, and west to Mesquite.

Outside the hotel, children began to gather around the glowing yellow windows to look inside. What they saw was a ballroom floor that was cleared of tables and chairs, and a platform at the front of the room for the musicians.

Once they were inside, the excitement was all it promised to be. Several young women were gathered on one side of the room, giggling and turning their heads in embarrassment as young men, just as embarrassed, made awkward attempts to flirt with them. At the back of the dance floor there was a large punch bowl on a table, and Quince saw one of the cowboys look around to make certain he wasn't being seen, then pour whiskey into the punch from a bottle he had concealed beneath his vest. A moment later another cowboy did the same thing, and Quince laughed.

"What is it?" Stanley asked. "What are you laughin' at?"

"Nothin'," Casey replied. "I think I'll just get me some punch."

"Punch? I didn't come here to be drinking some ol' lady's fruit punch," Stanley said.

"Choose up your squares!" the caller shouted through his megaphone, and several couples hurried to their positions within one of the squares. Quince started toward Lucy but saw that she had approached the cook.

"I'll be damned," he said.

Stanley laughed. "You'd better watch out there, Quince. That old man is beating your time."

"Ah, it's nothin'," Quince said with a dismissive wave of his hand. "She said she was goin' to dance with him once. Come on, let's find us a pretty girl."

Quince and Stanley joined the cowboys who were advancing toward the unattached girls, and when they found a couple to accept their invitations to dance, they made up the final two sets for the square that had Casey and Lucy.

The music began; then, with the skirling of the fiddles loud and clear and the guitars providing the rhythm, the caller began to bellow out the calls. As he did so, he clapped his hands and stomped his feet and moved around on the platform as if in one of the squares himself. The dancers moved and swirled to the caller's commands:

> *Honor to your partner, swing your honey high and low,*
> *Allemande left with the corner, and dosido.*
> *Ladies make a left-hand star, go full around the set,*
> *Swing with the corner lady a little bit more than that.*
> *Take her home, swing about and dosido that girl,*
> *Allemande left, and give her a whirl.*

Around the dance floor sat those who were without partners looking on wistfully, those who were too old, and others holding back those who were too young. At the punch bowl table, cowboys continued to add their own ingredients, and though many drank from the punch bowl, the contents of the bowl never seemed to diminish.

At that moment two men, Harry Holder and Eric Durbin, came riding into town. They were covered with trail dust.

"Let's find us a saloon," Holder said. "My mouth is as dry as cotton."

"Pugh said we was supposed to send him a telegram soon as we got here."

"Hell, you think it's goin' to make any difference whether we have a drink first?"

"I reckon you're right," Durbin said.

"Damn, look at all the horses and rigs," Holder said. "There's somethin' goin' on in this town, that's for sure."

"It's a dance," Durbin said.

"What dance?"

"Didn't you see the sign when we come into town?"

"No, I didn't notice no sign," Holder said.

The two men dismounted in front of the Red Bull Saloon, then went in. Except for the bartender and one man standing at the far end of the bar, the saloon was completely deserted.

"What can I get for you gentlemen?" the bartender asked.

"Whiskey," Holder said.

"Yeah, me too," Durbin added.

"Coming right up."

"Where the hell is everyone?" Holder asked as the bartender put the drinks in front of them.

"They're all at the dance."

"I told you there was a dance," Durbin said. "I seen it on the sign when we come into town."

"Oh, yes," the bartender said. "The merchants like to advertise it. Ever' month the Merchants and Cattlemen Association holds a dance down at the Homestead Hotel. The merchants all say that it's good for business 'cause it brings ever'one into town. I don't know, it might be good for stores and such, but it sure ain't all that good for any of the saloons. Hell, everyone winds up down there and there don't nobody come in here."

"A dance, huh?" Holder said as he tossed his whiskey down.

"Hey, Holder, what do you say we go down to that there dance?" Durbin suggested.

"What for?"

"Damn it, Holder, think about it. If there's dancin' down there, there's bound to be women. Wouldn't you like to be around some women for a change?"

Holder smiled. "Yeah, you're right. Okay, let's go get us a couple of women," he said.

"Wait," Durbin said.

"What?"

"Don't you think we ought to clean up a bit? I mean, we're pretty trail worn."

Holder held his arm up and sniffed under it. "Hell, it ain't that bad."

Durbin sniffed under his own arm, then chuckled. "You're right," he said. "It ain't that bad."

The two men left and the bartender walked down the bar to the one remaining customer. "I'm sure those two boys are goin' to have the women just crawlin' all over 'em," he said.

The customer laughed.

When Holder and Durbin stepped into the hotel ballroom, the dance was well under way. Out on the floor, couples moved and skipped, swayed and bowed, as the music played and the caller called. In addition to the dancers, there were several people who weren't dancing but were standing around the sides of the room instead.

"Damn, what is it? All men? Ain't they no women?" Holder asked.

"There's some women that ain't dancin'," Durbin said.

Holder looked toward the women Durbin pointed out, then scowled. "Well, hell, you can see why they ain't nobody a-dancin' with 'em. I've seen better-lookin' pigs."

Durbin chuckled. "I'm thirsty. Come on, let's get somethin' to drink." He began to make his way toward the punch bowl table.

"You mean like fruit juice and shit? That ain't nothin' to drink."

"I just seen somebody pour some whiskey into that bowl. I wouldn't doubt but there ain't been a whole bottle or maybe two that's done been dumped into it. Come on."

Ordinarily the two men, being dirty and odorous, would not have aroused attention from anyone. But because everyone had "cleaned up" for the dance, Holder and Durbin stood out, and as they moved through the crowd toward the punch bowl, people began moving away from them.

Holder and Durbin either didn't notice the reaction they were getting or didn't care. Holder got a glass of punch, then took a drink.

"Damn," he said with a broad smile. "You're right, this ain't bad."

The set ended and the couples left the floor. Holder finished his drink, then wiped his hand across his mouth.

"I don't know about you," he said, "but I'm goin' to go get me a good-lookin' woman."

"What good-lookin' woman? They ain't no good-lookin' women. Leastwise, there ain't none that ain't dancin'."

"I see me one, right now," Holder said.

CHAPTER TWENTY-FOUR

★

Lucy and Quince were just leaving the floor.

"Lucy, I hope you don't mind, but I promised Stanley I'd ask you to dance with him," Quince said. "He's so ugly and shy that he's a-scairt of even askin' a woman to dance."

"Oh, don't be cruel, Quince. He isn't all that ugly. And of course I'll dance with him," Lucy said, starting toward Stanley.

"While you're dancin' with him, I'm goin' to, uh, step out back for a couple of minutes," Quince said.

"You've been drinking too much of the punch, haven't you?" Lucy said.

"Uh, yeah," Quince replied, obviously embarrassed by the fact that Lucy realized he was going to have to go relieve himself. "I'll be back in before this dance is over, and don't be dancin' with anyone else but me."

"I don't belong to you, Quince Anders," Lucy said.

Quince smiled. "Yeah, you do. You just don't know it."

Lucy smiled and went over to where Stanley was standing. "Stanley, would you like to dance with me?" she asked.

A broad smile spread across Stanley's face. "Yes, ma'am!" he said.

Holder stepped in. "Get yourself another woman, cowboy. This here'n will be dancin' this dance with me."

"No I'm not," Lucy said. "I've already agreed to dance with this gentleman."

"Like I said, he can get hisself another woman."

Lucy very pointedly turned away from Holder.

"Don't you be turnin' away from me when I'm talkin' to you!" Holder said angrily. He reached out and grabbed Lucy, pulling her back around.

"Keep your hands off her!" Stanley said. Emboldened by his anger, he swung at Holder, knocking him down.

Casey was talking with Murdock Felton when he and everyone else in the ballroom saw what happened.

"Oh, damn," Felton said. "That's one of my cowboys. What's he getting himself into?"

"More than he wants to handle, is my guess," Casey said. Picking up a candleholder, he blew the candle out, then pulled it from the holder. He put the holder in his pocket and walked over to the point of excitement.

By now, nearly everyone else on the dance floor had backed away, leaving only Stanley and Holder as if they were performing onstage.

Holder got up quickly and, with an angry scowl and his hand hanging loosely over his pistol, stared at Stanley.

"Mister, you done stepped into it," Holder said. "You had no call to hit me like that."

"You had no call to grab Miss Lucy like you done," Stanley replied.

The scowl turned to an evil smile. "So, you decided to be a hero for the woman, is that how it is? Well, let's see just how big of a hero you really are. Draw."

"Draw?" Stanley replied. "What the hell, mister, don't you see that I ain't wearin' no gun?"

"Get yourself a gun," Holder said. "I'll wait."

"Where am I goin' to get a gun? There ain't nobody else in here got one, either."

"Why not? Are you all a bunch of cowards?"

"No, they are all gentlemen," another voice said. "Gentlemen don't come to a social engagement such as this carrying a pistol."

Turning, Holder saw a man whose hair was gray. His eyes were a dull shade of the same color, and there was a scar on his face running from just below his left eye to just above the corner of his mouth.

"Stay the hell out of this, you scar-faced old bastard, unless you're wantin' to deal yourself a hand into it," Holder said, the words little more than a snarl. He turned back to Stanley.

"Now, how about it, cowboy? You want to settle with me? My friend has a pistol, he'll lend it to you."

"I believe I will just deal myself a hand in this," Casey said, stepping up behind Holder.

Holder felt the barrel of a pistol pressed into his back.

"What the hell?" he said. "I thought you told me gentlemen didn't bring guns to the dance."

"That's right," Casey said. "But I'm not a gentleman. I'm just a cook."

"A cook? You're nothin' but a cook and you want to face me down?" Holder asked in disbelief.

"Oh, no, I'm afraid you misunderstand. I have no intention of facing you down. You see, I'm holding a .44-caliber derringer in your back. When I pull the trigger, the bullet will sever your spine and you'll collapse to the floor in excruciating pain. The pain will be so bad that you'll want to kill yourself to stop it, but you won't be able to, because when your spine is severed, you'll be completely paralyzed, unable to move so much as a finger. Also, you will be unable to control your bowels and kidneys, so you will probably soil your pants. Then, after several moments of agonizing pain, you will die."

"You're all talk. You won't pull the trigger."

"Son, I was in the war. You may have heard about it, it was in all the papers. I killed a lot of men in that war. They were good men: husbands, fathers, and sons. And the only reason I killed them was because they were wearing a different-color uniform. Now, do you think that, after killing good and decent men, I would hesitate for one second before I killed a polecat like you?"

The music had stopped, and the attention of everyone present was drawn to Casey and the armed stranger who had interrupted the dance.

"Take that gun out of my friend's back!" Durbin said, pointing his pistol at Casey.

"Mister, I'm going to count to three, and if you haven't dropped that gun by then, I'm going to pull the trigger," Casey said. "If you shoot me, I'll still live long enough to pull the trigger. And even if I don't live long enough, my last reflexive action will pull the trigger. So what's it going to be?"

"Drop the gun, Durbin! Drop the damn gun!" Holder said.

Durbin hesitated, and Casey began to count. "One . . ."

"*I said drop the damn gun!*" Holder screamed in fear.

Durbin dropped his pistol.

"Mr. Goff, would you kindly retrieve Mr. Durbin's pistol?" Casey said.

"Yes, sir," Stanley said, hurrying over to pick up the dropped weapon.

"And if you don't mind, I'll just take your gun," Casey said as he slipped the pistol from Holder's holster.

"You got no right to take our guns," Holder said.

"Oh, I beg to differ with you, sir. I have every right. You came into a peaceful gathering and began to make trouble. Marshal Wallace?"

The marshal, like everyone else in the room, had watched the drama unfold.

"Would you take charge of these men's weapons?"

"Yes," Wallace said, suddenly realizing that, as a

peace officer, he should have taken a more active role earlier.

Stanley gave the weapons to Marshal Wallace, and realizing that there was little chance of gunfire breaking out, everyone breathed easier.

By now Quince had returned to the ballroom and he, too, was watching intently.

"All right, you two galoots, get out of here," Marshal Wallace ordered.

"When do we get our guns back?" Holder asked.

"When I say you can have them back."

"What about the gun this man is holding?" Holder asked. "Are you goin' to take his gun from him?"

"I'm not holding a gun," Casey said.

"What do you mean, you ain't holdin' a gun? What's that you was holdin' pressed against my back?"

Casey raised his hand to show Holder and everyone else what he was holding.

"Oh, you must be thinking of this candleholder," he said. "Yes, I imagine it did rather feel like a pistol when I shoved it against your spine."

"What?" Holder bellowed. "You mean all this time it wasn't nothin' but a candleholder?"

The crowd in the ballroom laughed uproariously, and Holder, his face red with fury, glared at Casey.

Casey was neither smiling nor frowning. His demeanor and expression, like his words, were as calm as if he were discussing the weather. "I think you and Mr. Durbin should leave now," Casey said.

"Yeah? Well, what if we decide not to leave? Do you think you can run us out with a candleholder?" Holder challenged.

"He won't need a candleholder, mister," one of the cowboys said. "There are about twenty of us who don't appreciate you two fellas comin' in here disturbin' the decent folk. And I reckon we won't have any trouble throwin' you two out on your backsides."

Holder and Durbin glared at the others for a moment; then, because they had no other choice, they turned to leave, chased out of the hall by the combined laughter of every man and woman at the dance.

"Let's hear it for the cook!" someone shouted.

"Yeah!" another added, and everyone present cheered and applauded.

"I wonder what that son of a bitch's name was," Holder asked, his voice an angry growl.

"I don't know his name, but seems to me like he said he was a cook," Durbin said.

"A cook? A damn cook did that to me? You should have shot the son of a bitch when you had the chance."

"Maybe you don't recollect," Durbin said, "but you're the one told me to drop the gun."

"Yeah," Holder said. He stopped just before they went into the Red Bull Saloon and looked back toward the hotel. "Well, I'm goin' to find out that son of a bitch's name, and he'll be hearin' from me again."

Holder and Durbin pushed through the batwing

doors and saw the same two men still in the saloon, the bartender now standing at the far end of the bar, engaged in conversation with the lone customer. The two men looked at Holder and Durbin when they came in.

"Decided against goin' to the dance, did you?" the bartender asked, moving along the bar toward them.

"Yeah, we went," Holder said, his response little more than a growl.

"This here ain't a very friendly town," Durbin said. "We wasn't exactly welcomed."

"Well, I suppose it takes a little time to get to know people. Whiskey?"

"Yeah," Durbin said.

The bartender got the glasses out.

"Speakin' of knowin' people," Holder said. "There was a fella down there that said he was a cook. Do you know who that would be?"

"Well, just about every ranch around has a cook, and I expect most of 'em is at the dance tonight, so that would be hard to say."

"This here fella has him a scar from his eye damn near down to his mouth," Holder said, tracing the path of the scar along his own cheek.

"Oh, well, I expect that would be Ken Casey," the bartender said. "And he is one jim-dandy of a cook, I'll give him that. He cooks for Little Man Lambert. You'll have to eat there while you're here."

"Ken Casey, huh? Well, maybe I will pay him a visit."

The bartender set the drinks in front of the two men, took their money, then returned to the other end of the bar to resume his conversation.

"You ain't goin' to do nothin' till this business with Pugh is settled," Durbin said. "You heard what he said. They's twenty-five hunnert dollars apiece in this job. I ain't never even had me five hunnert dollars all at one time in my whole life, let alone twenty-five hunnert, and I ain't goin' to lose it now 'cause you're wantin' to settle some score with a cook."

"All right, all right," Holder replied. "I won't do nothin' yet. But as soon as this is over, me'n that cook is goin' to have a settlin' up."

CHAPTER TWENTY-FIVE

★

On Monday morning Casey went downstairs to start breakfast. Soon the kitchen was filled with the aroma of coffee and sausage, and he began mixing the batter for pancakes rather than biscuits.

Little Man came in still rubbing the sleep out of his eyes, then he poured himself a cup of coffee. Taking a swallow of his brew, he stared at Casey for a long moment over his cup. Casey was aware of Little Man's studious contemplation but he said nothing about it. Finally, Little Man spoke.

"Mr. Casey, about last night," he said. "Why did you do what you done?"

"It looked like that man was ready to shoot the young cowboy," Casey said.

"Oh, don't get me wrong. You had every right to interfere, and as far as I'm concerned, the whole town owes you a vote of thanks. No, sir, what I mean is, why did you take a risk like that? What if he had turned around and seen that you didn't actually have a gun?"

Casey's laugh was low and self-deprecating. "I would have been up the creek, wouldn't I?"

"Didn't you think about that before you tried something so foolhardy?"

"No, that was my problem: I didn't think until it was too late. Then I was standing there behind him, holding a candleholder, scared to death."

Little Man laughed out loud. "You may be right that you didn't think about it. But you'll never convince me that you were scared. I've never in my life seen anyone as calm and collected as you were."

"Looks can be deceiving," Casey said.

Little Man took another swallow of his coffee as he continued to study Casey over the rim of his cup.

"You got that right," he said. "Looks can be damn deceiving."

"I thought I would make pancakes this morning instead of biscuits."

"Yeah, good idea," Little Man said. "Guess I'd better be gettin' out there into the dining room. Folks will be comin' in pretty soon."

Breakfast business was brisk most of the morning. Casey stayed glued to the stove, flipping pancakes, while Little Man was behind the counter, handling the money. Lucy was waiting and busing tables when she saw the two men come in who had been the cause of the trouble the night before. She looked at her father, who also saw the two men. Little Man walked around from behind the counter and up to the pair.

"I hope you men aren't here to cause any trouble," he said.

"Are you Mr. Lambert?" one of the two asked. This was the one who had accosted Lucy at the dance.

"I am, and it was my daughter that you were rude to last night."

"Yes, sir, I'm real sorry about that. I'd been drinkin' and what I done was stupid. I come over here to apologize to the young lady, and also to your cook."

"And to have breakfast," the other man said, smiling. "We hear that you got the best cook in town."

"I probably do," Little Man said. He turned toward Lucy, who was standing in the back of the restaurant, watching with a wary eye. He raised his hand, bidding her to come over, and hesitantly she did so.

"Lucy, this gentleman has something to say to you," Little Man said.

"Yes, ma'am, I do. I want to apologize to you for what I done last night. Like I told your pa, I had been drinkin' and I wasn't thinkin' none too good."

"Your apology is accepted," Lucy said, though she spoke the words without a smile.

"Show our customers to a table," Little Man said, and as Lucy took the two men to an empty table, he went back into the kitchen.

Casey was mixing up another batch of pancake batter with a big wooden spoon when Little Man came in.

"Your friends from last night are here," he said.

"What friends?"

"The ones you accosted with the candleholder."

Casey laid the wooden spoon to one side and wiped his hands on his apron. "Are they causing trouble?"

Little Man shook his head. "No, in fact they said they've come to apologize. They've already apologized to Lucy."

Casey picked the wooden spoon up and started beating the batter again. "Good."

"They probably want to apologize to you as well."

"I don't need their apology."

Little Man chuckled. "No, I don't reckon you do," he said. "I just thought I might let you know."

After Little Man left, Casey stepped up to the kitchen door and looked out over the dining room. He saw the two men, and saw also that they had gotten their guns back, but it didn't look as if they were there to cause any trouble. And as he had told Little Man, he didn't need their apology. He returned to the stove and began pouring out another batch of pancakes.

At about nine o'clock, Little Man stepped into the kitchen.

"The rush is over," he said. "Let's have breakfast together out in the dining room."

"Sounds good to me." Casey and Little Man worked together to get three plates ready. A couple of minutes later Casey, Little Man, and Lucy were having their breakfast in a dining room that was now empty of customers.

"Mr. Casey, I swear these pancakes are so good and so light that it's a wonder they don't just rise up off my plate and fly away," Lucy said.

Casey laughed. "Lucy, my girl, it's not only your beauty that wins friends and admirers, it's your kindness and willingness to bestow compliments."

"Ha! You are the one who is kind and complimentary," Lucy said.

At that moment the front door opened, and Quince and Stanley came into the restaurant.

"Hello, boys," Little Man said. "Breakfast hour is over, but if you want, I'll go back and cook up some pancakes for you myself."

"No, sir, Mr. Lambert, there ain't no need for you to do that," Quince said.

"Well, how about some coffee?"

"Yes, sir, coffee would be fine."

Quince and Stanley came over and sat at a table that adjoined the one where Casey and Little Man were sitting. Lucy had gotten up to get coffee for them.

Quince stared at Casey for a long moment. It wasn't a challenging stare but one of curiosity. But it was Stanley who spoke first.

"Mr. Casey, I come into town today to thank you for savin' my life," he said.

"Oh, I wouldn't go so far as to say that I saved your life," Casey said. In truth, however, Casey had seen similar situations grow out of hand before, and he had known last night that there was a very good possibility that the belligerent cowboy might very well have pushed the incident to a fatal conclusion.

"Well, sir, I think you did. And I'm grateful."

"How come a cook like you had the nerve to do something like that?" Quince asked.

Casey shook his head. "I don't know," he replied. "As I think about it this morning, I realize what a foolish thing it was. If anyone ever sees me try something like that again, please stop me."

"Stanley said that you told that fella you was holdin' a candleholder to that you was in the war. Was you really in the war?" Quince asked.

"Yes."

"Whose side was you on?"

"Quince, that war was over when you were still a toddler, so maybe you don't know," Little Man said, "but that's not a question you ask people. Feelings are still too high."

"I wish I had been old enough to have been in the war," Quince said.

"Why would you wish that?" Casey asked.

"For the glory of it."

"There is no glory in war."

"Yeah, well, maybe not for you. More'n likely you never even seen any battle."

Casey stared at Quince for a long moment. He didn't glare at him; instead, his face remained expressionless. But there was something deep in his eyes that made Quince blink, then look away.

"Then maybe you did see some battle," Quince said. "I was just sort of spoutin' off, is all."

"Mr. Lambert," Casey said, "if you don't mind, I've

got some business to take care of this morning. I'll be back in time to start dinner."

"Sure, Mr. Casey, go ahead," Little Man said.

"Mr. Casey," Quince called to him just before he reached the door. Casey stopped but didn't turn around.

"I didn't mean nothin' by what I said. I hope you ain't took it the wrong way. I'm real grateful to you for what you done for my friend last night."

Casey gave him a slight wave, then left.

"You didn't have no call to talk to him like that, Quince," Stanley said after Casey left. "Most especial after he saved my life like he done last night."

"I told 'im I didn't mean nothin' by it, and I told 'im I was real grateful to him for savin' your life," Quince said. "Sometimes I just sort of shoot off my mouth without thinkin'."

"Yes," Little Man said. "Sometimes you do."

Quince stood up. "Look, me 'n' Stanley got to get back. Mr. Lambert, Lily, you tell Mr. Casey I . . . well, just tell 'im I don't want no hard feelin's betwixt us. Truth is, I think he's a good man, and I'm sorry I spoke out like that."

Little Man smiled, then reached out and put his hand on Quince's shoulder. "Don't worry about it. If I know Mr. Casey, he's already forgotten it."

Casey walked up the front steps to the church, tried the door, and, finding it open, went inside. It was a nondenominational Protestant church, so there was no font of holy water in the narthex, nor was there an altar or a cross in front. Nevertheless, Casey crossed himself, then walked up to the front pew. There were no kneelers in this church, so Casey just sat on the front pew and bowed his head.

The Reverend E. D. Owen heard someone come in and, stepping to the door of the pastor's office, looked out into the nave. He wasn't surprised to see Ken Casey; he had seen him here many times before. He would come and sit for several minutes, then he would leave. But he always came during the week. He had never come for a Sunday service.

Owen watched Casey until he crossed himself again, then just as Casey stood, Owen walked out of his office.

"Sir, can you wait for a moment?"

Casey stopped, and when Owen approached, he stuck out his hand. "Hello, Reverend Owen," he said.

"Please, won't you have a seat?" Owen invited, and Casey sat down again.

"You are Mr. Casey, aren't you? The cook at Little Man's?"

"Yes."

Owen smiled. "I've eaten there a few times since you started. I must say—and this is in concurrence with just about everyone I know who has eaten there—you are certainly an asset to this town. You are an excellent cook."

"Thank you."

"I've seen you come in here several times, Mr. Casey, but I've never seen you at one of our Sunday services."

"No," Casey said.

"I see that you cross yourself, which of course isn't a regular ritual of this church. But even though you may be Catholic, you would certainly be welcome at our service."

"I'm Episcopalian," Casey said.

"Yes, well, all the more reason," Owen said with a smile. "You are Protestant, and because this is the only church in town, we are quite ecumenical."

"I hope my private visits aren't an imposition," Casey said.

"No, no, of course not!" Owen said. "This is God's church and you are welcome anytime."

"Thank you." Casey got up to leave; then, looking up in the corner, he saw an obvious water stain on the wall, indicating that the church had a leaky roof.

"Mr. Casey, I mean that. You don't have to come on Sunday if you don't wish to. As I said, you are welcome anytime you choose to visit."

Casey nodded. "Thank you," he said.

From the church, Casey went back to his room and opened the trunk at the foot of his bed. Removing the contents of the trunk, he lifted out the false bottom and there, in the bottom, were bound packets of twenty-dollar bills, one hundred in each packet. He had twenty such packets, reward money from his days as a bounty hunter. He took five hundred dollars from one of the packets, then closed his locker. Going out again, he went to the post office and got an envelope and a piece of paper.

He wrote on the paper:

Matthew 6:3–4—When you give to the needy, do not let your left hand know what your right hand is doing, so that your giving may be in secret . . .

Then, without signing it, he wrapped the paper around the five hundred dollars, dropped it in the envelope, and addressed it to the church.

CHAPTER TWENTY-SIX

★

Wardell was filled with the "come to town on Saturday" visitors when Angus Pugh and six others rode in just before noon. Because the town was crowded with horses and carriages on the street and pedestrians walking up and down the boardwalks, the arrival of so many men riding together didn't arouse any curiosity. And only one curious little boy noticed Luke Draco.

Draco saw the boy looking at him, and he stared back at him menacingly, opening his eyes wide to emphasize the red pupils.

The boy, frightened, grabbed his mother's legs and buried his head in her dress.

"Matthew, what has gotten into you?" his mother asked, irritated by his action.

"Red eyes," Matthew said. "That man has red eyes."

"Red eyes, does he, sonny?" a nearby man asked. "Well, he probably just had a bout with demon rum, is all."

The seven men rode on down to the far end of the street, then dismounted in front of the marshal's office.

"Draco, you stay out here. I don't want the marshal to see you yet. No need in playing our hand before we have to."

Draco nodded but said nothing.

"The rest of you, come in with me," Pugh said.

Harold Wallace was sitting at his desk when the front door opened and several men came in, all of them wearing badges.

"Here, what is this?" he asked. "Who are you?"

"Marshal, my name is Angus Pugh. We are licensed detectives of the Texas and Pacific Railway, and we are here to do a job."

"What sort of job?"

"Next Saturday a train will be passing through Wardell carrying a money shipment for a bank in San Diego, California. I have orders for my men and me to meet that train."

"Oh, I see," Wallace said. "You are going to provide guards for the money for the rest of the way to San Diego, are you?"

"No, Marshal, we are going to take delivery of the money."

"What? You mean you are going to take the money off the train?"

"Yes."

"I don't understand. Why would you do that?"

"Perhaps these letters will clarify our position," Pugh said, putting two letters on his desk.

Office of the Governor
State of Texas
Austin, Texas

September 5, 1887

To Whom It May Concern:
   Be it known that the carrier of this letter is authorized to act on my behalf with regard to the transfer of railroad funds.

                     L. S. Ross
                     Governor

P.S. The bearer is acting in accordance with gubernatorial directive and is hereby authorized to supersede any and all local law officials until such time as the transfer of funds is made.

Wallace read the letter, then looked up. "This doesn't say anything about taking money off the train."

"No, but I have a letter from Colonel Scott that does say that."

"Who is that?"

"You'll see when you read the letter."

Texas and Pacific Railway Company
Fort Worth, Texas
To Express Messenger
    This office is in receipt of credible information that an attempt will be made to rob the train of the one hundred thousand dollar shipment, marked as T&P order number 648.
    Because of that, you are instructed to turn the money over to Angus Pugh, at the Wardell Depot. Pugh and his detectives will continue the transfer.
                    Thomas Scott
              President, T&P Railway

"I don't know about all this," Marshal Wallace said. "I'm the city marshal, why wasn't I contacted?"

"Because as of now your position as city marshal is superfluous," Pugh said.

"It's what?"

"The fact that you are city marshal is meaningless. From now until the train arrives, I, and the railroad detectives who are with me, will act as the law. You and your deputies are hereby suspended from duty until such time as we have the money and leave your city."

"The hell you say! Mister, I was appointed to the position by the city council! You are a detective for a private company, the Texas and Pacific Railway. I am a public servant, and you have no authority over me."

"Oh, but I do, Marshal. I point out to you the last paragraph in the governor's letter." Pugh read the last paragraph aloud: "P.S. The bearer is acting in accordance with gubernatorial directive and is hereby authorized to supersede any and all local law officials until such time as the transfer of funds is made."

"Let me see that again."

Pugh handed the letter to Marshal Wallace. "I particularly call your attention to the part that says 'supersede any and all local law officials.' That specifically gives me and my men authority over you. So, I say again, you and your deputies will have no legal function to perform until this operation is completed."

"All right, let's say that is true in as far as your dealing with the railroad and the money shipment is concerned. But what about routine law enforcement? What if there is a domestic disturbance? What if there is a murder or a robbery in town while you are here? What if there is a drunk and disorderly? *What if someone spits on the street?*" Wallace literally shouted the last line.

"As I said, we will function as the law for the next few days."

It wasn't until then that Marshal Wallace looked at the others who had come in and he recognized Durbin and Holder.

"Those two," he said, pointing. "Are you telling me that they are railroad detectives?"

"Yes."

"Well, mister, all I have to say is, the railroad sure ain't very particular about who they hire as detectives, are they?"

Pugh looked toward the two men and they both looked down at the floor.

"What do you mean?" he asked.

"They were here a few days ago, interrupted a town dance, and caused a lot of trouble. I had to take their guns away from them; I gave them back the next morning but I should have thrown them in jail. If I had known you were going to bring them here wearing badges, I damn sure would have thrown them in jail."

"Yes, well, as I said, Marshal, none of this is your concern now. Not until we secure the money to prevent a possible holdup. Until then, we will act as the local constabulary, and you and your deputies—"

"I have no deputies, which you should have known if you had done any research at all before coming in here to take over."

"Well, for the next week, Marshal, you can just relax."

Marshal Wallace got up and reached for his hat.

"Where are you going?" Pugh asked.

"You told me to relax, didn't you? I'm going somewhere to relax."

Wallace went outside and he saw Luke Draco leaning against the porch support with his arms folded across his chest. He stopped for a moment to stare at him.

"What are you looking at?" Draco asked, his voice a sibilant hiss. When he spoke he moved his arms, and Wallace saw the badge on his shirt.

"You're Luke Draco, aren't you?"

"Yes."

"Are you with Pugh?" Wallace asked.

"Yes."

"I thought you were a bounty hunter. What is a bounty hunter doing wearing a badge?"

Draco stared without speaking. Looking into those red-dotted crystal eyes, Wallace grew uncomfortable and looked down. He shook his head, then walked away. The first place he went to was the Red Bull Saloon.

"Walter, give me a shot of whiskey," he said.

"Marshal, you sure you want whiskey?" Walter asked. "You don't normally drink at this hour of the day, you say you are on duty."

"Yes, well, that's just it, you see. I'm not on duty."

"What do you mean, you aren't on duty?"

"I've been relieved by a group of detectives from the Texas and Pacific Railway."

"Wait a minute, they can't do that, can they? I mean, the railway is a private company and you are a public official."

"I tried that argument, but it didn't work. There are seven of them."

Before Walter could respond, Durbin and Holder came into the saloon.

"What are you boys doing back here?" Walter asked. "I was pretty sure that when you left, you'd had enough of our little town."

"Yeah, well, that was then, and this is now. And now we're in charge," Durbin said. Making a fist with his left hand, he put his thumb on the badge that was pinned to his shirt.

"What the hell? What do you mean, you're in charge?" Walter asked.

"You tell 'im, Marshal," Durbin said. Durbin and Holder stepped up to the bar. "Whiskey," Durbin said.

"Yeah, me too," Holder added.

Walter made no move to respond.

"Didn't you hear what we ordered?"

"I don't see any money on the bar," Walter said.

"Let's just call this special service for the law," Holder said. He pulled his pistol and pointed it at Walter.

"Here, what do you think you're—" Marshal Wallace started, but he stopped in mid-sentence when he saw Durbin pointing his gun at him.

"I'll just take your pistol," Durbin said. "Seein' as you aren't the law anymore, you won't be needin' it."

Wallace pulled his pistol out gingerly and handed it over to Durbin.

"Ha! Last time we had to give our pistols to you. How does it feel now that the shoe is on the other foot?"

Wallace stared at him for a moment, then left the saloon. As soon as he stepped outside, he got an idea and walked hurriedly to the depot, which was also the location of the Western Union office. There was no train due for two more hours, so the depot was empty except for Max Wood, the telegrapher, and Earl Cook, the ticket seller. They were playing a game of checkers.

"Hello, Marshal," Wood said, looking up with a smile. "Take a look at this board, will you? I've got Cook up against the wall. He's beat and he knows it."

"Max, I need you to send a telegram for me back to the T&P headquarters in Fort Worth."

"All right, I'll do that," Max said, standing. He pointed to the board. "Earl, I want you to know I've got the location of every piece memorized. Don't you even think about movin' 'em around on me."

"What, do you think I'd cheat you?"

"Damn right I think you would, if you thought you could get away with it."

"Ha, how do you know I haven't already cheated?"

"What do you mean? You mean you *have* cheated?"

"I'm not saying," Cook said with a little chuckle.

Wood turned his attention back to Marshal Wallace. "What are you sendin' a telegram to my boss for? You ain't plannin' on gettin' me fired, are you?"

"No," Wallace said.

The answer was short and said without a smile, and that left a puzzled expression on Cook's face, because he had actually asked the question jokingly.

"Give me pencil and pad," Wallace ordered.

Wood complied, and Wallace wrote the message he wanted sent:

HAS THE T AND P AUTHORIZED PRI-
VATE DETECTIVES TO REMOVE A
MONEY SHIPMENT FROM A TRAIN?
HAVE THEY BEEN AUTHORIZED TO
RELIEVE LOCAL AUTHORITIES? HAR-
OLD WALLACE CITY MARSHAL
WARDELL TEXAS

Wood read the message, then looked up at Wallace. "What's this about, Harold?"

"Just like it says," Wallace replied. "Seven men have arrived in town and they say they have the authority to remove a money shipment from a train that will be passing through here."

"Oh, I can't see the T&P authorizing anything like that," Cook said.

"I can't, either. That's why I'm sending the telegram. That is, if I can get you to actually send it."

"Well, yes, I'll send it now," Wood said. Sitting down at his table, he reached for the telegraph key and began the transmission.

Elliot Crabtree was sitting at the telegrapher's table in the Texas and Pacific Depot in Fort Worth when the telegraph key started clacking. He smiled as soon as he recorded the opening, indicating that the message was from the T&P Depot in Wardell. He knew exactly what the message was about, because he had been anticipating it. As soon as the message was completed, he started tapping out the return.

"Damn," Wood said as the return message started clicking. "They must've been ready for it. I've never gotten a response this fast. And on a Saturday too."

Wood transcribed the message.

DETECTIVE ANGUS PUGH OUR FINEST MAN IS AUTHORIZED TO REMOVE MONEY SHIPMENT FROM THE WESTBOUND TRAIN DUE THROUGH WARDELL ON SATURDAY OCTOBER 22 STOP DETECTIVES ARE TO RELIEVE LOCAL LAW AUTHORITIES UNTIL SUCH TIME AS MONEY TRANSFER IS MADE STOP THOMAS SCOTT PRESIDENT T AND P RAILWAY

"I'll be damned," Wood said after he received the message. He looked up at Wallace with an expression of disbelief on his face. "Here's your message, Marshal. It's all true."

Leaving the telegraph office, Marshal Wallace walked back to Little Man Lambert's Restaurant. As he did so, he saw that the railroad detectives were already out, patrolling the streets. He had the telegram clutched in his hand when he went inside.

"Hello, Harold," Little Man greeted warmly. "You're a little late for breakfast and a little early for lunch, but I'll gladly fix whichever one you want."

"A cup of coffee will be enough," Wallace replied.

"All right, a cup of coffee coming. . . . Harold, where's your pistol? Did it fall out of your holster?"

"No," Wallace said. "The railroad detectives took it."

"Railroad detectives? What railroad detectives?"

"Here, this will tell you all about it," Wallace said, showing Little Man the telegram he had just received.

Little Man read it. He thumped his finger on the message. "I don't care what it says here, the T&P is a private organization. They have no right to usurp authority from duly appointed public law officials."

"Yeah, well, I would think so too," Wallace said. "But this isn't the only thing. Pugh also has a letter from the governor saying that he and his men are authorized to supersede all local authority."

"How sure are you about that letter from the governor?" Little Man asked. "What I mean is, have you actually seen the letter?"

"Yes, I've seen it, and it looks real enough to me. I recognized the governor's signature."

"I don't know," Little Man said. "There sure is something fishy about this."

CHAPTER TWENTY-SEVEN

★

NOTICE
TO ALL RESIDENTS OF WARDELL:
THE CARRYING OF WEAPONS
IS PROHIBITED

The weapons prohibition sign was posted at either end of Broad Street, and badge-wearing railroad detectives were busily enforcing the order.

"What do you mean by imposing a prohibition on carrying weapons?" Wallace demanded when he went into his office. Pugh was sitting behind the desk, and he looked up at Wallace.

"It should be simple enough for you to understand," Pugh said. "I am responsible for the safe delivery of that money shipment. In order to make certain that nothing unforeseen occurs, I've decided to prohibit anyone from carrying arms." He held up his finger. "But don't worry, that will only be until after the transfer of the money. Once that happens, we'll be on our way, and the town of Wardell can return to normal. In the meantime, you just relax. Go to one of the saloons and have a few drinks."

Pugh smiled, but it wasn't genuine. "Start running a tab. I'll pick it up before we leave."

Just as Wallace returned to the Red Bull, three cowboys arrived in Wardell and were riding up Broad Street. Stopping in the middle of town, they dismounted and tied off their horses at one of the centrally located hitching rails.

"You know what we ought to do, don't you, Poke?" one of the three asked as he looped his horse's reins around the hitching rail. "We ought to go down to Big Kate's place and get young Marvin broke in."

"What are you talking about, get me broke in?" Marvin asked. Marvin was noticeably younger than the other two.

"You ain't never had no woman, have you?" Poke asked.

"Well, not actual," Marvin said.

Poke laughed. "'Not actual'? What does that mean, 'not actual'?"

"Well, I mean I've kissed girls. And I don't mean just kissin'. We, uh, well, like I say, I never, uh, actual done it, but Marilyn Jamison let me, uh, well, I told her I wouldn't tell."

"Like I said, we need to take you down to Big Kate's place and let her break you in."

"I don't know what you mean."

Poke laughed. "Tell him, Andy. Tell him about Big Kate."

"You know who Big Kate is, don't you, Marvin?" Andy asked.

"Well, yeah, I've seen her around. She's that real big woman that owns the Gentlemen's Club."

"You do know what the Gentlemen's Club is, don't you, Marvin?" Poke asked.

"I've heard it was a whorehouse. Only, I ain't never been there, so I don't know for sure."

"Oh, yes, it's a whorehouse all right. And here's the thing: if you ain't never been with a woman before, Big Kate always gives you the first time free," Poke said.

"Really?" Marvin said, breaking into a broad smile.

"Yeah, really. Are you interested? Because if you are, why, we might just pay a visit to Big Kate's place."

"Well, yeah, I'm interested," Marvin said excitedly.

"They's only one thing that maybe you ought to know about," Andy said.

"What's that?"

"If it's your first time, and you're doin' it for free, why, Big Kate is the one who breaks you in her own self."

"What?"

Andy and Poke laughed out loud.

"Yep!" Andy said. "You'll get all three hundred pounds of her, all to yourself."

"No! I don't want my first time to be with someone like her."

"Why not? She'll teach you tricks you ain't never even heard of," Poke said, and again he and Andy laughed at young Marvin's expense.

The three men had just started across the street, when Draco walked out and held up his hand to stop them.

"What do you want? What are you stoppin' us for?" one of the cowboys asked.

"I'll be taking your guns," Draco said.

"The hell you will. What do you mean, you'll be takin' our guns?"

Draco pointed to the end of the street to the sign. "Didn't you see the sign when you come into town? It says ever'one has to give up their guns. It's the law."

"I ain't never heard of no law like that. If you want me to give up my gun, I'm goin' to have to hear it from Marshal Wallace his own self."

"As far as you three are concerned, Wallace isn't the law. I am."

"What do you mean, you're the law? Where's Marshal Wallace? What's goin' on here?"

Draco pointed to a barrel sitting at the corner of the boardwalk. "Do you see that barrel? If you are going to stay in town, walk over to that barrel and drop your guns into it. Otherwise, turn around and go back," Draco said.

"Mister, maybe you ain't never worked on a ranch. Maybe you don't know how you look forward to comin' to town whenever you get the chance," Poke said. "Well, we're in town, and we ain't goin' to turn around and go back. And we ain't givin' up our guns, neither, so just get the hell out of our way."

"You have three choices," Draco said. "Give up your guns, leave town, or die."

"Die? Why, you dumb son of a bitch, there are three of us. Do you really think you can scare three of us?" Poke asked. "Now, you white-faced bastard, get out of our way or go for your gun."

Draco stretched his lips into what might have been a grin, but his face was so pale that it had the effect of making his head look like a skull.

"All right, have it your way," Draco said.

Draco drew his pistol then and fired three times. The draw was so unexpected, and so fast, that none of the three cowboys had the opportunity to even make a move toward their own guns.

The conversation that had been going on between Draco and the three young cowboys had been so quiet that nobody else on the street had overheard it, so when three shots suddenly rang out, it caught everyone by surprise. Looking toward the sound of the shots, they saw the three young cowboys crumple and fall to the ground.

Marshal Wallace was in the Red Bull when someone came running in. "Marshal, that white-faced bastard just shot three cowboys."

"What? Why?"

"I don't know, it just happened."

"Damn," Wallace said.

"Harold," the bartender called toward him. "Be careful."

"Hell, Walter, I can't be anything but careful. You may have noticed, I don't even have a gun now."

By the time Wallace reached the scene, there were already twenty or more of the town's citizens gathered around, looking on in morbid curiosity. Draco was still there, joined now by Holder and Durbin. They would have been the only three who were armed had it not been for the three dead cowboys. All three had their pistols still in the holsters.

"What happened here?" Wallace asked.

"It's none of your business," Durbin said.

"The hell it isn't. I'm still the marshal of this town, and whether you people have taken over until the train arrives next Saturday or not, I still have some responsibility for the safety of our citizens. Now, I demand to know what happened."

"You *demand*?" Holder asked mockingly.

Draco held his hand out toward Holder. "I killed them," Draco said.

"You killed them? Why?"

"I told them that they would have to give up their guns as long as they are in town. They refused to do so."

"So you just shot them down in cold blood?"

"They went for their guns," Draco said.

Marshal Wallace looked pointedly at the three young men.

"What do you mean, they went for their guns? Why, mister, all three still have their pistols in their holsters."

"I was faster," Draco said calmly.

Wallace had to take several breaths to control his anger. Finally, he spun around on his heel and walked quickly to the marshal's office—*his* office, although he no longer occupied it. Pugh was sitting at his desk, playing chess with one of his detectives.

"Pugh, I need to talk to you."

Pugh held up his hand as if holding Wallace back while he studied the chessboard. He moved a bishop. "My, my, Mr. Taylor, it seems that you are going to have to make a decision between your rook and your knight. You are going to lose one of them."

"A clever move, Mr. Pugh, a clever move," Taylor said.

"Now, Marshal, what is it?"

Wallace pointed back toward the middle of town. "That milk-faced deputy of yours just murdered three innocent men," the marshal said angrily.

"What do you mean, he murdered them? Why would he do such a thing?"

"He said that when he tried to disarm them, they went for their guns. I know that isn't true."

"How do you know it isn't true?"

"Because I saw them. All three of them still had their pistols in their holsters!"

"Well, that doesn't prove anything. If my deputy said they were going for their guns, I tend to believe him. But even if they weren't, just carrying a gun in town now represents a threat. If my deputy told them to surrender their weapons and they failed to do so, he had every right to shoot them."

"No, he doesn't have a right to shoot them!"

"Marshal, you have seen the letters and, I'm told, you have even sent a telegram back to my boss—over my head, I might add—to inquire as to whether I have the authority to relieve you. And I'm told that the answer you received from the headquarters of the Texas and Pacific completely validates everything I have told you. Now, will there be anything else?"

"Why have you given the order to confiscate everyone's gun? You don't have the right to do that."

"Oh, but I do have the right. The precedent of having a town free of guns has been established all over America. But don't worry about it, Marshal. As I have explained to you, after this Saturday everything will go back as it was. You will be in charge again, and if you wish to let just anyone carry a gun, well, you go right ahead and do so.

"But before you judge, I ask you to consider what I'm facing here. I have to make certain that the money shipment is safe, and I can't take a chance on somebody robbing the train before we can secure the money."

"How likely is that to happen, anyway? Before you came here, nobody even knew that the train would be carrying a money shipment."

"Oh, you've put my queen in jeopardy," Pugh said. "Good move."

"You are supposed to be the law now, you took the job from me. What are you going to do about this shooting?"

"I'm not going to do anything about it, Marshal," Pugh said as, with a knight, he took out the piece that was challenging his queen. "Don't you see? If those men had not been wearing guns, or if they had given up their guns as they had been ordered, none of this would have happened."

Frustrated and so angry that he feared he might project this argument further than he wanted to, Wallace turned and left the office. As he did so he saw the mortician, Gene Welch, with his wagon down at the scene of the shooting. Some of the townspeople were helping him load the bodies into the wagon. The white-faced deputy, Holder, and Durbin were standing to one side, talking and laughing as they watched.

"Yes, I heard about it," Little Man said. "They said it was three of Dewey Gimlin's cowboys."

"Yes, Poke Crowe, Andy French, and Marvin Gillespie. They're good boys. That is, they *were* good boys. I've never had any trouble with them," Wallace said. "Marvin couldn't have been older than seventeen or eighteen," he added.

"Yes, I know those boys. They generally come in here for a meal every payday."

"I just don't think Pugh has the right to take everyone's gun away from them unless there has been a city ordinance passed that specifically authorizes such a thing. And even then you wouldn't have the right to kill someone unless you actually were in danger. And no matter what that white-faced, red-eyed bastard said, there's no way they could have been drawing against him. Not one man even had his pistol out."

"What white-faced, red-eyed man?" Casey asked.

"Luke Draco," Wallace said. "I swear, he's about the ugliest human I've ever seen. Why, he's white as a sheet; I mean, it don't look natural at all. And his eyes—there's no color to them except his pupils, and they're red."

"That's actually the blood you are seeing," Casey said. The cook had come out of the kitchen and was listening to the conversation. "Albinos have no color at all: no skin color and no eye color. And Luke Draco is fast enough that he could have killed all three before they could get their guns out."

"Nobody is that fast, are they?"

"There are people that fast," Casey said. "Quince Anders is that fast."

"I've seen Quince draw and shoot, and he is fast, but I don't know how anyone could be fast enough to draw and shoot three men before any one of them could even get their guns from their holsters."

"A Dutch physiologist named F. C. Donders has done a lot of research in reaction time," Casey said. "He discovered that it takes more time for your brain to tell your hand to move than it does for your hand to move. So if Draco had already told his hand to move, he would quite easily draw and shoot before any of the three cowboys—who would first have to see him make his draw, then tell their hands to react—could actually get their guns out."

"Whooee, Mr. Casey, that's a bit more than I can comprehend," Little Man said.

"No need to have to understand anything more than that it is possible."

"So you're saying it was a fair fight?" Wallace asked.

Casey shook his head. "No, I'm not saying that. It was murder. It might have been legalized, but it was murder."

"We really are in trouble if someone like Draco is put in authority," Wallace said. "As far as I know, he isn't a wanted man. I don't know how he has avoided it, though. If the stories about him are true, he has killed a lot of people."

"The stories about him are true," Casey said.

"Then how has he avoided the law?" Little Man asked.

"Same way Ded Axton, the fella they called Death's Acolyte, managed to avoid the law," Wallace explained. "Axton probably killed as many men as Draco has killed, but there were always witnesses, and it was always a fair fight."

"Well, this isn't right," Little Man said. "I don't care what the T&P says, and I don't care what the governor says, this isn't right. I'm sure this is against some law."

CHAPTER TWENTY-EIGHT

★

There were four saloons in Wardell: the Red Bull, the Ace High, the Gilded Cage, and the Hog Lot. Of the four, the Red Bull was generally considered to be the most genteel, while the Hog Lot was the most indecorous. It was this, the indecorous atmosphere of the Hog Lot, that was the attraction for Angus Pugh's "deputies."

Warren Canby was standing at the bar in the Hog Lot when he saw a cowboy come in who, in obvious disregard of the signs posted around town, was wearing his gun. Although Luke Draco was the deputy with the widest-known reputation as a gunman, Canby was also very good, and he was looking for a chance to make a name for himself when the opportunity arose.

"Cowboy, didn't you see the signs telling you that you couldn't come into town carrying a gun?" Canby asked.

The cowboy glanced at Canby but paid him no attention beyond a quick glance. He turned back to the bartender.

"I'll have a beer," he said.

"Cowboy, I'm talkin' to you."

"I got a name and it ain't 'cowboy.'"

"Oh? Well, what *is* your name?"

"The name is Jim Trout. Not that it's any of your business."

"Oh, but it *is* my business," Canby said. "You see, you are wearing a gun, and I intend to take it from you."

"What gives you the right to take my gun from me?"

Canby pointed to the badge on his shirt. "This gives me the right."

Trout looked at the badge. "Hell, that ain't nothing but a railroad detective badge, mister. And maybe you ain't noticed, but there ain't no tracks runnin' through this here saloon." He laughed out loud at his own joke.

"I'll be takin' your gun," Canby repeated.

"Mister, you'll take this gun from me over my dead body," Trout said resolutely.

A broad smile spread across Canby's face. "Funny you would say that," he said. "Because that is just exactly what I have in mind."

Up until that moment Trout had been belligerent and challenging. But there was something in the way Canby was talking, and handling himself, that put him on his guard.

"Wait a minute," he said, holding up his hand. "I think maybe this little talk between us is beginning to get out of hand. Let's stop and start all over."

"All right, give me your gun," Canby said, obviously

displeased that his adversary seemed to be defusing the moment.

Trout shook his head. "No, I ain't goin' to do that," he said. "But this is what I *will* do. I'll just have my beer, then I'll just leave town and there won't be no need for any trouble."

Canby smiled. Maybe this was going to work out for him after all. "I tell you what, Mr. Trout. Since you're wearing that gun, we may as well get this settled." He stepped away from the bar and looked at the cowboy through cold, ruthless eyes. "I'll let you draw first."

"Draw? What draw? I told you, soon as I drink my beer I'll be leavin' town. There ain't no need for anyone to be drawin' on anyone."

"I said draw," Canby repeated in a cold, flat voice.

The others in the saloon knew now that the cowboy had carried things too far. They knew there was about to be gunplay and they began, quietly but deliberately, to get out of the way of any flying lead.

It wasn't until that moment, when he saw the others move out of the way, that Trout actually began to get a sense of the seriousness of his situation.

"Look, mister, if you're figurin' on forcin' me into a fight, you can just figure again, 'cause I ain't goin' to draw against you."

"Why not? You're wearin' your gun."

"That don't mean I'm goin' to get into a gunfight with you."

"You had your chance. All you had to do was hand

me your gun, but you didn't do it. Now you're goin' to have to use it."

"All right, all right, I'll give you my gun," Trout said.

"How are you goin' to do that?"

"What do you mean, how am I goin' to do it? I'll just give it to you, like you said."

"Huh-uh, it's too late for that. If you reach for your gun now, how will I know you aren't drawing on me?"

"'Cause I'm tellin' you I ain't."

"I can't take that chance. If you touch that gun, I'm goin' to figure you're drawin' on me. So you might as well do it."

"I ain't touchin' my gun, and I ain't drawin' on you," Trout said. He picked up his drink, but his hand was shaking so badly that some of the beer sloshed over.

"Draw," Canby said.

By now a vein was jumping visibly in Trout's neck, and his hands were shaking almost uncontrollably.

"Canby, for heaven's sake, leave him be," the bartender said. "Look at him! He can't draw on you. You want his gun, reach over and take it, there ain't nothin' he can do to you."

"Stay out of this, barkeep. Or else, get yourself a gun and become a part of it."

"What? No, I ain't goin' to get into no gunfight!"

"Then keep out of it."

"Please, Mr. Canby," Trout said. "It's like the bartender said. If you want my gun, take it."

"Draw," Canby said again.

"No, I ain't goin' to. No matter what you do, you can't make me fight."

"You think not?"

Canby jerked his pistol from his holster. The draw was so sudden that it looked like no more than a twitch of his shoulder before the gun was in his hand. He pulled the trigger and there was a flash of light, then a roar of exploding gunpowder. That was followed by a billowing cloud of acrid blue smoke.

At first everyone thought Canby had killed Trout, but when the smoke drifted away, Trout was still standing, holding his hand to the side of his head with blood spilling through his fingers. Canby's bullet had clipped off about a quarter-inch of Trout's earlobe.

"Draw," Canby ordered again.

"No."

There was a second shot and Trout's right earlobe, like his left, turned into a ragged, bloody piece of flesh.

"Stop it! What are you doing?" the bartender called.

Canby drew his pistol again, cocked it, and pointed it at the bartender. "Do you really want a part of this?"

"No, no!" the bartender said, moving away from Canby and down toward the end of the bar.

Canby holstered his pistol and looked at Trout, who now had a bloody hand covering each ear.

"Draw."

"No!" By now tears of pain, humiliation, and fear were streaming down Trout's face.

"I'm going to count to three," Canby said. "At three

I'm going to draw and I'm going to shoot you whether you draw or not. One, two . . ."

Before Canby could get to the count of three, a loud explosion filled the room. Canby was knocked forward and fell facedown on the floor. There was a big gaping hole in his back, the result of buck-and-ball. The bartender was standing at the far end of the bar, holding a double-barreled twelve-gauge shotgun with smoke curling up from both barrels.

"You son of a bitch!" the bartender shouted at Canby's body. "Why did you make me do this, you son of a bitch?"

The gunfire had attracted Poindexter to the saloon, and when he saw Canby lying facedown on the floor, his back a bloody pulp, and the bartender holding a smoking shotgun, he drew his pistol and pointed it at the bartender.

"Marshal," Fred Keaton said, coming into the Red Bull. "Those deputies have put Emmet Reardon in jail." Keaton, who was the Keaton of McKnight & Keaton, was also a member of the City Council.

"The bartender at the Hog Lot? What for?"

"Emmet killed one of the deputies. He shot him in the back with a double-barrel shotgun."

"That doesn't sound like Emmet," Walter said. "He worked over here for a while. He's a pretty levelheaded man, for all that he wound up at the Hog Lot."

"Why did he shoot the deputy?" Wallace asked.

"It had something to do with Jim Trout—you know, that cowboy that rides for Burt Rowe? Trout's down at the doc's now, getting his ears looked at."

"What do you mean, 'getting his ears looked at'?"

"The deputy shot 'em both off before Emmet shot him."

When Wallace went into Dr. Urban's office, he saw the young cowboy sitting on a chair while Dr. Urban was bandaging his ears. Dr. Urban was a tall, thin man, bald, with a neatly trimmed mustache, and rimless glasses.

"Damn! You really did get your ears shot off?"

"Just the earlobes," Dr. Urban said. "He won't look all that pretty for the ladies, but it won't hurt his hearing any."

"You want to tell me what happened?" Wallace said.

"Where were you when I needed you?" Trout asked accusingly. "When that son of a bitch was shooting my ears off because I wouldn't draw on him, why weren't you there?"

"I'm sorry, son," Wallace said, "but I have to be honest with you: I don't know that I could have done anything if I had been there."

"Then what kind of a marshal are you?"

"I don't know that I can answer that," Wallace said frankly.

From the doctor's office, Wallace went straight to the marshal's office, where he saw Pugh.

"I understand that you have one of our citizens in jail," he said.

"Yes, I have one of the town's citizens in jail. He's in jail for the murder of one of my deputies, Warren Canby."

"From what I have been able to determine, Emmet killed Canby to save the life of another man. He was about to kill young Jimmy Trout, a cowboy."

"A cowboy who refused to surrender his gun," Pugh said.

Wallace shook his head. "That's not true. He tried to surrender his gun and Canby wouldn't take it. He said if Trout touched his gun he would consider it as drawing against him."

"Well, I suppose it will all come out in his trial, won't it?"

"What trial?"

"Oh, Friday we'll hold his trial."

"Who will hold his trial?"

"I will, I and my deputies."

"And what if you find him guilty?"

"We'll hang him," Pugh said breezily..

"What? You don't have any right to do that!"

"We have assumed martial law over the town of Wardell. That gives us absolute authority to do anything we want," Pugh said. "Now, do you have any other questions?"

Wallace opened and closed his fist several times, then turned and left the office.

★   ★   ★

WEDNESDAY, OCTOBER 19, 1887

A hearse was standing in front of the red doors of the church while a steady rain was falling. The black curtains of the hearse had been pulled aside, but the windows were so rain streaked that nobody could see inside. If they could, they would have seen that the hearse was empty. Two well-mannered black horses stood quietly while the rain pelted them, as if the animals knew the sad task they were about to perform.

Inside the church, at the very front, three open caskets were resting on sawhorses. The occupants of the three caskets were Poke Crowe, Andy French, and Marvin Gillespie. All three men were wearing suits, something that none of them had ever worn during their life.

Practically the entire town and all the cowboys from the ranches in the area turned out for the funeral, and they were now sitting inside the church. The atmosphere was somber, the flickering candlelight partly dispelling the darkness in the nave as a result of the storm.

It had begun raining shortly after the funeral started, and the Reverend E. D. Owen continued the service for as long as he could, hoping that the rain would stop soon so they could proceed to the cemetery. Ken Casey looked up into the corner where the leak had been and was pleased to see that it had stopped. Evidently Reverend Owen had made good use of the money he had sent him.

Casey was sitting in the same pew as Little Man Lambert, Lucy, Quince, Stanley, and Mr. and Mrs. Murdock Felton. Mr. and Mrs. Dewey Gimlin, along with the other cowboys from the ranch where the three cowboys had worked, were sitting in the front. There, a pew had been marked off with purple rope as "family," the Gimlins and the other cowboys being the closest thing to family that Poke, Andy, and Marvin had. None of the railroad detective deputies were present in the church, nor did anyone expect them to be.

Finally the rain eased up somewhat, although it didn't stop. Taking that as his cue, Reverend Owen brought the service to a close. The cowboys, not only from Dewey Gimlin's ranch but from neighboring ranches as well, lined up to act as pallbearers. They carried all three coffins, now closed, out to the hearse, where they stacked them inside. The rain continued to fall as they went out to the cemetery, where, dressed in black and standing under black umbrellas, they endured the rain for the graveside service.

In the far corner of the cemetery a lone gravedigger was closing the grave over Warren Canby's pine box. There had been no service of any kind for him, nor had any of the other deputies come out to the cemetery for the burial. A few of those who were there for the interment of the three cowboys looked over to see the gravedigger but nobody showed any sympathy, or even any interest.

Finally the graveside services were concluded and

the townspeople left the cemetery, some on foot, a few on horseback, and many in buggies, surreys, buckboards, and wagons. A large number of them showed up at Little Man Lambert's, Dewey Gimlin having arranged for a repass meal to be served in the restaurant. Casey had put on a very large steamboat round beef roast the previous evening, cooking it all night so that it was tender and succulent for the meal.

During the conversation, Wallace spoke about Emmet Reardon being in jail. "Pugh says he plans to put him on trial Friday, then hang him."

"I'm sure he doesn't have the right to do that," Little Man said.

"He says he does, and he does have that letter from the governor."

"Why don't you go talk to Fielding Potashnick?" Little Man said. "He used to work in the state attorney's office. I'll bet he can tell you if there is some law against it."

"Yeah, that's a good idea," Casey said. "I think I will go talk to him."

CHAPTER TWENTY-NINE

★

Fielding Potashnick was a small man, bald except for a circle of gray hair just above his ears. Leaning back in his chair behind his desk, he puffed on his pipe as he listened to Marshal Wallace.

Removing the pipe from his mouth, Potashnick held it by the bowl and pointed the stem toward Wallace.

"Are you telling me that you saw the governor's own signature on a letter that authorizes the railroad detectives to supersede your authority?"

"Yes."

Potashnick shook his head. "That just doesn't seem plausible to me. I know Governor Ross; I knew him when he was General Ross. Hell, he's a former Texas Ranger and a former sheriff. He also took part in the Texas State Constitutional Convention. No, sir, I just can't see him authorizing such a thing. You're sure it was his signature? I mean, would you recognize it?"

"Yes, I've seen it many times. He always signs with his initials, L. S. Ross. And there it was, right above his P.S."

"Above his P.S.? What P.S.?"

"What we are talking about, Fielding. The P.S. that said that the railroad detectives would have authority over all local law officials until the transfer of funds."

"What was above his name? Do you remember?"

"Yes. It said that the bearer of that letter was authorized to act on his behalf in regard to the transfer of railroad funds."

Potashnick put the pipe back in his mouth and clenched the stem in his teeth.

"Hmm," he said. "That's it? He didn't specifically mention the train that was coming through on the twenty-second?"

"No."

"That's not like the governor, either," Potashnick said. "So here you have a letter that has a nonspecific reference to transferring railroad funds, then a P.S. passing all authority over to private detectives. Harold, you know what I would do if I were you?"

"What?"

"I think I would send a telegram to the governor, ask him if he specifically meant to transfer all authority from duly appointed municipal law officers to these railroad detectives. And also explain to him what's going on, especially the fact that three of our citizens have already been killed by one of these detectives."

"Yes," Wallace said. "Yes, that's a good idea. I'll do that."

Fifteen minutes later, Marshal Wallace showed up at the telegraph window at the depot.

"Max, I need to send another telegram. This time to L. S. Ross, governor of the state of Texas."

"Sorry, Marshal Wallace, but I can't do it," Wood said.

"What do you mean, you can't do it? Why the hell not?"

"They've taken my telegraph key from me. I can't send any telegrams without the key, which means they have to authorize anything that I send. And even then I have to route all my telegrams through the home office in Fort Worth."

"What? No, this has gone too far. I'm not going to put up with this. I'm going down to see Pugh and I'm going to have this out once and for all."

Pugh, Taylor, and Poindexter were engaged in conversation when Marshal Wallace returned to his office.

"What is it now, Wallace?" Pugh asked, the tone of his voice showing obvious condescension.

Wallace held out his hand. "I'll thank you for the telegrapher's key," he said.

"Why do you want the telegrapher's key?"

"It's obvious, isn't it? I want to send a telegram."

"You've already sent one telegram to the T&P Headquarters. Do you think if you send another telegram, that you will get a different answer?"

"I won't be sending this telegram to the Texas and Pacific," Wallace said, resolutely.

"Where will you be sending it?"

"I'll be sending it directly to the governor, asking him to withdraw his order that railroad detectives assume the responsibility for civil law. In fact, I'll be doing more than asking him: I will be challenging him. The constitution of the state of Texas does not grant him the authority to replace civil authority with private detectives. What's more, I'm sure he knows that. I don't believe he intended for you to interpret his letter as you have done."

Pugh leaned back in his chair, sighed, and ran his hand through his graying hair.

"Marshal Wallace, I didn't want to do this, but you have given me absolutely no choice. Taylor, Poindexter, put the marshal under protective custody until after our business here is concluded."

"What the hell are you talking about? What do you mean, protective custody?"

"He means we're puttin' you in jail," Poindexter said.

"Pugh, you won't get away with this!" Wallace said as Poindexter grabbed him by one arm and Taylor by the other. They took him to the back of the jail, opened one of the cells, then shoved him in.

"Do you hear me, Pugh? You won't get away with this!"

After everyone had left the restaurant, and while Casey, Little Man, and Lucy were cleaning up, Fielding Potashnick came in.

"Hello, Fielding. We missed you at the repass dinner," Little Man said.

"I didn't come; I figured there would be enough of their friends, the other cowboys and such, that I didn't want to add to the crowd. What did Harold find out from the governor?"

"What do you mean?"

"After he left my office, he went to the depot to send a telegram to the governor to inquire about his letter. He didn't come back to see me, so I was just wondering what he found out."

"Well, I don't know. He didn't come back here."

"Why don't we go see the telegrapher and find out from the horse's mouth?" Potashnick suggested.

"That's a fine idea."

"Lucy, if we get any supper customers, tell them it's roast beef or nothing," Little Man said.

"All right, Papa," Lucy replied as her father left the restaurant with Potashnick.

"I didn't send the telegram," Max Wood said.

"What do you mean, you didn't send it? Didn't Marshal Wallace come over here?" Potashnick asked.

"Oh, yes, he came over here all right," Wood said. "He said he wanted to send a telegram to the governor, but I told him I couldn't send any telegram without Pugh's permission. Pugh has the telegraph key."

"I'll be damned," Potashnick said. "Now, I know he doesn't have the right to do *that*. There is no city ordinance nor even a state law that can prevent telegrams from being sent. Hell, the federal government can't even prevent it. That comes under the First Amendment of the U.S. Constitution. It's called freedom of speech."

"Maybe so, but I can't do anything without my telegraph key."

"I think it's time we paid Mr. Pugh a visit," Little Man said.

"All right, let's do that," Potashnick agreed.

"Gentlemen, you are making a mountain out of a molehill," Pugh said when Potashnick and Little Man visited him to ask him about his interference with the free exchange of telegraph messages. "As I have explained many times to the marshal, this will all be over by noon Saturday. Then we'll take control of the money that is being carried by the train, make certain that it gets to its intended destination, and go on our way. Everything here will return to normal."

"In the meantime, by preventing us from sending a telegram to the governor, you are violating the First Amendment," Potashnick charged.

Pugh chuckled. "Hardly, sir. No less an authority than Justice Oliver Wendell Holmes declared that speech could be suppressed if it be used for criminal conspiracy. I sincerely believe that someone might use the telegraph to organize an attempted robbery of the train, and it is my duty to prevent that."

"Where is Marshal Wallace?" Little Man asked.

"Why, I have him in protective custody," Pugh said.

"What do you mean, protective custody?"

"He has been relieved of his duty, and because he is not currently an officer of the law, he is also prohibited from carrying a weapon. I am holding him for his own protection. I am sure that he has made some enemies while serving as the city marshal, and there may be some who, seeing him unarmed, might wish to take advantage of that fact to do him harm. Therefore, for his own safety, I have put him in protective custody."

"May we visit him?"

"No."

"I am his lawyer," Potashnick said. "I have a right to see my client."

Pugh stared at Potashnick for a moment, then he nodded. "Mr. Taylor, please accompany this gentleman back to the cells so that he may visit with Marshal Wallace."

Taylor nodded, then started toward the door that led to the rear of the building. Both Potashnick and Little Man started with him, but Pugh pointed to Little Man.

"Not you. You aren't his lawyer."

Taylor led Potashnick to the back of the jail. There, in the last cell, Marshal Wallace was lying on the cot with his fingers laced behind his head.

"Harold?"

"Fielding!" Wallace said, sitting up quickly.

Potashnick turned to Taylor. "I can handle it from here."

"I'll just wait here for you," Taylor said, not leaving.

"I didn't get the telegram sent," Wallace said. "Pugh has the damn telegraph key."

"Yes, so I've heard. Are you all right? Have they mistreated you?"

"Other than locking me in my own jail, you mean? No, they haven't hit me or anything like that. Fielding, is there anything you can do to get me out of here?"

"I'm going to do what I can," Potashnick said. "I'll get with Mayor Felker and we'll have a city council meeting to discuss what we should do."

"Thanks."

Mayor C. E. "Daddy" Felker was quite a colorful figure. During the last mayoral campaign, he had dressed as Paul Revere and ridden a white horse up and down every street in town at least three times on the day before the election, ringing a bell, and calling out, "Vote for 'Daddy' Felker!"

His rather unique campaigning method had won the election for him, and the barber turned politician was always quick to respond to the needs of his constituents.

"As soon as I finish with Mr. Culpepper's haircut, I will convene a meeting of the city council," he told Potashnick. "Perhaps you would be good enough to inform the members of the council?"

"I will," Potashnick said.

One hour later the council was convened in the meeting room of the city hall.

"Gentlemen, I have convened this special meeting of the city council to discuss a problem that can be no secret to any of you," Felker began. "As I am sure you are aware, our fair city has been invaded—and yes, that is the only way to describe it—invaded by a group of men wearing the badges of detectives of the Texas and Pacific Railway. They have killed three of the county citizens, they plan to have a trial for Emmet Reardon on Friday, they being the entire court, and they have put Marshal Wallace in jail. In doing all this, they have usurped authority not authorized by any ordinance, law, or federal statute, and I think we should do something about it."

"What can we do, Daddy?" Hodge Deckert asked. Deckert took tickets at the town theater and music hall.

"Well, the first thing we must do is pass an article of censure, expressing our—"

"All right, let's break it up in here!" Taylor said, coming into the room with two other armed deputies.

"What are you men doing here?" Felker demanded angrily. "This is a closed meeting of the city council and you have no authority here. Absolutely none."

"That's where you are wrong, Felker," Taylor said. "We have the power of both the Texas and Pacific Railway and the governor of the state of Texas to act with complete authority. That is the same thing as having martial law declared, and that means we—and not the city council—will run this city until such time as that authority is withdrawn."

"And when will that be?" one of the members of the city council asked.

Taylor smiled a smile that was a cross between triumphant and patronizing.

"We will be out of here by noon Saturday. You only have to put up with us for three more days."

"Why the hell do we have to put up with you at all?"

"Because it has been decided by wiser heads than anyone present in this room that this will be the safest and most effective way to carry out the transfer of funds from the train to our hands. Now, gentlemen, I urge you to adjourn this meeting. There is no need for it, you can accomplish nothing, and if you resist, there is always the possibility of someone getting hurt. But I shouldn't have to remind you of that; after all, there was a funeral today for three young men who refused to follow a lawful order."

"I move we adjourn," Deckert said. "Hell, it's only for three more days. I say, let's put up with it and be done with all this."

"I second," one of the other councilmen said.

Mayor Felker sighed. "Very well, this special meeting of the city council is hereby adjourned." Felker rapped his gavel on the table.

CHAPTER THIRTY

★

When Holder awakened, he was aware of two things: One, that he had an enormous headache, and two, that there was a woman lying beside him. For just a second he wondered where he was, then he remembered that he and Durbin had spent the night in Big Kate's Gentlemen's Club.

He groaned, put his hand to his head, and looked over at the woman who was lying beside him. It was too warm for cover, so she was naked, and he could see the blue and red veins of her swollen breasts. She had a large stomach, and there was a disfiguring scar on her nose.

What the hell? How did he wind up with this woman? Surely there had to be someone in this whorehouse who was better looking. She was as ugly a crone as he had ever seen. He turned in the bed and his head started spinning. Damn, he must have been awfully drunk last night.

He saw a fly buzzing around and he started to brush it away, then saw it land on one of the woman's ponderous breasts, so he rose up on one elbow and rested his head on his hand and watched.

The woman twitched, and Holder smiled.

The fly flew away and Holder caught it, then pulled a wing off and put the fly back on the woman's breast.

The woman twitched again, and this time she slapped her breast hard. Holder snickered.

"Uhmm, what is it? What happened?" the woman asked.

"There was a damn fly that's been botherin' us," Holder said. "He landed on you, and you got him. Good for you."

"Yeah, when it's this hot and you have to leave the windows open, the flies get in," the woman said. She smiled up at Holder, and he saw that she was missing most of her teeth. "What time did we get to bed last night, honey?"

"I don't know."

"I don't know, either. I don't even remember coming to bed. But I bet we had a lot of fun." She giggled.

"I have to take a piss," Holder said.

"There is a privy out back."

"Hell, I don't want to get dressed just to go out and take a piss. Ain't you got a chamber pot?"

"Yes, but I don't ever let the men use it."

Looking around, Holder saw a potted plant sitting over in the corner. "All right," he said.

The woman closed her eyes again and Holder got out of bed and walked over to the potted plant. He started peeing on the plant, the stream making a splattering sound as it hit the leaves.

"What? What are you doing?" the woman asked, opening her eyes in surprise and anger.

"What's it look like? I'm waterin' your plant," Holder said. "Don't you ever water it? Hell, it was as dry as a bone," he added with a chuckle.

"Get your clothes on and get out of here!" the woman demanded.

"Don't worry, I'm goin'. Hell, if I had seen last night how ugly you was, I wouldn't've come up here in the first place."

"Get!" she shouted.

Holder got dressed and went downstairs, where he saw Durbin sitting in a chair. "What are you doin' down here?" he asked.

"Waitin' on you so we could go get some breakfast."

"Yeah, that sounds good."

"So how was Fifi?" Durbin asked.

"How was who?"

"Fifi."

"Who the hell is Fifi?"

Durbin laughed. "Why, Fifi is the beauty you took to bed with you last night."

"Damn," Holder said. "If I took a good-lookin' woman to bed with me last night, I don't know where she went. 'Cause I sure as hell didn't wake up with her this mornin'."

Durbin laughed. "I didn't think you was goin' to be too happy about it this morning."

"Well, why didn't you stop me?"

" 'Cause Fifi and Gladys was the only two that was here, and neither one of 'em was anything worth lookin' at. But Gladys was a little better lookin' than Fifi, and you was a little drunker'n me, so that's how it turned out. Come on, let's go get some breakfast."

When Holder and Durbin went into the restaurant, it was empty except for Little Man and Lucy.

"Damn," Durbin said. "Ain't you got no customers? What kind of place do you run here?"

"Our breakfast hours are over," Little Man said, "and our lunch hours haven't started yet."

"What will we do if we want breakfast?" Holder asked.

"The Red Bull normally keeps a jar of pickled eggs on the bar in the morning," Little Man said. "If you buy a beer, you can have a boiled egg."

"That's a good idea," Durbin said. "Most especial since we don't have to pay for our beer."

"You know what, little lady? Me 'n' you never did get that dance, did we?" Holder said.

Lucy didn't answer.

"Well, I tell you what. We'll just have to have that dance here, real soon."

"I have no intention of dancing with you. Not now, not ever," Lucy said resolutely.

Durbin laughed. "You know what, Holder? I don't think she loves you. You'd better go back and see if you can talk Fifi into dancing with you."

"Hey, wait a minute. Isn't this where that cook works? The one that put a gun in my back?" Holder asked.

"Gun, hell! He got your bluff with a candleholder," Durbin said, laughing again.

"I think I'll just go back in the kitchen and—"

"You don't have to come into the kitchen," Casey said, stepping out into the dining room. "I'll come to you."

"Yeah, me 'n' you are—" He stopped suddenly when he saw Casey holding a pistol.

"As you can see, this isn't a candleholder," Casey said. "It is, in fact, a Colt .44." Casey pulled the hammer back and it made a loud, ominous click as the sear engaged the cylinder and rolled a cartridge in line with the barrel.

"Now, what exactly did you have in mind?" Casey asked.

"Nothin'," Holder said. "I didn't have nothin' in mind."

"I didn't think so," Casey replied. "I believe you said something about going down to the saloon to have some pickled boiled eggs?"

"Yeah," Holder said. "Yeah, I'm goin' to get breakfast."

Holder and Durbin left the restaurant.

"Ha, I guess you showed them," Little Man said.

"Shh," Casey said. "You and Lucy get into the kitchen. I want you out of the line of fire."

"Line of fire? What are you talking about?"

"Now!" Casey said sharply. "Take Lucy with you!"

"Come, Papa," Lucy said, and the two of them moved quickly into the kitchen.

Suddenly the front door to the restaurant opened and Holder came bursting in, a pistol in his hand.

"You son of a bitch!" Holder shouted. "I'm going to—"

That was as far as he got before Casey pulled the trigger. Holder, shot in the head, fell forward. Casey ran to the front door and looked outside, but he didn't see Durbin.

When he came back, he saw both Little Man and Lucy standing in the dining room, looking on in shock. Lucy had her fist raised to her mouth and was biting on it to keep from crying out.

"How did you know he was going to do that?" Little Man asked.

"Get the wheelbarrow brought up to the back door," Casey said. "I need to get rid of the body."

"Oh, yes, yes," Little Man said.

Casey grabbed Holder by his arms and pulled him across the floor toward the back door.

"Oh, there's blood on the floor," Lucy said in a weak voice. "I'll—I'll get it cleaned up."

"Good for you," Casey said.

By the time Casey got Holder's body to the door, Little Man had brought the wheelbarrow. Casey put Holder's body in it, then covered it with wood.

"I'll take care of it later," he said.

★ ★ ★

It was at least an hour before Durbin came back into the restaurant.

"Ah, there you are," Little Man said. "We're about ready to serve lunch now, if you'll have a seat. Will your friend be with you?"

"My friend?"

"The man who came in with you earlier," Little Man said. "Will he be having lunch with you?"

"I don't know, that's why I'm here now, I'm lookin' for him. Have you seen him?"

"Well, yes, of course. Both of you were here this morning."

"No, I mean, have you seen him since then?"

Casey came out of the kitchen. "Where is your friend?" he asked.

"That's what I was about to ask you," Durbin said.

"How would any of us know where he is?" Casey asked.

"I don't know what happened to him." He smiled. "He might have gone back down to Big Kate's."

"Yes, I would say that would be something he might do," Casey said. "If you see him, tell him I said to stay away from Miss Lucy. Do you understand that? I'll not have him bothering Miss Lucy."

"Yeah, yeah, I'll tell him," Durbin said, turning to leave.

"I have to tell you, Mr. Casey," Little Man said after Durbin had left. "You are one cool character."

"Sometimes you have to be," Casey said.

★ ★ ★

"Something has happened to Holder," Durbin told Pugh when he went back to the marshal's office.

Pugh was in a discussion with Draco and Taylor.

"What do you mean, something has happened to him?"

"I mean he's just disappeared."

"Yeah, well, I can't be worried about that now. I have another problem I need to deal with," Pugh said. He turned his attention back to Draco and Taylor.

"How many are they sending?"

"Two, is what I've found out," Taylor said. "They're going to Malone, and they plan to send a telegram from there."

"When are they planning to leave?"

"Right after lunch."

"All right, you two take care of them."

Draco smiled and nodded.

"Maybe we should take care of just one of them," Taylor suggested.

"Why just one?"

"If we let the other one come back, I think he'll be able to convince the rest of the town that we mean business."

Pugh stroked his chin for a moment, then nodded. "Yes," he said. "Yes, that might be a good idea."

"Let's go," Taylor said, and he and Draco left the office. A moment later the sound of their horses could be heard.

"Now," Pugh said, "what is this about Holder missing?"

"We went into the Red Bull about an hour or so ago. Then he said he had something to do and he left. But he never come back."

"Did you look for him?"

"Yeah, I looked down at Big Kate's. I looked in the Hog Lot, the Ace High, the Gilded Cage. He wasn't in none of them places."

"Maybe he just decided to leave, have you thought about that?"

"I checked his horse, and it ain't gone."

"Well, we don't have time to worry about him," Pugh said. "If he shows up, fine. If he doesn't, we'll just divide his money up among the rest of you, like we're doing with Canby's share."

"Huh-uh," Durbin said.

"What do you mean, 'Huh-uh'?"

Durbin smiled. "He was my friend. If he don't show up, I should get his share of the money. I'm sure that's what he would want."

Pugh laughed. "Are you, now? All right, that's fine with me," he said. "In the meantime, I'll have the others look for him."

"No need to be lookin' for him," Durbin said. "Like as not, he's just decided to wander off somewhere. Holder, he's kind of like that."

"Whatever you say, Mr. Durbin. After all, as you said, he is your friend."

CHAPTER THIRTY-ONE

★

Fred Keaton and Joe Cravens had been charged by Mayor Felker with going to Malone to send the telegram from the mayor to the governor. Like Fred Keaton, Joe Cravens was a member of the city council. They were five miles south of Wardell and discussing the plan that Mayor Felker had in mind. "I think it was smart of Felker to ask the governor to send some Texas Rangers," Keaton said.

"Yes," Cravens agreed. "Especially since he used to be a Texas Ranger himself."

"To tell you the truth, I don't know how the hell we let these people get in here in the first place."

"It's not like we let them," Cravens said. "Damn, we just looked up one day and there they were. Seven of them. It was like they was a small army or something."

"But . . . I don't know, maybe Deckert is right. Maybe we should just let things be until Saturday. That's only the day after tomorrow. Then they'll be gone. I mean, when you think about it, even if the governor does send a Ranger, I'm not sure he would get here in time, anyway."

"Yes, but what if they decide not to leave Saturday?

It would be nice to have a Ranger as a backup, don't you think?" Cravens asked.

"Yeah, if you put it that way, I guess so," Keaton said.

Suddenly two men rode out from behind a rock outcropping, blocking the road in front of them. They didn't have to ask what the two men wanted. They recognized them right away, especially Draco.

"Where are you two men going?" Taylor asked.

"What difference does it make?" Cravens asked. "You might control the town, but you don't control the entire state."

"By controlling the town, we control everyone *in* the town," Taylor said. "And that means we control the movement of everyone in town. You don't go anywhere without getting permission to go."

"The hell you say," Cravens said. "I'd like to see you stop me."

Suddenly, and to Keaton's complete shock, Draco, who had not said a word during the entire time, drew his pistol and fired. Cravens was knocked off his horse.

"Are you crazy?" Keaton shouted in fear and anger. He dismounted and knelt beside his friend. He held his hand to Cravens's neck.

"He's dead," Draco said.

"How do you know he's dead?"

"I know because I intended to kill him," Draco replied.

"I—I can't believe it! You had no reason to shoot him!"

"Go back to town," Taylor said. "Go back and let everyone know what happened here."

"What? You mean you want me to tell them that you killed Joe for no reason?"

"Oh, we had a reason all right," Taylor said. "It was to show the town, once and for all, that we are in charge."

"You didn't have to kill him."

"And you didn't have to try and send a telegram."

"How . . . how did you know that's what we were going to do?"

"We know everything," Taylor said. He shook his head. "I don't understand you people. All you have to do is just keep out of our way for two more days. Now, how hard can that be? Two more days and we'll be gone. You go back now and tell them that. You tell the town that I killed Cravens to show that we mean business."

"He's dead. Joe Cravens is dead. Draco killed him," Keaton told Felker and Potashnick when he got back to town. The two men were sitting at a table in Little Man Lambert's, drinking coffee and discussing conditions in the town. They had shared with Little Man and Casey, who was there as well, that they had sent the two men out of town to get a telegram off to the governor.

"What? Why? Why did Draco kill Cravens?" Felker asked.

"Intimidation," Potashnick answered.

"I don't know about that," Keaton said. "But he said it was to show the town that they mean business."

"As I said, intimidation."

"Intimidation, yes," Casey said, nodding his head. He smiled. "Perhaps it's about time we did a little intimidating of our own."

"What do you mean?" Felker asked.

"You'll find out what I mean when it's done," Casey said cryptically.

"Hello, Mr. Pugh."

The man who spoke had rimless glasses perched on his nose. He was wearing a three-piece suit with a gold chain stretched across his chest.

"Crabtree," Pugh said when the telegrapher came into the office. "When did you get here?"

"I arrived on the morning train," Crabtree said. "Now that our operation is about to come to fruition, I decided I would like to be here when it happens."

"Would you, now?"

"Yes. It isn't that I don't trust you, you understand. It's just that, since this was all my idea, I think I would like to see it played out. I suppose you could call it a matter of pride."

"Yes, but you do know what they say about pride, don't you?" Pugh asked. "'Pride goeth before a fall.'"

"What's that supposed to mean?" Crabtree asked, his voice displaying a bit of anxiousness.

Pugh chuckled. "You know what? I never could figure that out, either."

"Mr. Lambert, I've made a big pot of ham and beans and some corn bread," Casey said. "Since the noon meal is prepared, I wonder if you would mind if I took off for an hour or so."

"No, no, of course not. I don't mind at all," Little Man said.

Casey nodded, then he went out the back door. Curious as to why he had gone out that way, Little Man went over to take a look. He saw Casey pushing the wheelbarrow down the alley—the wheelbarrow into which he had put the body of the railroad detective this morning.

"Good," Little Man said under his breath. He had no second thoughts about Casey killing the deputy, but he was glad that the body was being moved from the back of his place.

At that moment four deputies came in and ordered lunch. Lucy served them, not with the warm smile as she generally had when she served the other customers, but with an expressionless, all-business demeanor.

Little Man recognized two of them, Durbin and the albino. By now everyone knew Draco. From their conversation he learned the names of the other two: Taylor and Poindexter.

"Well, miss, that was a very good meal," the one called Taylor said. He dabbed a napkin at his lips. "We'll be back for supper."

"Your meals were twenty-five cents each," she said. "That will be a dollar."

"No it won't," Taylor said. "As long as we are here, the meals will be free."

"What? What are you talking about? Of course the meals aren't free."

"Maybe you didn't get the word," Poindexter said. "As long as we are in town, all meals and all drinks are free."

"Not here, they aren't," Lucy insisted.

Little Man, seeing then that his daughter was in some kind of altercation with the railroad deputies, hurried over to the table.

"What is it? What's going on here?"

"These men don't want to pay for their meal," Lucy said.

"But of course you will pay for your meal. Four bowls of beans; that will be a dollar," Little Man said.

"Until Saturday, we are the law," Taylor said. "Are you trying to tell me that Marshal Wallace doesn't get his meals free here?"

"Not exactly free," Little Man said. "Marshal Wallace doesn't have to pay for his meals, but the city council pays for them. That is part of his compensation package from the town."

"Yes, well, you can just consider this a part of *our* compensation package."

"No. I don't even want you people here, and I certainly won't subsidize it by providing you with free meals."

★ ★ ★

As Little Man, Lucy, and the deputies were engaged in discussion about whether or not the deputies should have to pay for their meal, Casey was also busy. Removing Holder's body from the wheelbarrow, he sat it down on the ground and leaned it back against one of the signs that had been posted, informing all of the weapons ban. On the sign, he posted his own message.

> *Woe, woe, woe to those who dwell on the earth,*
> *at the blast of the trumpet*
> *which the avenging angel is about to blow!*

He was paraphrasing a quote from the Book of Revelation, but as far as Casey was concerned, it illustrated his point.

He returned to the alley, then started pushing the wheelbarrow back to the restaurant. No one had seen him put the body in front of the sign, but when he looked between the buildings after he reached the restaurant, he saw that people were just beginning to gather around it.

He leaned the empty wheelbarrow up against the back wall of the restaurant, then went inside. He found Little Man, Quince, and Stanley Goff in a very animated conversation.

"What is it?" he asked. "What's going on?"

"They took her!" Little Man said with an expression of terrified anger on his face. "They took Lucy."

"Who took Lucy? Where?"

"Draco and three others. They arrested her because she wouldn't give them their meals for free. Mr. Casey, they put her in jail!"

"She ain't goin' to be in there long," Quince promised. "I'm about to call Draco out."

Casey shook his head. "No, Quince, don't do that."

"What do you mean, don't do it? You think I'm just going to let Lucy stay in there and rot?"

"No, but there's nothing to be gained by going off half-cocked, either."

"What are we supposed to do? Just sit around and twiddle our thumbs?"

"No need to twiddle our thumbs," Casey said. "I've already started something to work on their minds."

"What do you mean?"

"Take a look at the sign down at the south end of Broad Street. The sign that says no weapons allowed."

"Yeah, I saw that sign," Quince said. He patted the pistol in his holster. "But if you notice, I didn't pay any attention to it."

"Hey, Quince," Stanley said from the front door. "Somethin's goin' on down there around that sign. There's a lot of people there."

"Yeah? What?"

"I don't know. Let's go down there and see."

"Hey, Pugh, we found Holder," Canby said. "Me 'n Poindexter found 'im."

"Oh? Where has he been?"

"Dead," Poindexter said. "That's where he's been. He's been dead. Somebody's got him propped up against the 'no guns' sign down at the south end of the street."

"Poindexter is right. He's there all right, with a bullet hole right in his forehead. And this here was stuck to the sign."

Canby handed a sheet of paper to Pugh. Pugh read it, then gasped. "No," he said. "It can't be."

"What? What is it?" Crabtree asked.

"Canby, where's Draco?"

"Last I saw him, he was down at the Hog Lot."

"Get him here. Fast. I need to talk to him."

"What is it?" Crabtree asked. "What's going on?"

"Nothing that concerns you," Pugh said.

"That's where you are wrong, Mr. Pugh. Everything that happens from now until we have the money safely in our hands concerns me."

CHAPTER THIRTY-TWO

★

Quince and Stanley went down to the far end of the street to see why a crowd had gathered. That was when they saw a body sitting propped up by the sign. The mouth was open and so was one eye. There was a black hole in the middle of the forehead.

"Hey, Quince, you know who that fella is? That's the—"

"Yeah, he was one of the two at the dance."

"Do you think the cook shot him?"

"The cook?" Quince scoffed. "What makes you think the cook shot him?"

"Well, you might remember, the cook bluffed him out at the dance. And he's the one who told us to come down here and check the sign."

"Yeah, well, maybe he saw the body here and thought we might be interested 'cause of what happened at the dance. Anyhow, I don't care about him. I'm goin' to get Lucy out of jail."

"How are you goin' to do that?"

"You just watch," Quince said. "Come on, let's go down there now."

"I don't know, Quince. You heard what the cook

said. He said this'll all be over in a couple of days, so why don't we just wait it out?"

"You wait it out if you want to," Quince said. "Not me."

Quince started walking down the center of the street, heading toward the jail. That was when he saw Draco and Canby coming toward the marshal's office from the other direction.

"Draco!" Quince shouted. "Draco, you son of a bitch! I'm coming for you!"

"Quince, no!" Stanley pleaded. He reached up to grab Quince by the arm, but Quince pushed him aside.

"Stanley, if you ain't with me, then get the hell out of my way!" Quince demanded. "Draco!" he called again.

"Oh, damn! Quince, please, don't do this!" Stanley said.

"I told you, get out of my way," Quince said with a dismissive wave of his hand.

Stanley moved quickly to get out of the middle of the road. Others, seeing what was going on, gathered to watch. Quince and Draco continued to approach each other, stopping when they were separated by about twenty yards.

"Were you calling me, cowboy?" Draco asked.

"I tell you what, Draco," Quince said. "You go into that jail and turn Lucy loose, and I'll let you live."

Those who were close enough to hear Quince's words gasped and felt a degree of hope that perhaps this young man would be their salvation. Quince's speed and prowess with a pistol were well-known. Was he faster than Draco? He had to be: he had put on shooting demonstrations that defied belief.

"I'm told you are fast," Draco said. There was a hissing quality to his voice, and he spoke so quietly that everyone had to strain to hear him.

"I'm fast enough," Quince said. Unlike Draco's quiet hiss, Quince's voice was much louder, defiant, and challenging.

"Show me," Draco said.

Quince drew, and as everyone hoped and many suspected, he had his pistol out in a split second, clearly beating Draco to the draw. He smiled triumphantly and started to thumb back the hammer and fire, but why? Draco had to know he was beaten. Surely he could stop now. Sparing Draco would make him more cooperative. He relaxed just a little.

All those thoughts took place in Quince's mind in just a split second, just in the time it took Draco to continue his own draw, pull back the hammer, and fire.

Quince was surprised by the sudden and unexpected outcome. He felt the heavy shock of the bullet going into his chest. Then an excruciating pain radiated out from the bullet's point of entry.

Quince dropped his pistol and slapped his hand over the chest wound, then felt the world spinning around him as he fell.

"Quince!" Stanley shouted, running into the street toward his friend.

Draco fired a second time and Stanley fell, his out-stretched hand just inches short of his friend.

"Quince Anders and Stanley Goff are dead," Fielding Potashnick reported when he walked into Little Man's restaurant a few minutes later. "Draco killed both of them. What's more, their bodies are lying out in the street, and the deputies are saying that the bodies are going to have to stay there until after they leave town Saturday."

"Did you hear that, Mr. Casey?" Little Man asked. "What kind of monster would give an order like . . ." Little Man looked around, but Casey was already gone. He stood up and walked back to the kitchen. "Mr. Casey?"

"Who are you looking for, your cook?" Potashnick asked.

"Yes."

Potashnick shook his head. "You aren't going to find him. I saw him go up the stairs a moment or so ago. I expect he's so frightened now that he's going to stay out of sight until after they are gone. That might not be a bad idea for any of us if you ask me. It's only . . . Lord in heaven, what is that?"

Potashnick pointed to the back stairs. Coming toward them in full ecclesiastical vestments was Ken Casey.

"Mr. Casey?" Little Man said, shocked by what he was seeing.

Casey said nothing, but when he walked out of the restaurant, both Little Man and Potashnick hurried to the front door. Looking out, they saw him walk out into the now deserted street and head directly for the bodies of Quince and Stanley.

"Who is that?" someone standing on the side of the street asked.

"You know him. That's the cook at Little Man's."

"You mean Ken Casey? What's he all done up like that for?"

"I don't have the slightest idea."

Casey reached the two bodies and looked down at them. "Quince, I told you that you couldn't do this. You couldn't do it because you hadn't lost your soul."

Casey made the sign of the cross over the two young cowboys.

"O Almighty God, with whom do live the spirits of just men made perfect, after they are delivered from their earthly prisons: I humbly commend the souls of these thy servants, my brothers Quince and Stanley, into thy hands, as into the hands of a faithful Creator and most merciful Savior. I most humbly beseech thee, that it may be precious in thy sight."

That done, he turned and started back toward Little Man Lambert's.

"Hey, cook! What was that all about?" someone shouted.

Casey didn't answer. When he entered the restaurant, Little Man and Potashnick looked at him in shock.

"Mr. Casey, why did you do that? Are you a priest?"

"No," Casey said. In his mind, he wasn't lying. He had abandoned all rights to ever again refer to himself as a priest.

Without saying another word to either of the two men, Casey went back upstairs.

"Now, that's the damnedest thing I've ever seen," Little Man said. "I mean, if he's not a priest, why does he have on those . . . whatever you call them?"

"They are called vestments," Potashnick said. "Little Man, how much do you know about him?"

Little Man shook his head. "Nothing, really. He's always been a little strange and quiet. But now Lucy—she noticed something about him right away, about how smart he was and . . . Lord in heaven, what now?"

Casey reappeared, no longer wearing vestments, but now was wearing trousers and a shirt. There was something else different about him. He was wearing a holster and pistol.

"Mr. Casey, what is this? What are you planning on doing?"

"Something I should have done before now," Casey said. "I'm going to kill Draco."

"Have you lost your mind? What chance would someone like you have with Draco? You saw what happened to Quince. My God, there was no one faster with a gun than he was, but not even he was fast enough."

"Oh, he was fast enough," Casey said. "But he wasn't a killer."

"And you are?"

"I've enjoyed working for you, Mr. Lambert. Tell Miss Lucy I'm sorry about Quince. I think he would have made a good husband for her. But she is a beautiful, intelligent, and wonderful young woman, and I know some lucky man will find her, and they will have a good life."

Casey started for the door.

"Casey, no! Come back here! Don't be crazy!"

When Casey was halfway to the marshal's office, he was met by two of the deputies. He recognized one of them as Durbin, but he didn't know the other one.

"Hey, mister, what are you doin' wearin' a gun? Ain't you seen the signs?"

"Do you mean like the sign that Mr. Holder is leaning up against?" Casey asked.

"Yeah, that sign. Take that gun out of your holster now and drop it over there in one of them barrels."

"No."

"What do you mean, no?"

"Is that a word you don't understand? I have no intention of divesting myself of this firearm."

"Of di . . . what?"

"Mr. Durbin, would you be interested in knowing what happened to your friend?"

"I think I know," Durbin said. There was nothing challenging about his voice.

"Durbin, quit talking to this old fool. Let's take his gun and be done with it."

"Shut up, Poindexter."

"What?"

"I said shut up," Durbin said, louder this time. "What do you want, cook? What are you doing out here wearing a gun?"

"I've come for Draco and Pugh," Casey said. "It is my belief that if I kill both of them, the rest of you might leave. If you don't, I'll kill all of you too."

"Why you ignorant old . . ." Poindexter shouted while at the same time starting to pull his gun. Casey drew, fired, then put his pistol back in his holster, doing it all so quickly that those who were watching weren't entirely sure of what they had seen.

"How . . . ?" Poindexter muttered, his face drawn into an expression of pain and surprise. He fell to his knees, stayed there for just a second, then flopped forward, facedown into a horse apple.

"Now, Mr. Durbin, would you be so kind as to ask Draco and Pugh to come out here?"

"What do you want with them?" Durbin asked.

"I want to kill them," Casey said, his words almost conversational.

"Who is it that's calling us out?" Pugh asked. "The cook?"

"Yeah, he cooks for Little Man Lambert's Restaurant."

"What the hell does the cook want with us?" Pugh asked.

"He said he wants to kill you."

"He wants to kill me?"

"No, he said he wants to kill both of you," Durbin said. "You and Draco."

"Ha! The cook wants to kill both of us, does he?"

"He's the one that kilt Holder. And he just kilt Poindexter too. You should have seen 'im! Why, he kilt Poindexter before Poindexter could even clear leather."

Draco chuckled. "Poindexter? You're impressed because he killed Poindexter? Hell, I saw Poindexter draw once. It took him a month of Sundays to get his gun out. Don't worry, Pugh, I'll go take care of him."

"He said he wanted to see both of you," Durbin said.

"Yeah? Well, he isn't the one givin' the orders around here." Draco started toward the door.

"Draco, wait," Pugh said.

"Wait for what?"

Pugh picked up the piece of paper that had been posted on the sign above Holder's body. He read the words again.

"There's something about this that's not quite right. I think I should go with you. And, Taylor, you come too."

Taylor chuckled. "You want me too?"

"Yes."

Pugh pulled his pistol and spun the cylinder to check the loads.

"Why are we doing all this for a cook?" Taylor asked.

"If it's who I think it is, it'll take all three of us," Pugh said.

"All right, if you say so," Taylor said, and loosening his pistol in his holster, he joined Draco and Pugh as they walked outside.

By now there were dozens of people on both sides of the street. They had seen the body of one of the deputies earlier, then many of them had witnessed the cook kill Canby. Now Draco was coming to meet him—the same Draco they had seen kill Quince not more than half an hour ago.

When Casey saw Pugh for the first time, he gasped in surprise. "Nate? You're the one they've been calling Pugh?"

"Hello, my old friend," Nate said. "It looks like we've both been flying false flags, haven't we?"

"So it would appear."

"I understand you plan to kill us."

"Yes. I'm sorry you are one of them."

"Why are you sorry? You've been after me for a long time now, haven't you?"

"No, I put it aside long ago. I was learning to live with it, but this . . . this evil that you have perpetrated on this town has to be stopped. And I'm afraid there's only one way to do that."

"What's with all the talk?" Draco asked. "Let's get this done."

"Draco, before we proceed, I would like to introduce to you an old friend." He pointed. "That gentleman is Ded Axton."

"*Axton!*" The name was spoken in awe, moving quickly from person to person among those who were gathered to watch.

"*Axton!*"

"*Death's Acolyte!*"

Draco started to draw, but it was too late. Axton already had his gun out. *Where did that come from? How did he get . . .*

Draco couldn't finish the question, not even to himself, because Ded had drawn and fired quicker than it took to even think about it. And even before the albino hit the ground, Ded fired two more times, dropping Nate Walker and Mickey Taylor.

Both Draco and Taylor were killed instantly, but Nate was still alive. Was it an accident that he hadn't been killed as quickly as the other two? Or had something old, something remembered—some visceral connection from their past—caused Ded to pull his shot?

He moved quickly to Nate's side.

"Pray for me, Ded. If ever there was a man who needed prayer, it's me."

Ded holstered his pistol, pulled the stole from his pocket, draped it around his neck, then made the sign of the cross over Nate.

Suddenly Nate pushed Ded aside and, lifting his pistol, fired. Ded looked over and saw, to his shock and surprise, a small man wearing a suit and glasses and holding a shotgun. Nate's shot hit the small man in the neck and, dropping the shotgun, he clutched his throat and fell to the ground.

Ded looked at Nate with a questioning expression on his face.

"His name is Crabtree," Nate explained. "He works for the T&P and he's the one who set all this up."

"I guess I owe you my life."

"That's the second time I've saved your bacon," Nate said with a coughing chuckle. "Remember the riverboat on the Ohio?"

"I remember."

"Make it a good prayer, Ded," Nate said.

Nate had taken his last breath by the time Ded finished his prayer. When he looked up, he saw several of the townspeople gathered around him.

"Is it true what he said? Are you really Ded Axton?" someone asked.

Ded didn't answer. Instead he stood up and started walking back toward the restaurant. Half an hour later, Durbin, the only remaining railroad detective, was in jail, while Marshal Wallace, Emmet Reardon, and Lucy Lambert were released. The bodies of Nate Walker, Draco, Taylor, Poindexter, Holder, and Crabtree were laid out, side by side, in the middle of the street. And as the town gathered around the bodies for a macabre celebration, none of them saw Ken Casey/Ded Axton riding away.

★ ★ ★

Lucy hurried back to the restaurant, where she and her father embraced.

"What happened?" she asked. "Who killed all those men?"

"Mr. Casey killed them."

"Mr. Casey killed all of them?"

"Yes. Except his name isn't Casey. It's Axton. Ded Axton."

Lucy gasped and put her hand over her mouth. "Ded Axton. You mean he has been here, living with us, all this time?"

"Yes."

"I knew it," Lucy said. "I knew there was something very special about Mr. Casey."

"Yes, you did, darlin'. I have to give you credit for that."

"Where is he now?"

"I imagine he is in his room. He seemed uncomfortable with everyone wanting to congratulate him for the killing."

"I don't want to congratulate him, I want to thank him."

Lucy hurried up the stairs. "Mr. Casey?" she called. "Mr. Casey, I want to thank . . ." She stopped in mid-sentence when she saw that his door was standing wide open.

"Mr. Casey?" she said quietly, stepping up to the door and looking in his room.

He was gone, but there was an envelope on his bed,

and when she walked over to it, she saw that her name was on the outside. Quickly she opened the envelope and pulled out the letter.

Miss Lucy,

> *By now you know who I am, and knowing that, you also know why I can't stay here any longer. I am very sorry about what happened to your friends Quince and Stanley. They were two decent young men, and in the end, that's what did them in.*
> *Knowing your love of poetry, I leave you with these lines from Henry Wadsworth Longfellow.*

> *"Athwart the swinging branches cast,*
> *Soft rays of sunshine pour;*
> *Then comes the fearful wintry blast;*
> *Our hopes, like withered leaves, fall fast;*
> *Pallid lips say, 'It is past!*
> *We can return no more!'"*

> *And like the poem, my dear, lovely Miss Lucy, my days here are past, and I can return no more. I hope that, from time to time, you will think kind thoughts about me.*

> *Sincerely,*
> *Ded Axton*

After reading the letter, Lucy ran quickly back down the stairs, then out onto the front porch.

"Mr. Casey!" she called, but he was nowhere to be found.

By now the celebration in the street had grown larger and more frenzied, and a fiddle, guitar, Jew's harp, and jug added music to the scene. With barely a glance toward the revelers, Lucy went back inside.

"He's gone," she said. She showed the letter to Little Man. "Why did he have to leave? I know that everyone in town would love him for what he did for us."

"No, darlin', he had to go. You know it, and I know it."

The devil had found Ded and he could no longer stay in Wardell. He was wearing his sheepskin coat, and he pulled the collar up around his neck as he rode away from the town. Winter was coming on, and it would be cold up in the high country.